Winter Park Public Library
460 East New England Av
Winter Park, Florida 327
Renewals: (407) 623-3300
or www.wppl.org

P9-DHA-012

DISCARD

# SPELL BOUND

## A HEX HALL NOVEL

Previous books in the Hex Hall series:

*Hex Hall*

*Demonglass*

# SPELL BOUND

## A HEX HALL NOVEL

## RACHEL HAWKINS

HYPERION
NEW YORK

Copyright © 2012 by Rachel Hawkins

All rights reserved. Published by Hyperion, an imprint of Disney Book Group. No part
of this book may be reproduced or transmitted in any form or by any means, electronic or
mechanical, including photocopying, recording, or by any information storage and retrieval
system, without written permission from the publisher. For information address Hyperion,
114 Fifth Avenue, New York, New York 10011-5690.

First Edition
1 3 5 7 9 10 8 6 4 2
G475-5664-5-12034
Printed in the United States of America

Library of Congress Cataloging-in-Publication Data
Hawkins, Rachel, 1979–
    Spell bound  :  a Hex Hall novel / Rachel Hawkins.  —  1st ed.
       p.   cm.
    Summary: Just as Sophie Mercer has come to accept her magical powers as a demon,
the Prodigium Council strips them away and leaves her alone, defenseless, and at the mercy
of her enemies the Brannicks, a family of warrior women who hunt down the Prodigium.
    ISBN 978-1-4231-2132-9 (alk. paper)
    [1. Demonology—Fiction. 2. Magic—Fiction. 3. Supernatural—Fiction.] I. Title.
    PZ7.H313525Sp 2012
    [Fec]—dc23                                                    2011020494

Reinforced binding

Visit www.hyperionteens.com

SUSTAINABLE
FORESTRY
INITIATIVE

Certified Fiber
Sourcing
www.sfiprogram.org

THIS LABEL APPLIES TO TEXT STOCK

*For Agent Extraordinaire Holly Root, for
her support, her ability to talk Certain
Authors off ledges, and for finding Sophie
and me the perfect home!*

3/12

# PART I

"I wonder if I've been changed in the night? Let me think: *was* I the same when I got up this morning? I almost think I can remember feeling a little different. But if I'm not the same, the next question is, Who in the world am I? Ah, *that's* the great puzzle!"

—*Alice's Adventures in Wonderland*

# CHAPTER 1

There are times when magic really sucks.

Sure, it's awesome when you're using it to change your hair color, or fly, or turn day into night. But for the most part, magic tends to end in explosions, or tears, or with you flat on your back in the middle of nowhere, feeling like a tiny dwarf is mining for diamonds inside your head.

Okay, so maybe that last bit was just me.

One of the drawbacks of traveling by Itineris—a kind of magical portal that can take you from one place to another—is how rough it was on your body. Every trip I'd ever taken through one had left me feeling like I'd been turned inside out; but this time was particularly bad. I was actually shaking. Of course, that might have been from all the adrenaline. I felt like my heart was trying to throw itself out of my chest.

I took a deep breath and tried to calm my racing pulse. Okay. The Itineris had dropped me off . . . well, somewhere. I hadn't quite worked out where yet, mostly because I still didn't feel capable of opening my eyes. Wherever it was, it was quiet and hot. I ran my hands over the ground under me. Grass. A few rocks. Some sticks.

I took a ragged breath and thought about lifting my head. But the very idea of trying to move made every nerve ending I had scoff, *Yeah, don't think so.*

Groaning, I clenched my teeth and decided now was as good a time as any to take stock.

Up until this morning, I'd been a demon and in possession of some pretty freaking-awesome magic. Thanks to a binding spell, that magic was gone. Well, not gone exactly; I could still feel it fluttering inside me like a butterfly under glass. But I couldn't access any of my powers, so it might as well have been gone.

Also gone? My best friend, Jenna. And my dad. And Archer, the guy I was in love with. And Cal, my fiancé. (Yeah, my love life was complicated.)

For a second, the pain in my head was nothing compared to the pain in my chest as I thought about the four of them. Honestly, I wasn't sure who to worry about more. Jenna was a vampire, which meant she could take care of herself, but I'd found her bloodstone crushed on the floor at Thorne Abbey. The bloodstone's main job was to protect Jenna from all the side effects of vampire-dom. If it had been taken from her in the daylight, the sun would kill her.

Then there was Dad. He'd been subjected to the Removal, which meant he was even more powerless than I was now. At least I still had my magic, useless as it was. Dad's powers were gone forever. The last time I'd seen him, he'd been lying in a cell, pale and unconscious, covered in dark purple tattoos from the Removal. Archer had been with him, and as far as I knew, they had both *still* been locked in that cell when Thorne Abbey was attacked.

Still been trapped there when the Council used Daisy, another demon, to set Thorne Abbey on fire.

Cal had gone into the burning mansion to save them, but not before telling me to take the Itineris to find my mom, who was, for some reason, with Aislinn Brannick, leader of a group of monster hunters. And since the Brannicks saw *me* as one of those monsters, I couldn't figure out why Mom would be with them.

That's how I'd ended up lying flat on my back, Archer's sword still clutched in my hand, my head aching. Maybe I could just lie here and wait for Mom to find *me*. That would be convenient.

I sighed as the wind rustled the leaves overhead. Yep, that was a solid plan. Lie here on the ground and wait for someone to come to me.

A bright light suddenly seared against my closed eye-lids, and I winced, raising my hand to ward off whatever it was. When I opened my eyes, I honestly expected to see one of the Brannicks standing there, maybe with a torch or a flashlight.

What I wasn't expecting was a ghost.

The ghost of Elodie Parris, to be exact, standing at my feet, glaring down at me, arms crossed. She was glowing so brightly that I squinted as I sat up. Elodie had been murdered by my great-grandmother nearly a year ago (long story), and thanks to a little shared magic between us before she died, her ghost was now tied to me.

"Oh, wow," I croaked. "I was just lying here think-ing this night could not get any worse, and then it totally did. Huh."

Elodie rolled her eyes, and for just a second I thought her glow got a little brighter. She moved her mouth, but no sounds came out. One of the drawbacks of being a ghost—she couldn't talk. From her expression and the little bit of lip-reading I could do, I thought that was probably a good thing.

"Okay, okay," I said. "Now is not the time for snarking."

Using Archer's sword as a crutch, I managed to get to my feet. There was no moon out, but thanks to Elodie's luminescence, I could see . . . well, trees. Lots of them. And not much else.

"Any idea where we are?" I asked her.

She shrugged and mouthed, "Forest."

"You think?" Okay, so the whole "no more snark" thing wasn't off to a *great* start. I sighed and looked around. "It's still night, so we must be in the same time zone. That means we couldn't have gone too far. But it's hot. Like, way hotter than it was at Thorne."

Elodie's mouth moved, and it took the two of us several tries before I could decipher what she was saying. Finally, I worked out that it was: "Where were you trying to go?"

"The Brannicks'," I told her. At that, Elodie's eyes went wide, and her lips started flying again, undoubtedly telling me what a freaking idiot I was.

"I know," I said, holding up a hand to cut off her silent rant. "Scary Irish monster hunters, maybe not the best plan. But Cal said my mom was with them. And no," I said, as her ghostly mouth opened up yet again, "I don't know why. What I *do* know is that apparently the Itineris sucks, because the only scary redhead I see around here is you." Sighing, I rubbed my free hand over my eyes. "So now we just—"

A howl split the air.

I gulped, and my fingers tightened on the sword's hilt. "Now, we just hope that whatever that is, it doesn't come this way," I finished weakly.

Another howl, this one closer. In the distance, I could hear something crashing through the underbrush. For a second I thought about running, but my knees were so rubbery that just standing was a challenge. No way could I outrun a werewolf. Which meant staying and fighting.

Or, you know, staying and getting mauled.

"Awesome," I muttered, lifting the sword, the muscles in my shoulders groaning. I felt my powers stir in the pit of my stomach, and a sudden terror shot through me. I was normal, I reminded myself. Just a regular seventeen-year-old girl, about to face against a werewolf with nothing more than . . . Okay, well, I did have a big-ass sword and a ghost. That had to count for something.

I glanced over at Elodie. She was staring into the woods, looking vaguely bored.

"Um, hi," I said. "Werewolf headed this way. Are you even a little bit concerned about that?"

She smirked at me and gestured toward her glowing body. I read her lips: "Already dead."

"Right. But if I get killed, too, you and I are *so* not becoming ghost BFFs."

Elodie gave me a look that said there was no danger of that happening.

The sounds got louder, and I hoisted the sword higher.

Then, with a snarl, something large and furry leaped through the trees. I gave a little shriek, and even Elodie jumped back. Well, floated back.

For a moment, all three of us were frozen, me holding the sword like a baseball bat, Elodie hovering a few feet off the ground, the Were crouched in front of us. I had no idea if it was a boy or a girl werewolf, but I thought it was young. White froth dripped from its snout. Werewolves are kind of drooly.

It lowered its head, and I clutched the sword tighter, waiting for it to spring. But instead of leaping to rip my throat out, the werewolf made a low keening sound, almost like it was crying.

I looked in its eyes, which were disturbingly human. Yep, definitely tears. And fear. Lots of it. It was panting hard, and I got the feeling it had been running for a while.

Suddenly it occurred to me that maybe the Itineris didn't suck as much as I'd thought. Something had scared this werewolf, and there were only a few things I could think of that could do *that*. Scary Irish Prodigium hunters? Way up on that list.

"Elodie—" I started to say, but before I got anything else out, she winked out like a bitchy firefly.

The werewolf and I were plunged into darkness. I cursed, and the werewolf made a growl that sounded like the same word. For a few moments, just long enough to make me think that maybe I'd been wrong, the woods were quiet and still.

And then everything erupted at once.

# CHAPTER 2

There was a shout from somewhere in front of me, and the werewolf bayed. I heard a brief scuffle, followed by a sharp yelp. Then the only sound was my own breath, bellowing in and out of my lungs.

I caught a movement out of the corner of my eye, and instinctively stepped toward it, still holding the sword out in front of me.

Suddenly, a bright light, much brighter than Elodie had been, shone directly in my face. I closed my eyes, and stumbled. That's when something slammed into my outstretched hand, hard enough to make me cry out. My hand immediately went numb, and Archer's sword slipped from my fingers. Another hit, this one to the back of my legs, and suddenly I was on my back.

A weight settled on my chest as bony knees

pressed both of my arms to the ground. I felt a sharp stinging under my chin, and I fought the urge to whimper.

Then a high-pitched voice asked, "What are you?"

I opened my eyes gingerly. The flashlight that had blinded me was lying a few feet from my head now, which gave me just enough light to see what appeared to be a twelve-year-old girl sitting on my chest.

I'd gotten my butt handed to me by a *sixth grader*? That was embarrassing.

Then the cold metal at my neck reminded me this particular sixth grader had a knife.

"I'm . . . I'm not anything," I said, trying to move my mouth as little as possible. My eyes were rapidly adjusting to the dim light, and I could see the girl's bright red hair. And as weird as it may seem, what with a blade at my throat and all, my first thought was, *Oh, thank God.*

She may have been littler than I'd expected, but in a lot of ways, this girl was everything I'd imagined the Brannicks to be. They were a large family of women— always women, although I guess guys factored in there somewhere, seeing as how the family had been around for over a thousand years. Descended from a megapowerful white witch named Maeve Brannick, they'd dedicated themselves to ridding the world of evil.

Unfortunately, I fit their definition of evil.

The girl scowled. "You are something," she hissed, leaning in closer. "I can feel it. Whatever you are, it's not human. So you can either tell me what kind of freak you are, or I can cut you open and find out myself."

I stared at her. "You are one hard-core little kid."

Her scowl deepened.

"I'm looking for the Brannicks," I said in a rush. "And I'm guessing you are one because . . . you know, red hair and the violence and everything."

"What's your name?" she demanded as the stinging at my neck became actual pain.

"Sophie Mercer," I said through clenched teeth.

Her eyes widened. "No way," she said, sounding for the first time like the middle schooler she probably was.

"Way," I croaked.

For a second, she looked unsure, and the knife at my throat slid back, maybe an inch or so. It was all I needed.

I rolled hard onto one side. The move pulled something in my shoulder so badly that tears sprang to my eyes, but it still had the desired effect of dumping the girl off me.

She shrieked, and I heard a muffled thump that I really, really hoped was the knife hitting the ground. I didn't give myself time to check, though. On my hands and knees, I scrambled over to Archer's sword. My fingers closed around the hilt, and I dragged it toward me.

Using the sword for leverage, I pushed myself to my feet and turned back to the girl. She was still sitting on the ground, leaning back on her hands, her breath coming hard and fast. All traces of Badass Girl Scout were gone from her face; now she was just a scared little kid.

I wondered why. I mean, I was still leaning on the sword, not pointing it at her. My legs were trembling so much, I was sure she could see it, and I knew my face was streaked with tears and sweat. I couldn't have made a very intimidating—

And then I remembered her face when she'd heard my name. She knew me, or at least knew of me. Which meant she probably knew what I was.

Or used to be.

I tried to give her my best "I Am A Demon Princess" look, which was quite the challenge, seeing as how my hair was hanging in my face and my nose was running. "What's your name?" I asked.

The girl kept her eyes on me, but her hands were moving restlessly over the ground around her, no doubt searching for the knife. "Izzy," she said.

I raised both my eyebrows. Not exactly a name to strike fear into the heart.

Izzy must've read that in my expression, because she frowned. "I'm Isolde Brannick, daughter of Aislinn, daughter of Fiona, daughter of—"

"Right, right, daughter of a bunch of fierce ladies, got it." I ran a hand over my face, my eyes aching and gritty. I wasn't sure I'd ever been so tired in my life. My head felt like it was filled with cement, and even my heartbeat seemed heavy and sluggish. There was also this weird, niggling feeling at the back of my mind, like I was missing something important.

Shoving that aside, I turned my attention back to Izzy. "I'm looking for Grace Mercer." As soon as I said Mom's name, a thick, painful lump rose in my throat. I blinked as I added, "I was told she was with the Brannicks, and I really need to find her."

*And throw my arms around her, and cry for maybe a thousand years,* I thought.

But Izzy shook her head. "There's no Grace Mercer with us."

The words fell on me like blows. "No, she has to be," I said. Izzy wavered in front of me, and I realized I was seeing her through tears. "Cal said she was with the Brannicks," I insisted, my voice cracking.

Izzy sat up straighter. "Well, whoever Cal is, he was wrong. There are only Brannicks back at the compound."

Find Mom. That had been the only thing I'd focused

15

on from the moment Cal turned to run into Thorne Abbey. Because if I could find Mom, then somehow everything would be okay, and I'd be able to find everyone else, too.

My dad, and Jenna, and Archer, and Cal.

A wave of grief and exhaustion slammed into me. If Mom wasn't here, then I'd just put myself right in the middle of enemy territory for nothing. No powers. No parents. No friends.

In that moment, I let myself entertain the idea of just putting the sword down and lying on the ground. It would feel good, and really, if I'd lost everything, who cared what this tiny homicidal person did to me?

But just as quickly, I shut that thought right the heck down. No way had I survived demon attacks, and ghoul duels, and demonglass explosions to end up murdered by Raggedy Ann. Whether Mom was here or not, I was going to survive this.

My fingers tightened on the sword's hilt until I felt the metal cut into my skin. It hurt, but that was good. That might actually keep me from passing out, which in turn would keep Izzy from dissecting me, or whatever it was Brannicks did to demons.

Former demons. Whatever.

"So you guys have a compound," I said, trying to

will my brain into working. "That's . . . cool. I bet it has bunkers and barbed wire."

Izzy rolled her eyes. "Duh."

"Right, so this compound. Where exactly . . ." My words trailed off as the ground started swaying. Or was it me weaving from side to side? And was everything getting dimmer because the flashlight was dying, or was it my eyes that had stopped working?

"No. No, I am *not* going to faint."

"Um . . . okay?"

I shook my head. "Did I say that out loud?"

Izzy rose to her feet slowly. "You don't look so good."

I would have glared at her if my eyes hadn't been involved in more important things like not falling out of my skull. A loud chattering noise filled my head, and I realized it was my teeth.

Great. I was going into shock. That was just . . . *so* inconvenient.

My knees started to give, and I held onto the sword's handle even tighter, trying hard to stay on my feet. *Archer's sword*, I told myself. *You can't pass out because you have to find him and help him. . . .*

But it was too late. I was slipping to the ground, and Izzy had turned around, obviously looking for the knife.

Suddenly, I noticed a faint glow coming from some-where behind me. Confused, I started to turn toward it, figuring it was probably a Brannick hunting party. And then I felt a powerful, almost electric buzz shoot through me. I recognized it immediately.

Magic.

I stood completely still, disoriented. Had my powers just—but no. Whatever was flowing through me, it didn't feel like *my* magic. I'd always felt my powers shoot up through my feet, rushing from the ground. This magic felt like something light and cold settling on top of my head. Like snow.

Like Elodie's magic.

*That's because it* is *my magic, moron,* Elodie's voice sneered inside my head.

"What?" I tried to say. But my mouth wouldn't move. One of my arms lifted from my side, but I wasn't moving it, either. And I certainly didn't shoot a golden bolt of power from my fingertips into Izzy's back.

Shrieking, Izzy tumbled to the ground.

I walked forward, the sword lifted high, but again, it was like I was a puppet. I could feel the grooved metal of the sword's hilt in my hands, and the pain in my shoulders from the strain of lifting it, but I had no control over what I was doing.

Izzy had managed to get to her feet and was stumbling

18

away from me. She backed into a tree with a thump, and I watched as I placed the tip of the blade at her throat.

Even as I began to wig out inside my own head, I could feel Elodie's triumph blazing through me.

*Get out!* I screamed silently. *I wouldn't even want to share a dorm room with you, much less my body.*

*No way,* was Elodie's only reply.

"I'm super over you right now," I heard myself snarl to Izzy. "So you can either tell me where my mom is, or I can shish kebab you. Your choice."

Izzy was panting, and there were tears pooling in her big green eyes.

*She's like, twelve, Elodie,* I thought.

*Whatever,* Elodie replied. I could practically hear the eye-roll in her voice.

"I—" Izzy said, her eyes darting to look somewhere over my shoulder.

I tried to turn my head to look, but Elodie kept my gaze riveted on Izzy.

"You know," I said, feeling my lips curve into a smirk, "a Brannick killed by a demon with one of L'Occhio di Dio's swords. There's something kind of delicious about that, don't you think?"

*There is something behind me, you crazy person!* I shouted inwardly. *Stop doing the creepy villain thing, and look!*

But Elodie ignored me.

I was still studying Izzy's face when her look of terror suddenly crumpled into relief. I wasn't sure which emotion was stronger, my panic or Elodie's confusion, both of which I could feel welling up from my stomach.

And then both feelings were eclipsed by an enormous bolt of pain as something crashed into the back of my skull.

# CHAPTER 3

I was dead. That was really the only explanation I had for the sensation that I was lying in a comfy bed, cool, clean-smelling sheets pulled up to my chin, and a soft hand stroking my hair.

That was nice. Being dead seemed pretty sweet, all things considered. Especially if it meant I got to nap for all eternity. I snuggled deeper into the covers. The hand on my hair moved to my back, and I realized someone was singing softly. The voice was familiar, and something about it made my chest ache. Well, that was to be expected. Angels' songs would be awfully poignant.

"'I was working as a waitress in a cocktail bar, when I met you . . .'" the voice crooned.

I frowned. Was that really an appropriate song for the Heavenly Host to be—

Realization crashed into me. "Mom!" I cried, sitting up. That was a mistake, because as soon as I did, agony exploded through my head.

Gentle hands eased me back onto the pillows, and suddenly she was there. Mom, leaning over me, her face etched with worry and streaked with tears, but looking so beautiful that I wanted to cry, too.

"This is real, right?" I asked, glancing around the room. It was tiny and dim, and smelled faintly woodsy, like cedar. Other than the bed and the cane-back chair next to it, it was completely bare. Bright golden-red light came in the one window, so I knew it was early evening. "This isn't a dream or some kind of concussion-related hallucination?"

I felt Mom's arm around my shoulders. Her lips were warm against my temple. "I'm here, sweetie," she murmured. "Really here."

And then I did cry. A lot. Big, wrenching sobs that hurt. Through them, I tried to tell Mom about everything that had happened at Thorne, but I knew I wasn't making any sense.

When the storm had finally passed, I lay against Mom, taking deep, shaking breaths. Tears were running down her face, too, wetting the top of my head. "Okay," I finally said. "That's the story of my crappy summer vacation. Your turn."

Mom sighed and hugged me tighter. "Oh, Soph," she

said in a very small voice, "I don't even know where to begin."

"Where are we?" I asked. "That's a pretty good starting place."

"At the Brannick compound."

Everything came back to me then. Izzy, and the sword, and Elodie turning my body into a murderous puppet.

*Elodie?* I asked silently. *You still there?*

But there was no reply. I was the only person in my head for now. Speaking of which . . .

"What happened to my head?"

"Finley—that's Izzy's older sister—went out looking for her. Izzy said you attacked her with your powers. I thought you said you couldn't do magic anymore."

"I can't," I said. "It's . . . I'll explain it later. So Finley cracked me over the head with what? A baseball bat? A Mack truck?"

"A flashlight," Mom answered, her fingers delicately parting my hair over what felt like a basketball-sized lump on the back of my head.

We were quiet then, both of us knowing what I was going to ask next: why in the heck was my mom, who'd spent most of her life running from All Things Magic, spending her summer vacay with a bunch of monster hunters?

But something told me that whatever her answer was, it was going to be complicated. And probably unpleasant. And even though I was dying to know what had brought her here, we could get to it later, preferably when my brain wasn't threatening to launch itself out of my skull.

"It was hot," I said. There are few topics less complicated and unpleasant than weather, right? "Outside. Where exactly is the Brannicks' place?"

"Tennessee," Mom answered.

"Okay, well that's . . . Wait, Tennessee?" I sat up to look at Mom. "I used the Itineris to travel from England to here. It's this magic portal thingie," I started to explain, but she was nodding like she already knew. "Anyway, I left Thorne at night, and I got *here* at night, so I couldn't have gone that far."

Mom was watching me very carefully. "Sophie," she said, and something in her voice made my stomach go icy. "Thorne Abbey burned down nearly three weeks ago."

I stared at her. "That's impossible. I was there. I was there last night,"

Shaking her head, Mom reached out and cupped my cheek. "Sweetheart, it's been seventeen days since we got word of what happened at Thorne. I thought . . ." Her voice cracked. "I thought you'd been captured or killed. When Finley brought you in tonight, it was like a miracle."

My mind was reeling.

Seventeen days.

I remembered stepping into the Itineris, remembered the crushing, still blackness. But I'd only felt it for a moment or two before I'd found myself flat on my back in the woods. How had *seventeen days* passed in the space of a few heartbeats?

Then another thought occurred to me. "If it's been that long since Thorne burned down, you must have heard something about Dad. Or Cal, or the Casnoffs."

"They're all gone," a voice said from across the room.

I whipped my head around, wincing as I did. A woman leaned against the doorframe, holding a steaming mug. She was wearing jeans and plain black T-shirt, and her red hair, darker than Izzy's, fell over her shoulder in a long braid.

"Vanished off the face of the earth," she continued, moving into the room. Beside me, I could feel Mom stiffen. "James Atherton, the warlock boy, the *other* warlock boy, those Casnoff witches, and their pet demon. We figured you disappeared with them until you showed up trying to kill my daughter."

I'd guessed this badass woman was Aislinn Brannick. Still, actually having her in front of me sent my stomach somewhere south of my knees. I cleared my throat. "In my defense, she pulled a knife first," I said.

To my surprise, Aislinn made a rusty sound that might have been a chuckle. She handed me the mug. "Drink this."

"Um, how 'bout, no," I replied, staring at the dark green contents. Whatever the liquid was, it smelled like pine trees and dirt, and seeing how this woman was Izzy's mom, I figured it was poisoned.

But Aislinn just shrugged. "Don't, then. No skin off my nose if your head hurts."

"It's okay," Mom said, never taking her eyes off Aislinn. "It'll make you feel better."

"By making me dead?" I asked. "I mean, I'm sure that would make my headache go away, but that's a heck of a side effect."

"Sophie," Mom murmured, a warning tone in her voice.

But Aislinn just regarded me shrewdly, a tiny smile playing on her lips. "She's got a mouth on her, that's for sure," she said. Her eyes flicked to Mom. "Must've gotten that from him. You were always quiet."

I looked to Mom, confused, but she was still watching Aislinn Brannick, her face pale.

"You need to get downstairs in five minutes," Aislinn said, moving to stand at the foot of the bed. "Family meeting."

I took a very hesitant sip from the warm mug. It tasted

even worse than it smelled, but as soon as it slid down my throat, I felt some of the pain in my skull recede. Closing my eyes, I leaned back against the headboard. "Why do you need us for that?" I asked. "Can't you guys just . . . Brannick it up without us?"

A heavy silence fell over the room, and when I opened my eyes, Mom and Aislinn were staring at one another.

"She doesn't know?" Aislinn asked at last, and a mix of dread and anger rose up in my chest. I didn't want to deal with this. I wasn't ready to deal with this, not yet.

But when Mom turned to me, I knew. I saw it in the fear and sadness on her face, in the way her hands were clutching the blanket. And I knew that whether I wanted to face it or not, there was a very simple reason for why she was here.

Still, I heard myself ask, "Mom?"

But it was Aislinn answered. "Your mother is a Brannick, Sophia. Which makes you one of us, too."

# CHAPTER 4

When the door clicked shut behind Aislinn, Mom lowered her face into her hands with a shuddery exhale. I downed the rest of the drink Aislinn had given me. Instantly, my head felt better. In fact, everything felt better, and I felt almost . . . perky, even though my mouth felt like I'd just licked a pine tree.

But the gross taste in my mouth was fine. That gave me something to focus on other than the fact that basically everything in my life had been a lie. Or that I'd somehow lost seventeen days. Or that I'd had a ghost inside of my body.

Suddenly, I missed Jenna so much that it was almost a physical ache. I wanted to hold her hand, and hear her say something that would make this whole situation funny instead of incredibly screwed up.

Archer would've been nice, too. He probably would've raised an eyebrow in that annoying/hot way he had, and made a dirty joke about Elodie possessing me.

Or Cal. He wouldn't say anything, but just his presence would make me feel better. And Dad—

"Sophie," Mom said, shaking me out of my reverie. "I don't . . . I don't even know how to start explaining all of this to you." She looked at me, her eyes red. "I meant to, so many times, but everything was always so . . . complicated. Do you hate me?"

I took a deep breath. "Of course not. I mean, I'm not *thrilled*. And I totally reserve the right to angst over all this later. But honestly, Mom? Right now, I'm so happy to see you that I wouldn't care if you're secretly a ninja sent from the future to destroy kittens and rainbows."

She chuckled, a choked and watery sound. "I missed you so much, Soph."

We hugged, my face against her collarbone. "I want the whole story, though," I said, my words muffled. "All of it on the table."

She nodded. "Absolutely. After we talk to Aislinn."

Pulling back, I grimaced. "So how exactly are you related to her? Are you guys like, cousins?"

"We're sisters."

I stared at her. "Wait. So you're like, a *Brannick* Brannick? But you don't even have red hair."

Mom got off the bed, twisting her ponytail into a bun. "It's called dye, Soph. Now, come on. Aislinn is already in a mood."

"Yeah, picked up on that," I muttered, shoving the covers off and standing up.

Mom and I left the bedroom and headed out to the dim landing. There was only one other room on this floor, and I suddenly found myself thinking of Thorne Abbey and all its corridors and chambers. It was still hard to believe a place that massive could just be . . . gone.

We headed down a narrow flight of stairs that ended at a low arch. Beyond the arch was yet another murky room. Did these people have something against overhead lighting?

I spotted an ancient green refrigerator, and a round wooden table positioned under a grimy window. The smell of coffee hung in the air and there was a half-finished sandwich on the counter, but the kitchen was empty. "They must be in the War Room," Mom said, almost to herself.

"Hold up; did you just say 'War Room'?" I asked, but Mom had already moved past the kitchen and was rounding a corner. I trudged after her, trying to get a sense of the house. The main word that came to mind was "spartan." At Thorne, there had been so much stuff—paintings, tapestries, knickknacks, freakin' suits of armor—that your

30

eyes couldn't process all of it. Here, it was like everything that wasn't completely necessary had been stripped away. Heck, even some things that *were* necessary seemed to be missing. I hadn't seen a bathroom yet.

There were no windows, just several fluorescent bulbs affixed to the ceiling, throwing a sickly light over everything. And by "everything," I mean the one dingy brown couch, some metal folding chairs, a couple of overflowing bookshelves, some cardboard boxes, and a huge, round table covered in papers.

Oh, and the weapons.

There were all kinds of scary instruments of death littered from one end of the room to the other. Next to the couch, I counted three crossbows, and there was a pile of what looked like those throwing star thingies on top of one of the bookcases.

Izzy was sitting cross-legged on the couch, a paperback book in her hands. She didn't look up when we came in, and I wondered what she was reading that had her so absorbed. *Monster Killing for Beginners*, probably.

The only other people in the room were Aislinn and a girl who looked around my age. When Mom and I walked through the door, both their heads shot up from a book they were studying. I saw a Maglite tucked into a holster around the girl's waist. So this was Finley, Wielder of Flashlights. I rubbed the crown of my head, and she scowled at me.

I turned to look at my quiet, bookish mother, a woman I had honestly never seen swat a fly. "I'm sorry, but there is no way you grew up here. It's not even possible."

There was a whirring sound, and I felt something pass by my face. Out of the corner of my eye, I saw Mom's hand go up, and suddenly she was holding the hilt of a knife—a knife that had apparently just been hurled at her head. The whole thing had happened in less than a second.

I swallowed. "Never mind."

Mom didn't say anything, but kept her gaze focused on Aislinn, who, I noticed, still had one hand slightly raised. She was smiling. "Grace was always the quickest of all of us," she said, and I realized she was talking to me. Smiling *at me.*

"Okay," I finally said. "Well, I didn't get that from her, in case you're wondering. I can't even catch a football."

Aislinn chuckled, even as Finley's scowl deepened.

"So you're the demon spawn," Finley spit out.

"Finn!" Aislinn snapped. Huh. So at least one of the Brannicks hated me. Weirdly, that made me feel better. That was normal. And if there was one thing I knew how to deal with, it was Mean Girls.

"I actually go by Sophie."

From the couch, I heard a snort of laughter, and we

all turned to look at Izzy. She covered her mouth and tried to turn it into a cough, but Finley still jerked her head and said, "Go on to your room, Iz."

Izzy closed the book and laid it on her lap, and I was surprised to see that it was *To Kill a Mockingbird*. "Finn," she protested. "I wasn't laughing like, *with* her." Izzy glowered at me. "She tried to kill me."

"Actually, I didn't," I broke in. There was a hard look in Aislinn's and Finley's eyes that scared the heck out of me. The last thing I wanted was to be held responsible for Elodie's actions, especially now that I was, technically, one of these women, and the words just came pouring out of my mouth. "See, I don't have powers anymore, because I was supposed to go through the Removal, and that sort of locked my magic away so that I can't use it. But there was this girl—well, this witch—Elodie, and because she passed her magic on to me when she died, we're connected. That means her ghost follows me around and stuff, so when you attacked me, she possessed my body. Which is new and, quite frankly, super freaky, and something that I haven't really processed yet. Anyway, *she* was the one who used magic on you. Oh, and held the sword to your throat, and said all that creepy stuff. I'm not creepy. At least not on purpose."

By now, all three Brannick women—all four, if you counted Mom—were staring at me. Man, what had that piney-tasting stuff been? The Brannick version of Red Bull?

"I'll, uh, stop talking now."

Aislinn wasn't smiling anymore. In fact, she looked kind of horrified. Finley leaned one hip against the table and crossed her arms. "What do you mean, you don't have powers anymore?"

I tried very, very hard not to roll my eyes. "I mean exactly what I said. I had powers, then the Council—they're the people who make all the rules for Prodigium," I explained, only to have Finley roll *her* eyes, and say, "Yeah, we know that."

"Awesome for you," I muttered. "So they did this ritual that didn't . . . well, it wasn't as intense as the Removal. My magic isn't gone forever." At least, I hoped it wasn't. But I didn't say that to the Brannicks.

Aislinn and Finley glanced at each other. "But for all intents and purposes," Aislinn said, "you're human."

"Except for when Elodie's ghost possesses me, yup."

I thought that would make them happy; after all, didn't they hate Prodigium? But Aislinn gripped the edge of the table with both hands and dropped her head with a long sigh. Finley laid a hand on her shoulder, and murmured, "It's okay, Mom. We'll figure it out."

My own mom rubbed my back, and said quietly, "Oh, honey. I'm so sorry."

I felt that urge to fall on the floor and start sobbing rise up, so I shrugged and said, "Hey, I went to London to get my powers taken away. It just didn't turn out the way I thought. But no tattoos, so score."

Aislinn pounded one of her fists on the table, and when she lifted her head, she suddenly looked every inch the Scary Prodigium Hunter.

"We are at war. Your kind is in the process of unleashing hell on the world, and you're making jokes?"

I didn't know what had brought on the sudden shift from Smiley Aislinn to Seriously Pissed-off Aislinn. I met her gaze and said, "In the past few hours, I've been possessed, nearly had my head caved in, and found out my mom is secretly a Prodigium hunter. And before that, I lost just about everyone else I care about, and discovered that people I trusted are secretly demon-raising creeps. My life sucks pretty hard right now. So, yeah. I'm making jokes."

"You're useless to us now," Finley said.

"I'm sorry, how exactly was I useful to you before?" I asked, even though I had a feeling I already knew.

Sure enough, Finley met my gaze and said, "You heard Mom. We're at war. And you were supposed to be our weapon."

# CHAPTER 5

I stared at her. "And you guys thought I would do that, why, exactly?"

"Torin said you'd fight for—" Izzy interjected, but Aislinn held up her hand.

"Enough, Isolde," she said. "It doesn't matter now, anyway."

"It matters to me," I said. "Who the heck is Torin? And what were you gonna do, use me like your very own magic bomb?" Mom's arm tightened around my shoulders. I shrugged her off and walked to the table to face Aislinn.

"That's what they wanted to do, you know," I told her. "The Casnoffs." My voice wavered a little as I thought about Nick and Daisy, the two demon kids I'd . . . well, *befriended* was a strong word—I'd gotten to know at Thorne Abbey. The last time I'd seen Daisy, she'd demoned out and tried to kill me, all thanks to Lara Casnoff. Same with Nick, who attacked Archer and nearly killed him. Because Lara had turned them into demons, Nick and Daisy were under her control.

There was a part of me that missed them, weird and homicidal as they'd been, which was probably why my voice got louder when I added, "The Casnoffs and the other members of the Council want to use demons to fight you and The Eye."

Aislinn didn't seem angry anymore. Just defeated. She ran a hand through her hair. "Is that really what you think, Sophie? That they're raising demons to keep mon—your kind safe?"

"I . . . yeah, I guess so. I mean, they were always saying you were going to kill us all."

A weird look crossed Aislinn's face, almost like she felt sorry for me. Finley gave a disgusted sound. "Right. The only reason those Casnoff chicks want to make demons is so that they'll have their own secret service. Having their very own demon army wouldn't be convenient or anything."

Thankfully one of those folding chairs was pretty close by, so I was able to sink into it.

"I don't get it," I said, looking over my shoulder at Mom.

Her mouth was set in a grim line. "Let's just say the Brannicks have never believed that Lara and Anastasia's father, Alexei, was so interested in creating demons to protect other Prodigium. That much power? He basically had the equivalent of a magical nuclear weapon under his control."

Alexei, with the help of another witch, had turned my great-grandmother, Alice, into a demon. She'd been just a regular girl, but once Alexei Casnoff was done with her, she'd become more or less a monster, the dark magic inside of her driving her insane.

So, yeah, you could create a demon, but controlling it wasn't that easy.

"The first night I ever spent at Hex Hall," I said to Aislinn, "Mrs. Casnoff showed us this big slide show of all the ways humans had killed Prodigium over the years. Not just Brannicks or The Eye, but regular people, too. Mrs. Casnoff basically made it seem like we Prodigium are under attack all the time."

"Yeah, because regular people stand a chance against monsters," Finley scoffed.

"Do you know how many Brannicks there are, Sophie?" Aislinn asked softly. When I shook my head, she said, "You're looking at them."

I stared at her. "What, just . . . just the three of you? And one of you is like, twelve?"

"I'm fourteen," Izzy called from the couch, but no one paid any attention.

"Four when we had your mother," Aislinn replied.

"Okay, but you've teamed up with The Eye," I said. A few months ago, the Prodigium Council Headquarters in London had burned down. Seven members of the Council had been killed, and according to Dad, it was L'Occhio di Dio working with the Brannicks.

Aislinn just laughed. "The Eye? Team up with us? There's no way. Our family is descended from a witch, remember? The Eye wants no part of that."

"So, what—The Eye attacked Council headquarters by themselves?" I asked.

"They didn't attack it at all," Finley said. "That was all your buddies, the Casnoffs."

I felt like I'd just been plunged into Bizarro World, and I shook my head again, like that would somehow make my brain work faster. "But why would the Casnoffs—" And then it dawned on me. "It's just like the slide show thing. Make everyone even more freaked out about The Eye and the Brannicks, and suddenly no one cares that you're turning kids into demons. Not if demons will keep them safe from The Eye, or all of you," I said, gesturing toward Aislinn and Finley.

Aislinn nodded. "Exactly. And now they've laid the destruction of Thorne Abbey and the possible death of your father on The Eye, too."

My chest ached at that, and I felt Mom's hand on my hair.

"So now it's like the Casnoffs have free rein to raise as many demons as they want," Finley said. "And no one will stop them."

"I will," I said automatically.

"How?" Finley scoffed. "You don't have any powers. They have the most potent magical weapons ever."

Inside my chest, my magic surged and shook. "We're people," I said, and to my horror, I felt tears spring to my eyes. I really, really did not want to cry in front of Finley. "Raising a demon just means pouring really dark magic into the soul of a regular person, or Prodigium, or whatever. That person, who they are, doesn't go away. Nick and Daisy. And me and my—my dad. We're not things you can use and destroy. We're not weapons." On that last word, I grabbed the edge of the table so hard, I broke one of my fingernails.

Mom stepped forward, wrapping her hand around my elbow. "Enough," she said. "The point is, we'll find some way of stopping the Casnoffs that doesn't involve using Sophie as anything."

"That isn't your decision, Grace," Aislinn said.

Mom whirled on her sister with a fierceness I'd never seen in her before. "She is my *daughter*."

"And we don't always get to pick the paths our family members take, do we?" Aislinn replied, holding Mom's gaze.

A low chuckle reverberated throughout the room, and the hair on the back of my neck stood up. Izzy jumped, and both Finley and Aislinn turned to glare over their shoulders. For the first time, I saw there was something hanging on the wall. I wasn't sure what exactly, because it was covered with a heavy piece of dark green canvas, but from its large, rectangular shape, I guessed it was a painting of some kind.

"Ah, Grace and Aislinn arguing. It's like old times again," a male voice said, sounding vaguely muffled. "Could someone take this blasted thing off so that I can see?"

Once again, my magic was thumping and bumping inside me, so I knew whatever was speaking, it wasn't human. Still, when Aislinn crossed over to the thing hanging on the wall and ripped down the canvas, I was taken aback by what I saw.

It wasn't a painting after all; it was a mirror, reflecting the dingy, gloomy room. It was weird seeing the tableau we made. Mom stood with her hand still on my elbow, her expression wary. Aislinn was looking at the mirror with something like disgust, while Izzy had gone even paler, and Finley was scowling. As for me, I was shocked by my reflection. I was thinner than I remembered being, and my skin was dirty, tears leaving trails on my dusty cheeks. And the hair . . . you know what? Let's not even go there.

But my looking like Little Orphan Sophie wasn't what had my powers going nuts. It was the guy.

In the mirror, he was sitting cross-legged in the middle of the round table, smirking out at all of us. Even though I knew he wasn't really there, I glanced at the center of the table anyway. The same maps and papers that were crumpled under him in the mirror were still unruffled and smooth. His shaggy hair was dark blond, and lace dripped from the cuffs of his shirt, brushing the papers on the table as he rested his wrists on his knees. He was also rocking some pretty impressive tall boots and ridiculously tight pants, so he was either way into Renaissance Faires over there in Mirror-Land, or he was very old. I was guessing the latter.

"So this is the girl all the fuss is over," he said, studying me. His voice was low, and I think he would've been hot if he weren't radiating this air of "I Am Super Evil—No, Really—And Not In The Sexy Way." Still, I was pretty sure he was just a regular warlock. Demons gave off a stronger, darker vibe, and while this guy was definitely bad news, he wasn't that dark or that powerful.

Aislinn whacked the frame of the mirror with her

hand, causing the table the guy sat on to rock and nearly tip over. The table in the room stayed still.

Clutching one side of the table, Mirror Boy frowned, then opened his mouth to say something. Aislinn cut him off. "You were wrong, Torin. She doesn't have powers anymore."

Torin shrugged. "Does she not? Well, that certainly makes things more interesting." He smiled. Maybe some women would've found it charming. I just found it skeevy. That must have shown on my face, because his grin quickly collapsed, and he turned back to Aislinn with a shrug. "It's no matter. I'm never wrong. I told you that Thorne Abbey would be consumed in fire, and it was. I told you this girl would be returned to you, and so she has been."

He pointed at Aislinn. The surface of the mirror bowed out around his finger, like a stretchy bubble. "And I told you that you would lose Grace to one of the beasts. No one wanted to believe that one," he said to me. "And yet, here you are. Proof that my prophecies are always correct. And what I told you is true, Aislinn," he added, turning to her. "This girl will stop the Casnoff witches."

A heavy silence fell over the room as we all stared at the guy in the glass, and I tried to wrap my mind around the fact that the Brannicks, witch killers extraordinaire, were listening to a prophecy-spouting warlock, and that said warlock had apparently tapped me to end this big freaking magical war that was brewing. Still, I didn't like my dad being referred to as a "beast," so I tried my best to look disdainful as I stood up.

"You guys have a magic mirror? You should've mentioned that earlier," I said to Izzy. "I mean, that's way cooler than barbed wire and bunkers."

"It isn't a magic mirror," Izzy replied, and I couldn't help but notice the way her eyes never moved from Torin. "He's our prisoner."

"Guest," Torin snapped, but everyone ignored him.

"How did you manage to trap a warlock when you don't use magic?" I asked.

"The Brannicks didn't trap him," Mom answered. "He did that all by himself."

Torin suddenly became very interested in straightening his cuffs, turning his back to us.

"He was attempting a spell that was just a little too big for him," Finley added. "Ended up stuck in there, back in 1589."

"1587," Torin corrected. "And the spell was in no way 'too big' for me. It was just . . . trickier than I'd expected."

Finley snorted. "Sure. Anyway, Avis Brannick found him . . . it, whatever, a few years later, and brought the mirror back to the rest of the family."

"When Avis discovered that Torin had the power of

prophecy, she realized he could be a useful tool. We've been his guardians ever since," Aislinn finished up. I wondered if they always told stories in a round like that. It reminded me of the three-way glances that Elodie, Anna, and Chaston used to do, and I felt another one of those weird pangs in my chest. It wasn't as if I'd liked those three, but now one of them was dead and two of them were missing. God only knows what had happened to them.

"They have been corrupted," Torin said, and I startled.

"What?"

"You were just thinking of two witches you knew back at your school, wondering what happened to them," he said. For the first time, I realized his eyes were so dark brown, they were nearly black. "You suspect the Casnoff women turned them into demons. They did."

"Wait, so you don't just tell the future? You know other stuff, too?"

He nodded, pleased with himself. "I know many things, Sophia Mercer. And you have so many questions, don't you? Where were you for those seventeen days? Whatever became of your little bloodsucker friend and your father . . . ?"

Without thinking, I crossed the room to stand right in front of the glass. "Is my dad alive? Is Jenna—"

I broke off as Torin started chuckling and backing

away. "I can't give away all my secrets," he said, spreading his hands wide.

Every ounce of magic inside of me wanted to leap through the glass and blast him into tiny pieces. I settled for just grabbing the frame and shaking it. "Tell me!" I shouted as he fell to the ground, the mirror-table finally turning over, papers spilling onto the floor.

Strong hands gripped my shoulders and pulled me back. I spun around, expecting to see Aislinn holding me, but it was Mom. "Cover that damn thing back up," Mom said to her sister. As Aislinn draped the canvas back over the mirror, Mom smoothed my hair away from my face. "We're going to find your dad, sweetheart. And Jenna." She shot a glare at the now-covered mirror. "And we're not going to use Torin to do it." Her eyes swung to Aislinn. "We never should have started listening to him in the first place."

"We don't have many choices left, Grace," Aislinn said. She sounded tired.

Whatever had been in that green drink was starting to wear off, and I could feel weariness seeping back into my bones. I was just about to ask if I could go back up to my room when Aislinn sighed and said, "We can talk about all of this later. It's nearly sunset." She motioned to Finley and Izzy. "Come on girls, time for patrol."

Without a word, the two younger Brannicks headed

for the door. I watched them go, and was plotting when I could sneak back in here to have a word (or a thousand) with Torin when Aislinn clamped a hand on my shoulder. "You too, Sophia."

"What?"

"All Brannicks under eighteen are required to patrol the grounds during evening shift."

She handed me something, and it took me a few seconds to realize what it was: a silver stake. I blinked at Aislinn, not understanding. She grinned, and it was terrifying.

"Welcome to the family."

# CHAPTER 6

"So neither massive head injuries, *nor* finding out you're a member of this family thirty freaking minutes ago—and therefore have *very little experience* handling weapons— gets you out of patrol?" I asked as I met Finley and Izzy by the backdoor.

After Aislinn had made her announcement, Mom had tried to argue on my behalf, saying that A) I was still processing the whole "being a Brannick" thing, and B) I had gone through a lot, so maybe I could use a nap. Or a snack.

Aislinn's answer was to give me ten minutes to take a shower, some of Finley's clothes, and a flask full of that Pine-Sol–tasting liquid. The shower had helped, even if it had been lukewarm; and while the clothes were both a little too long and a little too tight, I was happy to be out of my grimy, smoky stuff from Thorne Abbey. I slipped the silver stake into one of my belt loops and hoped it wouldn't sever an artery. Then I'd taken a few sips of the green stuff before heading downstairs, and while it still tasted awful, I was feeling better.

I took another hesitant swallow now as Izzy snorted and said, "I'm pretty sure decapitation wouldn't get us out of patrol."

I smiled, which earned me a glare from Finley. "I know it must be an adjustment after having faeries, or whatever, do your dirty work for you, but this is how we do things here," she said, shoving a black backpack at me.

"Please. You must never have met a faerie if you think they do *anything* dirty," I replied.

"We've met plenty of faeries," Finley snapped, but her shoulders were up around her ears, and Izzy shot her a curious look. Whatever. I had enough family drama of my own to deal with. But then I reminded myself that technically, Izzy and Finley *were* my family. Demons on one side, Prodigium hunters on the other. Was it any wonder I was so screwed up?

Finley turned to face the door, which was bolted with several different locks. I watched her spin the dial on two, open another with a key she wore around her neck, and unhook a latch at the top.

"Man, I bet it takes you forever to get into your

49

locker," I joked, but Izzy shook her head.

"We don't go to school," she said, and there was something so serious and mournful in her voice that I didn't have the heart to tell her I'd only been kidding.

Finley pressed her shoulder against the door, and it opened with an ominous creak. We stepped outside and into what appeared to be a playground designed by ninjas. There were two balance beams, both at least six feet above the ground. There was also a pull-up bar and a heavy iron cage at the very edge of the clearing. Near that, several targets were set up. I spotted arrows stuck in one, some gnarly knives in another, and throwing stars in the third.

Trees circled the clearing, and just beyond them, I could make out a few other structures. Following my gaze, Izzy nodded toward them and said, "Tents. They built this place back in the thirties, when there were still lots of Brannicks. They used to have gatherings here. That's what we called the big Brannick meet—"

"Shut up, Iz," Finley said, walking away from us. "She's not a freaking Brannick, so don't tell her all of our stuff, okay?"

For the record, she didn't really say "stuff." Or "freaking" for that matter. A few months ago I probably would've had a snotty comeback for her, but I decided to let this one go. I turned back to ask Izzy more about the Brannicks, and as I did, the setting sun glared off the small emerald pendant around her neck. Suddenly, the image of Jenna's shattered bloodstone flashed in my mind, and I made myself shove it away. Still, something must've shown on my face, because Izzy said, "She's normally not like that. Well, I mean, she *is*, but the bad words are a new thing."

I kind of wanted to ruffle her hair, but something told me she wouldn't take that very well. So instead, I just shrugged and said, "It wasn't that. I was just thinking about . . . Forget it. Anyway, I get why Finley isn't in the best of moods."

The setting sun burned brightly off Finley's copper hair as she stalked across the clearing and disappeared into the trees. Izzy and I followed, and I slung my backpack over my shoulder. It clanked, and I glanced at Izzy. "So what exactly does 'patrolling' entail?"

She shrugged. "Making sure the woods are clean of supes."

"Why would there be soup in—oh, 'supes'? Like for 'supernaturals'? Is that what you guys call us?"

Izzy didn't turn around, and it could have just been a trick of the light, but I thought the tips of her ears pinkened. "It's just something I made up," she mumbled, and I was very glad she had her back to me as a smile broke out over my face.

"I like that."

She spun around then, and I made sure my expression was deadly serious. "I mean it," I told her. "You know what we call ourselves, right? Prodigium." I made a derisive snort. "The only thing lamer and more pretentious than Latin is made-up Latin."

Izzy watched me for a moment and apparently decided I wasn't making fun of her, because she gave a little nod. For the first time, I saw that she had a cluster of freckles across the bridge of her nose, just like I did.

I'd lost sight of Finley by now, but Izzy seemed to know where we were going. For a long time, we made our way through the trees and underbrush in silence. Even though the sun was nearly down, I was sweating, and I tugged at the neckline of my borrowed black T-shirt. "Do you guys actually get a lot of, um, supes around here? Because in my experience, they don't really like to lurk around forests that surround the home of a bunch of people who want to kill them."

I came to a stop as a memory resurfaced. I'd been so busy freaking out over finding the Brannicks that I'd totally forgotten about the werewolf Izzy and Finley had been chasing. "What happened to that Were last night?" I asked Izzy now.

Izzy turned to me with a grin that reminded me way

too much of her mother. "What do you think we're hunting tonight?"

I twisted and pulled at my backpack until it was in front of me, then opened it. More silver stakes. Little glass bottles of holy water. And, oh my God, was that a *gun*?

My knees were wobbling as I zipped up the Bag O'Death and gingerly dropped it in the grass.

"What's wrong?" Izzy asked.

"Um, a lot? There is seriously so much wrongness going on right now. Namely, the fact that you people *are* teenagers with bags of *guns*."

Izzy stiffened a little at that. "We're not kids," she spit out. "We're Brannicks."

Sighing, I shoved my hands in my pockets. "I get that, but look, Izzy, I can't kill a werewolf. I know werewolves. I lived with some, and they're . . . well, they're gross and slobbery and super scary, but I can't kill one."

I waited for her to whip out a crossbow, or handheld cannon, or whatever other crazy killing implement she was no doubt packing. Instead, she tilted her head and asked, "You lived with werewolves?"

It was almost fully dark now, and I wished I could see her face better. "Yeah," I answered. "At Hex Hall. There were a few of them there. This one girl, Beth, was actually pretty nice. And then there was this kid, Justin, who wasn't much older than you are."

I knelt down to scoop up the bag again, only to have her shock the heck out of me again by asking, "What other kind of supes did you live with?"

Looking up at her, I said, "All kinds. Like I said earlier, faeries—and there were witches and warlocks. My roommate was—" I broke off and gave myself a second to swallow the lump that had risen in my throat. "My roommate was a vampire. Jenna."

"Holy crap," Izzy said, and once again, she sounded like a kid. Especially when she added, "Mom and Finley faced off against a couple of vampires last year. I didn't get to go because they said it was too dangerous. Weren't you scared she was gonna like, drink your blood when you slept?"

My impulse was to immediately defend Jenna, but I remembered how I'd felt that first night in our dorm room, when I'd come in to find her chowing down on a bag of blood. "A little bit. Before I got to know her. But once I did, I was never afraid that she'd hurt me. She was— *is*—my best friend." And then, before I could start crying again and risk death by dehydration, I stood up, holding the backpack out from my body. "Also, it's kind of hard to be scared of a vampire who's barely five feet tall and has pink hair, you know?"

Izzy was quiet for a moment before saying, "Pink hair?"

"Well, not over her whole head, but a stripe—" I said, before the way Izzy had said "pink hair" registered. I thought of all those papers, files, and boxes in the War Room. "Have you heard of her? Have you guys seen her?" I asked, my heart surging in my chest.

"No," another voice snapped, and I turned to see Finley standing behind me. "We haven't heard anything about a pink-haired vamp, and if we had, we'd be going over to England to stake her because that's what we do. Now, let's go."

"You're lying!" I hadn't meant for my voice to be so loud, but it seemed to reverberate through the dark forest. "And if I ever hear the word 'stake' in reference to Jenna again, I will—"

"What?" Finley shouted back. "Push me down? Pull my hair? You don't have powers. We lost everything because of you, and you're *useless*."

"Oh, I'm so sorry my lack of magic is inconvenient to you. And what do you mean you 'lost everything'?"

Finley stepped closer to me, and in the soft glow of the moonlight, I could see that her eyes were bright with anger. "There weren't always just three of us. In fact, about seventeen years ago, there were nearly fifty. It still wasn't a lot, but it was *something*." She stopped and rubbed at her nose. "Until the others found out that your mom got knocked up by a demon. My mom was supposed to be the next head of the family, but instead, they kicked her out. They elected some distant cousin to lead them, some chick who wasn't even a direct descendant of Maeve Brannick."

"Okay, well, I'm sorry if your mom didn't get to be Head Brannick-In-Charge or whatever, but all of that happened before we were even born. So I really don't see—"

"Three months after the new leader was elected, she led the entire Brannick family on a raid to the biggest vampire nest in North America. Do I need to spell out what happened next?"

Sick to my stomach, I shook my head.

"It was stupid and pointless, and Mom would've known that," Finley said, nearly spitting her words. "If *your* mom hadn't gotten *my* mom kicked out of the Brannicks, that raid never would've happened. But you know what? When Torin said you'd be the one to stop the Casnoffs, I thought, Hey, maybe there was a point in losing our entire family. At least this freak can do something for us. But you can't. So all those Brannicks died for *nothing*."

I didn't know what to say to any of that. So in the end, I settled on what seemed like the easiest thing. "I'm sorry."

She snorted, and reached down to fumble with

something at her waist. "Whatever. It doesn't matter. Now, let's finish this circuit before—"

She didn't finish her sentence. This time, there was no howl, no crashing through the bushes. There was just a large dark shape, leaping out of the night, and Finley's scream as the werewolf landed on her.

# CHAPTER 7

For a few seconds, everything descended into pandemonium. The werewolf was snarling, Izzy was yelling for Finley, and I had apparently dropped the backpack full of weapons again, since it wasn't in my hands anymore. As stupid as it sounds, I still waited a second, hoping to feel my magic swelling up from the soles of my feet. Would I ever get used to being . . . well, human?

My fingers finally closed over the strap of the bag, but even as I pulled it to me, I wondered just what I was going to do. I'd never fired a gun in my life, and I wasn't sure how exactly to stake something. Finley's and Aislinn's words echoed in my brain: *Useless, useless, useless.*

I glanced up to see Izzy holding the same knife she used on me last night, but as Finley and the Were scuffled in the dirt, Izzy wavered on her feet, obviously unsure of how to go after the creature without hurting Finley. I fished in the bag and drew out a handful of holy water vials. Rising to my feet, I chucked them at the werewolf's back with everything I had in me.

It turned out that wasn't a lot, because only one of the tiny bottles cracked. The others rolled harmlessly off its fur and onto the ground. Still, I got its attention.

It rose off of Finley and spun to face me, big strings of drool dripping from its muzzle.

I gulped as Finley scooted backward.

Last night I'd seen a spark of humanity in the were-wolf's eyes. Tonight, with the full moon rising, it was obviously more animal than human. Still, it didn't attack me. Instead, it lowered its nose and sniffed, cocking its head to the side.

"That's right," I said, wishing my voice wasn't shaking. "You know what I am." I might not be able to use magic, but I knew the Were could still sense I was more than just an ordinary human. "Now, look," I said, very aware of Finley and Izzy staring at me like I was a crazy person. "I know you're scared, and I know these girls have been hunting you. But if you hurt them, you're just going to give more people like them more reasons to want to kill you. So why don't you just, uh, scamper off?"

The Were considered me, and for the space of three breaths, I thought we might all get out of this unscathed.

And then it bared its teeth, a low growl rumbling out of its chest, and I knew I was screwed.

Out of the corner of my eye, I saw Finley loading a bolt in a mini-crossbow, but I knew how fast werewolves could move. There was no way she'd get off a shot before it was on me. And then I saw a bright flash. For a second, I thought maybe Izzy had fired a gun, but then that feeling of anger and pride and . . . *power* flooded through me. My hand lifted, my fingers twisted, and the werewolf froze, a sparkling net of magic holding it in place.

*There!* Elodie's voice exalted in my head, and if I'd been in control of my body, I would've gritted my teeth.

*I appreciate the save, but come on. This body-snatcher thing needs to stop.*

This time, there was no answer, but I felt even more magic pouring down over my head and shoulders. I watched my fingers move again, and the spell holding the werewolf pulsed, sending out blue sparks. And then, with a rush of air, the werewolf vanished.

*Where did it go?* I asked Elodie.

*Another dimension*, she replied, and I wondered how a voice inside my head could sound so flippant.

*What the—* I started to ask, but then I was turning around and facing the Brannick girls.

"Stop being bitchy to Sophie," I heard myself say.

Finley and Izzy looked at each other, then back at

me. "Um, why are you talking about yourself in the third person?" Izzy asked.

But Finley shook her head. "It's not Sophie, Iz," she said. "Remember what she told us? She can only do magic when a ghost possesses her. I'm guessing this is the ghost."

I felt myself nod. "Elodie," my mouth said. "And I'm serious. She's not exactly my favorite person, but she's been through a lot. It's not her fault your stupid club kicked Aislinn out and then got themselves killed. Crap happens." I stepped forward toward Finley, watched as my finger poked her in the chest. "So take your teen angst somewhere else, and cut the girl some slack."

I was speechless. Elodie Parris, defending me? Maybe in all this chaos, hell actually *had* frozen over.

Finley narrowed her eyes at me, but Izzy said, "She saved you, Finn. Before the ghost got in her. She fought a werewolf even though she didn't have any magic or any fighting skills. This ghost seems like kind of a jerk, but maybe . . . maybe she's right."

*See?* Elodie said in my head. *That's how you handle chicks like this.*

*I really don't need you to fight my battles for me,* I replied, and she snorted.

*Oh yeah, you totally had that werewolf.*

I was about to make a sarcastic comment right back,

but before I could, Elodie swooped away. I'd been unconscious the last time she did that, which, it turns out, had been a good thing. Because having a ghost in control of your body suddenly vanish? It's kind of traumatic.

I fell to my hands and knees, gasping at the sensation of having a Band-Aid ripped off my soul. I stayed there, breathing deeply and wondering how I was ever going to stand up again. And then I felt a hand slide under my arm. Izzy was helping me to my feet. Finley took my other arm, and between the two of them, they got me up and moving.

"Thanks," I mumbled.

To my surprise, it was Finley who said, "No problem." Then to Izzy, she added, "Let's get her back to the house."

We stumbled through the dark night. "So do you have any idea where she put the werewolf?" Izzy asked me.

"She said another dimension, so who the heck knows what that means?"

When we arrived at the house, Mom and Aislinn were sitting in the kitchen. They both had coffee mugs, and from the tension that hung in the air, I was guessing they'd been having some kind of intense conversation. As Finley rummaged around in the cabinets for antiseptic— the scratches on her arm looked red and angry—I filled Aislinn in on what had happened.

"That's a very powerful spell," she said, and even though the words *You think?* immediately sprung to mind, I bit them back. "If you can send creatures into other dimensions—" Aislinn continued, but I cut her off.

"I can't. Elodie can. And it's not like she's reliable." That was the nicest way I could think of to say, *Back off with this weapon stuff, because it ain't happening.*

Aislinn sagged back in her chair, the light fading from her eyes. "Right. That's a good point."

Mom said, "Okay, that's enough for tonight. Sophie needs her rest, and I'm sure Finley and Izzy do, too." She glanced around the kitchen. "Speaking of, where is Izzy?"

Finley winced as she patted her bandage into place. "She probably went upstairs already."

We all said good night then, bringing an end to what might have been the most bizarre twenty-four hours of my life (which said *a lot*). Aislinn told me I could keep the bedroom I'd been in earlier, and after hugging Mom—who was apparently going to stay downstairs to finish her discussion with Aislinn—I trudged back up the dimly lit staircase to my room.

Izzy was standing outside my door, a folder clutched in one hand. "Hey," she said, sounding a little sheepish.

"Hey. Look, Izzy, I'm really beat, so whatever you want to talk about—"

"Here," she said, thrusting the folder into my hands.

"I just . . . I wanted to say thank you. For trying to save Finley and for . . . I don't know. Being nicer to us than you had to be."

I smiled at her, and for a second, we did that "are we gonna hug?" dance, both of us moving in and out, our arms held at our sides. Good to know awkwardness apparently ran in the family. In the end, we just kind of patted each other's shoulders before Izzy went back downstairs, and I headed into my room.

I leaned against the door as I opened the folder Izzy had given me. That ended up being a good thing, because as soon as I saw what was inside, my knees gave out. I slid down the door, one hand over my mouth as tears flooded my eyes.

There were only two things in the folder. One was a grainy color photograph that looked like it was some kind of surveillance shot. The other was a piece of paper with a few lines typed on it. The photograph showed a vampire I knew well—Lord Byron. Yes, the poet. He'd been a teacher at Hex Hall, and once he'd left the school, I'd seen him at a club in London. And now here he was, strolling down a street, a scowl on his face. But he wasn't alone.

Jenna was walking next to him, looking nervously over her shoulder at something. She was thinner than normal, and paler, if that was even possible. But there was no mistaking that bright pink stripe. I ran my fingers over her image before looking at the paper.

*New vampire joined Lord Byron's nest,* the note read. *Female, age TBD, possibly one Jennifer Talbot.*

There was a date under that. Taking into account those three weeks I'd missed, the picture was taken less than a week ago.

Jenna was safe. Jenna was safe and not burned up. She was with Byron, who may have been a total jerk, but who would take good care of her.

I closed my eyes and hugged the picture tight to my chest. If Jenna was alive, then maybe Dad, Archer, and Cal were, too.

# CHAPTER 8

The next morning, Izzy took me on a tour of the compound. As promised, there was barbed wire and bunkers, but the main thing I took away from the place was how still and barren it was.

"We've always lived here, and the other Brannicks used it as sort of a halfway house. They came here for extra training, for strategy sessions, whatever," Izzy told me as we walked through the basement. There were a couple of cots down there, all covered with the same scratchy-looking blue blankets. Fluorescent lights buzzed overhead.

"Where's your dad?" I asked her, sitting down cross-legged on a cot. "I mean, you obviously have one."

Izzy fidgeted with her hair. "He's hunting supes on his own. Boys aren't allowed to live with Brannicks.

They just come for, uh, visits and stuff. We usually see him every three months or so."

"That's very . . . Amazon Woman of you."

She sat down next to me and began picking at the blanket. "It sucks," she muttered.

I caught myself going to take her hand and then pulling back at the last second. "Thank you for Jenna's picture," I said, changing the subject.

Blushing, Izzy suddenly became very interested in one of her nails. "It was nothing. When you said pink hair, I remembered that picture we'd gotten in last week, and I figured it was her."

"I don't guess you happen to have any other pictures lying around?" I was so relieved to know that Jenna was okay, but that didn't lessen the hollow feeling in my stomach whenever I thought about my dad, Cal, and Archer.

Izzy shook her head. "No, that one came in from a friend of Mom's that specializes in hunt—um, keeping up with vampires." She ducked her head, looking up at me from underneath her bangs. "You're still really worried about your dad, aren't you?"

My voice was a little strangled when I replied, "Yeah. I am. I'm actually worried about a lot of people. Do you think . . . That dude in the mirror, Torin. Would he really know where my dad is?"

Something flickered across Izzy's face, and she pulled back a little. "Maybe. But he'll just say a bunch of smart-ass stuff before *maybe* telling you anything real. That's what he does."

Standing, I said, "I think I can hold my own in smart-assery." I jogged up the basement steps, determined to go have a little word with Mirror Boy. Until I knew that all the people I cared about were safe, I couldn't even begin to wrap my mind around this whole Casnoff thing.

But when I got to the War Room, Mom was inside, leaning against the big table, arms crossed, facing Torin. Whatever they'd been talking about, they stopped as soon as I entered. I didn't like the expressions on either of their faces.

"Um, hey," I said, rapping my knuckles on the doorframe. "I was actually just coming to talk to you."

"Okay," Mom said, but I shook my head.

"Not you. I mean, we definitely need to talk, but first, I want to talk to *you*." I pointed at Torin.

He grinned at me. "Certainly. Although I'm guessing that your inquiries are the same as your mother's. Where is James, is he alive, is there any way to reach him . . ."

"You were asking him about Dad?"

Mom threw a dirty look at Torin. "I was. Not that it's doing much good. I'd forgotten just how annoying you were."

Still smiling, Torin rested his chin in his hand and said, "You know, if you'd just release me from this bloody mirror, I could go get James myself. Providing he isn't burnt to a crisp, of course."

I clenched my fists and called him a word I had never, ever said in front of my mom, but she didn't seem particularly offended. Instead, she muttered, "Agreed," and with a flick of her wrist, dropped the canvas covering the mirror.

"He's useless most of the time," Mom said, rubbing the back of her neck. The lines of worry around her mouth were even deeper. "Aislinn should've gotten rid of him years ago."

"I heard that!" Torin cried, his voice muffled by the canvas.

Mom rolled her eyes. "Do you want to get out of here for a little bit?"

I hesitated. What I'd *wanted* to do was talk to Torin, but I knew there was a lot of stuff Mom and I needed to hash out. Besides, it wasn't like Mirror Boy was going anywhere. "Sure."

We ended up going for a walk. It was weird how pretty and nonthreatening the forest around the Brannick compound looked in the daytime. For a long time, we were quiet. It wasn't until we reached the trunk of a huge tree, arching over a trickle of water too tiny to even be called a creek, that Mom said anything. "This used to be my favorite place to come and think. Back when I was your age."

"I bet you had a lot to think about back then."

She chuckled, but there was nothing happy about the sound. We sat down on the fallen tree. The tips of Mom's boots touched the water, but mine were still a few inches above it.

"Okay, talk," I said, once we were seated. "I wanna hear the whole story of how you went from Baby Brannick to Grace— Oh, wow." I turned and looked at Mom. "Mercer is just a made-up name, isn't it? You're Grace Brannick."

Mom looked a little embarrassed. "The night I ran away, the car that picked me up was a Mercedes. When the driver asked me my name, I . . . improvised."

Names are just words. I know that. But learning that the last name I'd used all my life was fake . . .

"So what should I call myself, then?" I asked. "Sophie Atherton? Sophie Brannick?" Both sounded weird and made me feel like I was wearing clothes that didn't fit.

Mom smiled and brushed my hair away from my face. "You can call yourself whatever you want."

"Okay. Sophie Awesome Sparkle-Princess it is."

Mom laughed then, a real laugh, and laced her fingers with mine. We sat there on that tree, my head on her shoulder, and Mom told me her story. It reminded me of when I was little and she'd read to me before bedtime. And her tale wasn't much different than the fairy tales I used to love, the really dark ones full of scary stuff and heartbreak.

"Growing up here, life was . . . Well, you've seen what it's like for Finley and Izzy. It was brutal. I loved my family, but it was just training, and fighting, and hunting, and more training." Mom sighed and pressed her cheek against the top of my head. "It just didn't seem like any way to live. So when I was twenty-one, I left. Went out for patrol one night, and just . . . kept walking."

She'd gone to England, hoping to do more research into the Brannick history, to see if there was some other way she could be useful to her family that didn't involve killing things.

"Then you met Dad," I said softly. Once again, I wondered where Dad was. How he was. *If* he was.

"Yes" was all she said.

"Did you know what he was?"

"No," Mom answered, her voice thick with tears. "What I told you about meeting your dad, all that was true. We were at the British Library and requested the same book about the history of witchcraft."

I gave a little laugh. "That should've been a clue."

"Probably," Mom said. "When I went over to his

table to ask if I could use it. . . ." She broke off with a sigh. "It was such a cliché. He handed me the book, our fingers touched, and that was that. I was a goner."

I thought about that first day I'd seen Archer leaning against a tree outside Hecate Hall. "I know the feeling," I muttered.

"We were together for nearly a year. And then one day, I woke up early and saw him conjuring breakfast out of thin air. Scared me to death."

"How could you live with him a whole year before knowing what he was? Izzy figured out that I wasn't human after, like, five seconds."

Pushing her hair off her forehead, Mom said, "That's Izzy. Not all Brannicks have the same abilities. I can't sense the presence of Prodigium the way she can. Anyway, when I realized that I'd been living with the very thing I was supposed to be fighting, I—"

"Flipped all the heck out?" I supplied.

"Big time. And then I realized I was pregnant with you, and . . . well, you know the rest. All the moving, all the hiding."

"But it wasn't Dad you were hiding from." The last puzzle pieces finally clicked into place. "At Thorne, Dad said that you had your reasons for always moving around." He'd also said that he was still in love with Mom. I wanted to tell her that, too, but something

72

stopped me. Maybe because I hoped that Dad would still have a chance to tell her in person.

"I had no idea how my family would react to the news that I was going to have a Prodigium baby. And not just any kind of Prodigium, but a demon. Now I understand that I should have given them the benefit of the doubt, but I was scared. And young. God, I was just six years older than you are now. That's terrifying." She raised her shoulder, nudging my head. "Please don't make me a grandmother in six years, okay?"

I scoffed. "Trust me, after the Boy Issues I've had, I'm becoming a nun."

"Well, that's good to know."

We stayed there, dangling our feet over the creek, talking, until the sun was high overhead. By the time we made our way back to the compound, I was feeling a little better. Sure, my life was still intensely screwed up, but at least I had some answers.

When we got back to the compound, Izzy and Finley were out doing chores. Or what the Brannicks called chores, anyway. Izzy was rearranging the targets on the training field. (I still called it the Ninja Backyard. Izzy laughed when I told her that.) Finley was set up in the converted barn just off the training field, sharpening knives. "You can help her," Aislinn told me, once I found her. She was down in the basement, changing the sheets on the cots. I wondered why she bothered, but decided not to ask.

"If it's all the same to you, I'm not really great with the knives," I told her. "Is there anything else I can do? Anything less . . . deadly?"

Shaking a pillow into its case, Aislinn shrugged and said, "You can go up to the War Room and check our files on Hecate Hall and the Casnoffs. See if there's any information we have wrong, or details you can add."

Ah, yes. Files. Books. Nothing with sharp edges. Perfect.

"Will do. Thanks."

I jogged back up the steps, stopping near the top. "Oh, and, um, thanks for letting me stay here. I mean, after everything my whole existence put you through."

When she just looked at me, I hurried on to say, "Finley told me what happened to the other Brannicks. She said it wouldn't have happened if you'd been their leader."

I stood there awkwardly while Aislinn studied me. She had Mom's eyes, so it was doubly weird to feel myself under such intense scrutiny. In the end, she just said, "You're family."

There was nothing really to say to that. I just nodded and hurried back upstairs.

The War Room was every bit as depressing and messy

as it had been yesterday, and after ten minutes of pawing through the papers on the table, and the big, heavy boxes on the floor, I hadn't found the files about Hecate Hall. Frustrated, I let out a long sigh.

"Problem?" a silky voice murmured.

I ignored Torin and turned my attention to the stack of notebooks near the couch.

"I am sorry for what I said about your father this morning," he said. "It was beneath me."

I still didn't say anything.

"Being trapped thus is incredibly frustrating for me, and occasionally I take it out on others. Again, I apologize. Now, if you'd like, I can help you with what you're seeking."

Knowing I'd probably regret it, I crossed the room and yanked the canvas off the mirror. As before, he was sitting on the table, smirking at me.

"Jackass, jackass on the wall, where's the info on Hex Hall?"

Torin laughed long and loud at that, and I saw that his teeth were slightly crooked. Seeing as how he was from the sixteenth century, I guess he was lucky to have any teeth at all.

"Oh, I do like you," he said, wiping tears from his eyes. "All these bloody warrior women are so serious. It's nice to have a real wit about the place again."

"Whatever. Do you know where the file on Hex Hall is, or not, Mirror Boy?"

He leaned forward and pointed under the table. In the mirror I saw a box pushed back in the shadows. No wonder I'd missed it.

As I dragged the box out, Torin said, "Is that all you want my help with, Sophia?"

I rocked back on my heels and scowled at him. "You made it pretty clear last night that you're big into being cryptic. I'm not in the mood to have my chain jerked right now."

He was quiet while I pawed through the box. I pulled out two big manila envelopes with CASNOFF scrawled across them. There were three separate folders labeled HECATE HALL, and I took those out, too.

"You were stuck in a void space," Torin said.

I was so busy flipping through the first Casnoff folder that it took a second for what he said to register. Once it did, I looked up at him blankly. "What?"

"Those three weeks you lost. You were stuck in a void between dimensions. That's how the Itineris works, traveling in and around other dimensions. Most of the time there are no problems. But you got stuck, probably because of what you are. Or aren't."

When I just kept staring at him, he clarified. "You're not a demon anymore, not completely, but neither are you human." Torin rested his chin in his hand, a heavy ruby ring on his pinkie winking at me. "You were a very confusing object for the Itineris to digest. So it held you for a bit. You're quite fortunate it eventually decided to spit you out."

The words "digest" and "spit" were more than a little unsettling. "Okay," I finally said. "That's, um, really awful to know. But thanks for telling me."

He shrugged. "It was nothing."

I went back to the folder, studying a picture of Mrs. Casnoff and her sister, Lara, when they were young, maybe in their late teens, early twenties. There was a man sitting with them who had black hair slicked back from his forehead, and a mustache every bit as elaborate as one of Mrs. Casnoff's hairdos. I guessed this was Mrs. Casnoff's father, Alexei.

"You know, I can see more than just the future or the past."

"Really?" I asked, paging through the papers in the file. "Can you also see the present? Because I can do that, too. Like, right now, I sense that I'm in a messy room with a total toolbox."

I didn't look up, but I could hear the scowl in his voice when he said, "No. In certain cases, I can see . . . let us say, alternative futures."

"What does that mean?"

"Time is not a fixed thing, Sophia. Every decision can lead us down a different path. So, occasionally, I see more than one possible outcome. For example, I told your aunt that you would be the one to stop these Casnoff witches from raising their demon forces. And I did see that. But it isn't the only future I saw for you."

I wanted to ignore him, but I found myself putting the file down and facing the mirror. "What was the other one?"

"It's quite the contradiction," he answered, ridiculously pleased with himself. "For in one scenario, I saw you defeating the Casnoffs. And in the other, I saw you joined with them. Of course I didn't share that vision with Aislinn. If I had, I doubt your welcome would have been quite so cordial. You should thank me, really."

All I could do was say, "Well, your vision was wrong. I would never be part of the Casnoffs' demon . . . whatever."

"Oh, you weren't part of it," he clarified, grinning. "You were leading it."

I turned away then; my hands were shaking. "You're just saying all this to screw with me."

"Believe that if you like, Soph—" He broke off, and I raised my head to see Izzy standing in the doorway. "Isolde!" Torin exclaimed. "How lovely to see you."

Izzy chewed on her lower lip. "Why are you talking to Torin?" she asked.

"I need help finding some stuff," I replied, holding up the folder so that she could see. "I figured he was useful for that, at least, since his prophecies seems to be on the fritz."

Torin made an offended noise. "They most certainly are not! I am never wrong." Sliding off the table, his gaze flicked to Izzy. "Never."

At that, Izzy crossed the room in a couple of big strides and draped the canvas back over the mirror. "Cover me up all you want, Isolde," Torin said, his voice now muffled. "It does not change anything."

Something flickered across Izzy's face, and I couldn't help but ask, "What's that all about?"

But she just shook her head and came to kneel next to me on the floor. "It's nothing. Just more of Torin's crap. So did you find what you were looking for?"

"Not sure yet," I said, turning back to the first page of the Casnoffs' file.

*Alexei Casnoff was born in 1916 in St. Petersburg (or, as it was called at that time, Petrograd), to Grigori and Svetlana Casnoff, and*

Before I could get any further, a loud pounding reverberated throughout the house.

I dropped the papers. "What the heck was that?"

Frowning, Izzy got to her feet. "I don't know. I think it's at the front door, but . . . no one ever comes here."

Together, we dashed out of the War Room and into the hallway. Aislinn had one hand on the doorknob and a dagger in the other. Mom was right behind her. Inside my chest, my magic shrieked and swirled, and I knew that whatever waited on the other side was powerful.

And as Aislinn slowly opened the door, I realized I was right.

Standing on the threshold, looking taller and older and a lot more exhausted than I remembered, was Cal.

And leaning against him, the purple marks on his face unnaturally dark against his pale skin, was my dad.

# CHAPTER 9

"James!" Mom gasped, and then there was total confusion as everyone started talking at once.

"What's he doing here?" Aislinn barked, just as Izzy laid her hand on my arm and said, "Who are those guys?"

"It's—it's my dad," I said, my voice breaking. And then I was shoving past Aislinn to throw my arms around Dad's neck.

His own arms came up to weakly encircle me. "Sophie," he murmured against my hair. "Sophie."

It was almost too good to believe, that he could be standing here, that Cal could be next to him. I squeezed my dad tight, tears spilling onto his shirt collar. "You're okay," I sobbed. "You're okay."

He gave a raspy chuckle. "More or less. Thanks to Cal, here."

I pulled back. Dad's eyes were red, and he looked like death warmed over. And the purple markings swirling all over his skin, signs of the Removal, were just as devastating to see as they'd been the night he'd gotten them.

But he was there, and that was all that mattered. My eyes slid over to Cal, who still hovered uncertainly beside Dad. "You're okay, too," I said softly, and he smiled. Well, he did that weird lip quirk that Cal called a smile. "Yeah," was all he said, but there was a lot of meaning behind that one word. Relief and happiness flooded through me, and I took a step forward, wanting to hug him, too. But for some reason, at the last moment, I just reached out and squeezed his arm. "I'm glad."

His hand briefly covered mine, his touch rough and warm. I could feel a blush spreading up from my chest, so I turned back to Dad. "How did you get here? Where have you been?"

"Can we go somewhere less . . . transitory to discuss this?" he asked, gesturing around the hallway. I felt like I might burst into tears all over again. *Transitory*. God, I'd missed him so much.

I'm pretty sure Aislinn was about to tell him no, but Mom stepped forward. "Of course. We can talk in the living room." For a moment, my parents held each other's gaze, and while normally your parents gazing at each other is kind of gross, I couldn't help but smile.

Like every room in the Brannick house, the living room was practically empty. There was a couch that seemed slightly better than the monstrosity in the War Room, and Dad and Cal sat there. I sat on Dad's other side, while Aislinn and Izzy hung out in the doorway, and Mom perched on the edge of the sofa nearest me.

Dad sighed, and his hand trembled a little as he laid it on mine. "I can't begin to say how good it is to see you."

I laced my fingers with his. "Same here. I mean, with me seeing you, obviously."

Smiling, Dad squeezed my hand. "Yes, I deduced as much."

"How did you find this place?" Aislinn asked, pretty much killing any hope for a nice family moment. "It's warded against your kind."

"There's a spot about three feet across in the north-west corner," Cal answered. "The wards are broken there. I can fix them if you want."

Aislinn was obviously taken aback, but she recovered quickly. "No need. I'll send Finley out to redo it tomorrow morning." Since the Brannicks were descended from a powerful White Witch, some of them still had residual powers. Apparently, this was the case with Finley. "You can go help her," Aislinn added, to Izzy. "It's time you learned to make wards."

"As for how we found you," Dad said, "it wasn't

easy. Cal told me that he'd sent you to the Brannicks, but when he tried to use his magic to get a lock on you . . ."

"It was like you had just disappeared," Cal said. "No locator spell worked, no tracing hex."

"It was the Itineris," I explained. "It didn't know what to do with me now that I'm de-magicked."

Dad nodded. "I suspected as much. Anyway, we've spent the past few weeks making our way here. Cal didn't think it was wise for me to travel by Itineris in my . . . current state, so I'm afraid we've had to travel the old-fashioned way."

"It took you three weeks to fly from England to Tennessee?" Aislinn asked, raising an eyebrow.

"We didn't come here right away," Cal answered, crossing his arms over his chest, a scowl on his face. "There was a lot of other stuff to deal with."

"What kind of stuff?" I asked.

Dad rose to his feet and started to pace. "After the Brannicks and L'Occhio di Dio attacked Council Headquarters in the spring, there were only five Council members left."

"That wasn't us," Aislinn retorted. "Or The Eye, for that matter."

Dad stopped his pacing and stared at her. "What?"

Briefly, Aislinn told Dad the same story she'd told me

last night, about suspecting that the Casnoffs had set the fire themselves, only to blame it on their enemies. When she was done, Dad seemed to have aged ten years. "I wish I could say that that's preposterous. But after what I've seen Lara Casnoff do . . . In any case, the other three members of the Council were killed when Thorne Abbey was destroyed."

I'd seen one of those three, Kristopher, killed, but it was a shock to learn the other two, Elizabeth and Roderick, were gone, too. "Lara and I are the only members still remaining," Dad continued. "I'm"—he gestured to his tattoos—"not exactly useful. I'm also dead."

"What?"

"A few days after Thorne Abbey burned down, Lara Casnoff called a huge meeting in London at the mansion of some bigwig warlock," Cal said to me. "I was able to do an invisibility spell and get in. There must have been hundreds of Prodigium there. Anyway, that's where Lara made the big announcement that your dad had been murdered by The Eye." He nodded toward Aislinn. "With the help of the Brannicks."

Aislinn swore under her breath, and Mom lowered her head.

"Okay," I said slowly. "Look, I get that that's bad, but can't you just pop up and be like, 'Hey, here I am! Totally not dead!'"

"I could," said Dad, "but if it suits the Casnoffs' purposes for me to be deceased, something tells me I wouldn't stay 'totally not dead' for long."

"What do you think the Casnoffs' purposes are?" Mom asked.

Dad glanced at her, then over to me. "To terrify the Prodigium population to the point where using demons seems like the only course of action. They have Daisy, and they may have managed to corral Nick. There haven't been any other attacks linked to him." The same night the Casnoffs had used Daisy to fight The Eye, Nick had gotten loose and gone on some kind of rampage. The thought of it still made me shudder.

"Did she say anything about the demons at this big meeting?" I asked Cal.

He shook his head. "Not specifically. All she said was that she and her sister had a plan to rid the world of the Brannicks and The Eye once and for all."

"Speaking of—" Dad broke in. "Sophie, have you had any contact with Archer Cross?"

Every eye in the room was on me, and I had this bizarre urge to cover my face. I knew everything I was feeling was painted all over it. "No. I thought maybe . . ." I turned to Cal. "Did you see him? When you went in to get Dad at Thorne Abbey?"

It's not like I expected Cal to go, *Yes, I did. In fact, I was keeping him in my pocket. Here you go.* But when Cal met my eyes and said, "Your dad was alone in the cell when I got there," the words physically hurt.

You're lucky, I reminded myself. Your dad is here. So is Cal. And Jenna is safe. What were the chances that you'd get everyone back?

"The cell door had been broken down," Cal continued, "so your dad and I figured The Eye took him."

"You don't remember anything?" I asked Dad.

A rueful expression was on his face as he shook his head. "I was unconscious, I'm afraid."

Shoving my hands into my pockets, I said, "I'm sure you're right. He's probably with The Eye." And they were either still keeping him as their pet warlock, or they'd found out about the two of us working together, and killed him. Either way, Archer was gone.

That thought was so painful, so loud inside my head, that it took me a minute to realize Dad was still talking. ". . . certainly not the only one to have vanished."

Aislinn had retreated back to the doorway, arms folded over her chest. "So the Cross boy is gone, and both those Casnoff women," she said, ticking off the names on her fingers. "As well as their demons."

"And Graymalkin Island," Cal said, so softly that at first I was sure I'd misheard him.

"Wait, what?" I asked.

"Hecate Hall and the island it was on are gone," Dad said.

"How is that even possible?" Mom asked from her spot on the couch.

Dad glanced back at her, and once again something passed between them. "No one knows," he said at last. "But a few days after Thorne Abbey burned down, the entire island seemed to vanish into thin air. One minute it was there; the next, nothing but empty ocean. It's my belief that it's not really gone, but that the Casnoffs are cloaking it for some reason."

"You think that's where they are?" I asked, once I'd found my voice again. I was remembering that feeling I'd had the day Cal, Jenna, and I had left Hex Hall. A premonition had come over me that we'd never go back. I shivered a little now remembering it.

"It makes sense," Dad said. "Graymalkin Island was where they were raising demons. It's been Anastasia's home for years. I can't imagine they'd just abandon it. And . . ." Dad trailed off, rubbing his eyes again. He went to move back toward the couch but stumbled. Mom leaped up and caught his arm while Cal moved to his other side. Together, they lowered him back to a seated position.

"The travel has wiped him out," Cal said. "I've done protection spells on him, but he's still pretty weak."

"Please don't speak of me as though I weren't here," Dad said, but the exhaustion in his voice canceled out any snappishness.

"That's enough for tonight," Mom said, and I noticed that she hadn't taken her hand off Dad's arm.

Aislinn nodded. "I need to tell Finley what's going on." A muscle worked in her jaw, and she muttered, "And have a word with Torin. You two," she said to Dad and Cal, "stay tonight. In the morning, we can decide where to go from here."

It cost her something to let them stay. I could see it in the tightness around her mouth. I think Dad saw it, too, because he gave a respectful nod. "Thank you, Aislinn."

"They can use the tents," Aislinn told me. I'd forgotten about those—the weird canvas structures extra Brannicks had used, back when there had been extra Brannicks. I thought about mentioning the cots in the basement, but maybe Aislinn wasn't down with too many Prodigium under her roof.

Aislinn left the room then, Izzy trailing after her. As soon as they were gone, Dad leaned back on the couch and closed his eyes. "You should stay in here tonight," Mom said to him. "Those tents are barely livable, and after all you've been through . . ." She cleared her throat. "Anyway, neither of you needs to brave the great outdoors tonight."

Dad just nodded without opening his eyes. But Cal shrugged and said, "I'm used to sleeping outside. Besides, you guys probably need, uh, family time."

He turned to go, but as he did, Dad said, "Sophie, why don't you show Cal to his accommodations? I wanted to speak to your mother in private for a moment."

"Oh," I said, shoving my hands in my pockets. "Okay. Right." The last time I'd been alone with Cal, he'd kissed me. It had definitely been a kiss of the "We Might Die, So This Is Just Us Saying Good-Bye (Maybe)" variety, but still. He was, technically, my fiancé (you know, as if Prodigium aren't weird enough, they also have arranged marriages). Being engaged brought a whole new level of weirdness to my and Cal's friendship.

Cal gave one quick glance back at me, and even though I couldn't be sure, I thought his gaze fell on my mouth for just a second. I tried hard not to gulp, and when he left the room, I followed him.

# CHAPTER 10

Cal and I made our way from the main house to the tents in silence. I'd stopped in the kitchen to grab one of the battery-operated lanterns the Brannicks apparently hoarded. My shadow and Cal's stretched out in front of us, nearly entwined, even though we weren't walking that close together. My thoughts were still so wrapped up with Archer that I didn't even see the semicircle of structures surrounding the compound until we were practically on top of them.

What the Brannicks called "tents" were actually pretty solid buildings. The roofs were made of heavy canvas, but instead of being on the ground, they were situated on wooden platforms. There were even stairs leading up into each one.

"Wow," I said as we came to a stop. "These aren't

really tents. They're more like cabins. Or like a tent and a cabin had a baby. A 'tenbin.'"

It was a bad joke. A stupid one, and my heart wasn't even a little bit in it. Archer would've laughed at it anyway, I thought, and once again, pain slammed into my chest, nearly leaving me breathless.

Cal didn't say anything, so I just swung my arm out, gesturing to the tents. "Pick any of them. They're all empty."

Still not looking at me, Cal moved toward the tent directly in front of us, and pushed back the flap. It occurred to me that I probably should have just given him the lantern instead of following him inside, but by the time I'd had that thought, he was already in the tent.

I climbed the steps and ducked through the canvas doorway. "Wow," I said to his back. "Not exactly the digs we had at Thorne, huh?"

There were two pieces of furniture on the scuffed wooden platform: a folding table and a low cot like the ones in the basement. Of course, that's about all there was room for. The tent was tiny, and I suddenly felt a little claustrophobic.

I put the lantern on the table, wishing the pool of light it cast were bigger. As it was, I could barely see Cal's face in the gloom. Then I shoved my hands in my back pockets and blew out a long breath. Cal sat down on the cot, and it squeaked slightly under his weight. He rested his elbows on his spread knees, hands clasped in front of him, but he still didn't say anything.

"Hey," I said, my voice way too loud, "if you're, uh, hungry or something, I can see what's in the kitchen. Running for your life and dragging a powerless demon all over the world probably works up an appetite, huh?" As soon as the words were out of my mouth, I mentally cringed so hard, I'm surprised I didn't sprain something.

"I'm not hungry," he replied in a low voice.

"Awesome," I said. "Then I'll leave you alone and let you get some sleep."

My cheeks flaming, I headed for the entrance.

And then, from behind me: "I thought about you. Every day."

I froze, my hand still holding the canvas flap.

Cal's voice was slightly hoarse as he continued. "Three weeks is a long time to wonder where someone is. All that time, I thought maybe I'd done the wrong thing, telling you to find the Brannicks."

I turned around then. I wanted to make a joke, or say something sarcastic, anything that would cut the tension enveloping us. Instead, I said, "I thought about you, too."

Cal glanced up, and I met his eyes. "Cal, you . . . you saved my dad's life. You tried to save Archer's." My chest ached, saying that out loud, but I made myself go on. "That's so huge, I don't even know where to start. 'Thank you' doesn't really cut it, you know? And I'm not sure there's a fruit basket big enough to—"

He rose to his feet, and suddenly his arms were around me and my face was pressed against his chest. He smelled good, and familiar, and tears sprang to my eyes as I put my hands on his back and pressed him closer. He stroked my hair. "He might be okay, Sophie," Cal murmured. "The Eye could've gotten him out."

I squeezed my eyes closed. "I know," I whispered. "It's not that. I mean, it *is* that, but not just that. It's . . . Everything is so screwed up, Cal."

His arms tightened. "I know. With Graymalkin being gone . . ." He blew out a long breath but didn't say anything else.

I hadn't even thought about that. How much Cal had loved the island. I remembered what he'd told me at Thorne, that Graymalkin had always felt like home to him. I was used to feeling vaguely homeless, but Cal had lived at Hex Hall since he was thirteen.

I pulled back to look in his eyes. "I'm so sorry," I told him. "For all of it."

On his face, I saw everything I was feeling. The

confusion, the helplessness, the loneliness. And I guess it was that last emotion that made me rise up on tiptoes and softly brush my lips over his. I hadn't meant for it to be a real kiss; it was more a gesture of thanks and comfort than anything else. But when I went to pull back, Cal cupped my cheek, and his mouth slanted over mine, and just like that, it was *definitely* a real kiss.

I kissed him back, my hands clutching at his T-shirt. For a minute, it felt nice. Well, better than nice, really. I felt safe and comfortable, and his arms were so warm around me.

And then, suddenly, I was pulling away, my face hot. "Oh, God, and now I'm sorry for *that*," I said, turning my back to him and wiping at my cheeks with trembling hands.

I'd only thought the atmosphere in the tent was tense before. Now I was practically choking on it. From behind me, I heard Cal sigh. "No, I'm sorry," he said. "We're both . . . We're in a weird place."

I turned back around then and gave him a shaky smile. "Both metaphorically *and* literally," I said, gesturing around the tent.

Cal gave a tiny smile back. "You should probably go. Check on your dad. We can talk more tomorrow when things aren't so . . ." His words trailed off, and finally he just shrugged.

I nodded. "Right. Tomorrow."

I could feel his gaze on my back as I left the tent, and it was like it stayed there, a hot spot between my shoulder blades, as I jogged back to the house.

*I kissed Cal. Again. For real.*

The words pounded inside my brain in time to my footsteps, and I wasn't sure whether it was guilt or giddiness jumping around in my stomach. My hands were still trembling when I opened the back door. The house was strangely silent, and I crept toward the living room. Dad was still on the couch, his eyes closed, his breathing shallow. Mom sat on the floor next to him, a steaming mug beside her. She was looking at Dad with such a strange expression: sad, and scared, and . . . something else. Her finger barely touched his skin as she traced the purple whorls on his hand.

I backed out before she could see me.

As I made my way upstairs, I felt shaky and hollow. Sometimes I think we have a limit to how many emotions we can feel at once, and I had clearly reached mine. Between Dad and Cal reappearing, and kissing Cal . . .

I pressed the heels of my hands against my eyes and took a shuddery breath. Yup. Definitely had all I could handle for one night.

When I opened my bedroom and saw a soft, ghostly

glow, I groaned. "Not tonight, Elodie," I sniffled. "I'm not in the mood."

The words died in my throat.

It wasn't Elodie's ghost standing in the middle of my room.

It was Archer's.

# CHAPTER 11

"Oh, good, it worked," Archer said, his ghostly face relieved. Unlike Elodie, his voice came in loud and clear, and so familiar that my heart broke all over again.

I stood frozen, my back against the door. Even though he was faint, I could see him smirk.

"Um . . . Mercer? Haven't seen you in nearly a month. I was expecting something like, 'Oh, Cross, love of my heart, fire of my loins, how I've longed—'"

"You're dead," I blurted out, pressing a hand against my stomach. "You're a ghost, and you think—"

All the humor disappeared from his face, and he held up both hands. "Whoa, whoa, whoa. Not dead. Promise."

My heart was still hammering. "Then what the heck are you?"

Archer almost looked sheepish as he reached inside his shirt and pulled out some kind of amulet on a thin silver chain. "It's a speaking stone. Lets you appear to people kind of like a hologram. You know. 'Help me, Sophie-Wan Kenobi, you're my only hope.'"

"Did you steal it from the cellar at Hecate, too?" Archer had collected all sorts of magical knickknacks back when we had cellar duty at Hex Hall.

"No," he said, offended. "I found it at a . . . store. For magical stuff. Okay, yes, I stole it from the cellar."

I rushed across the room and thrust my fist at his solar plexus. It went right through him, but it was still kind of satisfying. "You jerk!" I cried, striking at his head. "You scared me to death! Cal said The Eye probably had you, and I thought they'd found out about you and me working together, and killed you, you arrogant piece of—"

"I'm sorry!" he shouted, waving his translucent hands. "I—I thought the talking would give it away, and I didn't mean to scare you, but I'm not dead! So would you please stop hitting me?"

I paused. "You can feel it?"

"No, but it's still kind of unsettling to see your fist coming at my face."

We were inches away from each other. I let my arms drop to my sides. "You're not dead."

"Not even a little," he replied. And then he smiled,

99

a genuine, happy smile, and my cheeks started to ache. That's when I realized I was grinning, too.

"So hologram means—" I finally said.

"It means non-corporeal, yeah. Which sucks seeing as how there are a lot of *very* corporeal things I'd like to do with you right now."

My cheeks flushed hot as my gaze dropped to his lips. Then I remembered that ten minutes before, I'd been in another guy's arms. Kissing another guy's lips.

I spun away from him, hoping he hadn't seen, and went to sit on the bed. "So where are you?" I asked, drawing my knees up to my chest.

Even though he was all ghostly, I noticed a brief flicker of guilt on his face.

"Rome," he answered. "Or, if you want to get more specific, hiding in a closet in a villa in Rome."

It wasn't a surprise he was with The Eye. After all, hadn't that been the best case scenario as far as him getting out of Thorne went?

"Why are you making that face?" Archer asked.

I hugged my knees tighter. "What face?"

"Like you want to throw up or cry. Both, maybe."

Oh, the joys of having whatever the opposite of a poker face was. "It's just been an insane night. An insane few weeks, really." I didn't know how much time I had to talk to Archer, so I gave him the most bare-bones version of what had happened since I left Thorne. He stood there listening, and only looked surprised when I told him that my mom was a Brannick.

"So that's why we're here," I told him, "chilling with the Brannicks. And now my dad has shown up, and, uh, Cal, and now you. It's been kind of a busy night."

"How did Cal and your dad track you? I've been trying this magical GPS thing ever since I left Thorne, and it only locked on to you today."

"Cal had told me to come to the Brannicks when I left Thorne, so they were just hoping I'd be here. It may be the first time I've had any luck since . . . oh, 2002 or so."

Archer smiled and then began to flicker in and out. "Damn it," he muttered, tapping on the stone around his neck. "Okay, it's looking like I don't have much longer, so I'll make this quick. All The Eye knows is that the Casnoffs have disappeared. There haven't been any more reported demon attacks, but something is definitely stirring. They just don't know what."

"That's what Dad said, too."

"We're looking for the Casnoffs, but so far, no dice. It's like we're all in a holding pattern."

"Here, too," I told him. "So . . . what now, Cross? Are you going to stay with The Eye?"

Archer glanced over his shoulder at something. "I

don't know," he said when he turned back, his voice much quieter. "But it's not like I really have anywhere else to go."

"You could come here."

He smiled at that and reached out one ghostly hand. I pressed my fingertips to his, even though I couldn't feel him. "I wish I could," he said. "But they're watching me pretty closely these days. For now, it's probably safer for me to stay there. Toe the line a little bit."

I stared at our hands. "Am I ever going to see you again?"

"You better believe it," he said. "Didn't I promise you we could make out in a castle?"

Chuckling, I drew my hand back. "You did. And to take me on dates. Real dates with no swords or ghouls or angst."

"Well, there you go," he said. "As soon as we've saved the world from a demon invasion, it's you, me, and Applebee's."

I rolled my eyes, but I was grinning now. "Oh, the romance."

His smile slowly faded. "I will see you again," he said, serious this time. "I promise." He moved closer to me so that his translucent legs disappeared into the bed. "Mercer, I—"

And then, just like that, he blinked out and was gone.

"Oh, come on," I groaned to the empty room. Sighing, I flopped back against the pillows and shut my eyes. I'd been lying like that for a few minutes when I suddenly had the sense I wasn't alone anymore.

Sure enough, when I opened my eyes, Elodie was perched on the end of the bed, watching me with an unreadable expression.

Finally, she mouthed, "Do you love him?"

I took a moment before replying, "Yeah. I think I do."

She nodded, like that was the answer she'd expected. "I thought I did, too."

It suddenly occurred to me that if I ever did see Archer again, Elodie's new habit of popping into my body whenever she felt like it could be . . . awkward.

"He's sorry, you know," I told her. "For lying to you. And for the whole you-getting-killed thing."

She shrugged. "Not his fault I got killed." I was getting a lot better at reading her lips. She didn't have to repeat anything now. "That was Alice. And since the Casnoffs had a hand in making her a demon, I guess it was their fault in the end."

"We're going to stop them," I told her. "I don't know how, but we will."

Elodie gave me a look. "Will you? I heard what that magic mirror dude said, about seeing two futures for you."

"I would never help the Casnoffs," I said, automatically, but I couldn't help the little shiver that went up my spine as I remembered Torin's words.

I thought Elodie might have sighed. It was hard to tell since she didn't technically breathe. "Well, even if you don't go over to the dark side, you're still pretty screwed. Your dad doesn't have powers anymore. You might as well not have any, because I certainly can't keep taking over every time you run into trouble. Those two little girls can't even kill a werewolf, and Aislinn Brannick is just one woman. Your mom is better at books than she is at weapons, and Torin is both annoying and useless. Basically, the only thing you have going for you is Cal, who *might* be able to postpone the inevitable when the Casnoffs and their pet demons rip you to shreds. But, you know, good luck with that."

And with that inspiring little speech, she vanished.

# CHAPTER 12

The next morning, I found myself at what had to be the weirdest breakfast ever. I looked around the room and tried to take in everyone who was there: Me, Mom, Dad, all three Brannicks, and Cal. Oh, and Torin, since "breakfast" involved all of us eating Pop-Tarts in the War Room. Elodie's words from the night before circled my brain. Did we honestly think we stood a chance at defeating the Casnoffs?

"You have to know something," Aislinn was saying to Torin now.

"I do," he shot back. "I told you, those women are on their thrice-damned island."

"Which. Is. Where?" Aislinn asked for what had to be the fourth time.

"In. The. Bloody. Sea," Torin replied. He threw up

his hands, his lace cuffs falling back as he did. "I don't know why you can't find it. It's exactly where it always was."

"As I've told you, Aislinn, it's my belief that they've cloaked Graymalkin somehow," Dad said. He was leaning heavily against one of the folding chairs. Cal stood on one side of him, Mom on the other. My eyes met Cal's, and last night flashed in my mind. My fingers twining in his shirt, my mouth against his.

I suddenly gave my full attention to Torin. "So the Casnoffs are at Hex Hall," I said. "Probably with however many demons they've managed to create. What are they doing there? Throwing a hellacious slumber party?" When no one said anything, I added, "Get it? Hellacious? Because they're all . . . Forget it."

"I got it," Izzy said softly, and I threw her a grateful smile.

"I cannot tell what they're planning," Torin said. "Only that they're there." He frowned at all of us. "I don't know everything, you know. Only that this girl"—he pointed at me—"is the key to stopping them from using an army of demons to wipe humans off the face of the earth."

*Or leading the charge.* The thought popped into my mind, making my stomach twist itself into knots. Torin winked at me, and I wondered if thought-reading was another of his powers. Or maybe it was just my expression.

Shoving aside the image of me at the front of a demon army, I said, "The Eye doesn't know what they're up to, either."

Suddenly, every one in the room was staring at me as what I'd just said registered. "I, uh, saw Archer last night," I said, like I'd just bumped into him at Starbucks. "He used this communicating stone thingie to . . . drop by, and, um, say hello."

"And you just now decided to mention this?" Dad asked.

"When I got here, you guys were already yelling at Torin," I fired back. "I didn't exactly have a chance to get a word in. Besides, Archer didn't know anything, really. Or at least nothing more than we do. I didn't think it was a big deal. He was only here for like, five minutes."

"In your room?" Mom asked, eyebrows up.

"He was non-corporeal!" I cried. "And all . . . ghostly. Everything was totally G-rated, swear."

"One of L'Occhio di Dio is your *boyfriend*?" Finley asked incredulously.

Dad cleared his throat. "In any case," he said, saving me from answering Finley, "that's good information to have. It means that we're all on the same page as far as the Casnoffs are concerned."

"Right," I said. "Which is that no one knows what to do next. I'm not really seeing that as a good thing, Dad."

"So what *can* we do?" Finley asked. "Just sit here and wait for the Casnoffs to make their move?"

"We could go to Lough Bealach," Aislinn answered.

"Is that a place, or are you choking?" I asked, earning me a glare in return.

Dad made a strangled sound that might have been a laugh. He covered it with a cough and said, "Lough Bealach is a lake in Ireland. It was once a very sacred place to the Brannick family, if I'm correct."

"The most sacred place," Aislinn answered. "It was once the Brannicks' responsibility to guard it."

"What's there that needs guarding?"

"Supposedly, an opening to the underworld," Mom answered.

"If we're going to fight demons, it might be handy to have a lot of demonglass, seeing as how it's the only thing that can kill a demon," Aislinn said. "And the underworld is the only place we could get it."

"Like *literally* going to hell?" I asked.

Everyone ignored me. "We couldn't get in," Finley said. "There's not one of us here who could survive a trip into the underworld. You'd need dark, powerful magic to do that. If Sophie still had her powers, maybe it would be feasible, but without them . . ." She shook her head.

And then Dad said, "Sophie does have her powers."

"Well, yeah," I agreed. "I didn't go through the Removal. But they're stuck in here." I tapped my chest. "Whatever that word the Council said at my sentencing, it sealed my magic away."

Dad reached out and took my hand. "Do you remember when we studied the grimoire at Thorne Abbey? There was a spell in that book that I made you put your hand on."

I did remember. I hadn't been able to tell what kind of spell it was, but when I'd touched it, I'd felt a sold thump right in the middle of my sternum.

Which, I now realized, was the place where I always felt my powers swirling around.

"It was a protection spell," Dad said. "Ensuring that your powers could never be fully taken away from you. No matter what kind of binding spell is put on you, all you have to do is touch that particular spell, and your magic will be restored."

I squeezed his hand so tightly it must've hurt him. "Oh my God," I breathed. My magic back. No more feeling helpless. No more needing Elodie's ghost to do magic. A chance at actually stopping the Casnoffs. Hope and excitement surged through me.

And then, as if a cold bucket of water had been

thrown in my face, I remembered what Torin had said last night. Me, leading the Casnoffs' demon army. I'd have to have my powers to do that, wouldn't I? But no. No, he was lying about that. There was no way I'd ever, *ever* team up with the Casnoffs for something so awful.

I remembered something else. "I have to touch that spell. That spell that's in the grimoire. And the grimoire is where, exactly?"

Abashed, Dad looked down and admitted, "Undoubtedly with the Casnoffs."

I deflated. "Who are on an island that we can't find. I swear to God, this whole thing is like the world's most twisted riddle."

"Maybe there's another way," Finley suggested. "Don't you guys know any witches or warlocks who could restore Sophie's powers?"

"Perhaps," Dad said, but I'd known him long enough to know that when Dad said, "perhaps," it usually meant, "no freaking way."

"Couldn't someone just say the spell?" I asked. I knew I was grasping at straws, but if there was any chance for me to use my powers again, I was going to take it.

Dad shook his head. "No. That particular spell was woven to the paper with blood magic. It has to be touched. The words themselves don't have the same power."

"I may not have dark magic, but my powers are pretty strong," Cal offered. "If we *did* go to Ireland, is there any chance I could get in?"

Considering that, Dad ran a hand over the back of his neck. "It's possible, I suppose. But the potential risk—"

"We need to do something," Cal said quietly. "I'd rather take our chances at Lough Bealach than wait around here."

"The boy is right," Torin said, even though he and Cal were probably close to the same age (well, plus or minus five hundred years, I guess). "And the sooner, the better. We're in stasis now, but something is coming. I sense a—"

"Great disturbance in the Force?" I interrupted before I could stop myself.

Torin frowned. "I suspect you're mocking me, but I don't understand the reference. In any case, dark powers are stirring. The more prepared you are, the better."

"Then, let's go," I said.

"Perhaps we should explore some other options before swanning off to Ireland," Dad said, pushing his glasses up. "After all, Sophie, you've been through quite the ordeal."

"I'll nap on the plane. Look, we are dealing with the possibility of *an army of demons*. I don't know about you guys, but those words are right up there with 'root canal' and 'school on Saturdays' in terms of things that terrify me. We're already three weeks behind. We don't have time to just sit here and explore options or read more books or listen to more half-assed prophecies from this jerk," I said, pointing at Torin. He made a gesture that I think was the old-timey version of flipping me off.

"So, yeah," I continued. "Maybe this is a totally stupid idea. But if there's even a chance one of us can get into the underworld, then we have to take it."

"Okay, I do like you," Finley said, flashing me a grin. She looked at my dad. "She's right. If we can't figure out a way to stop these Casnoff chicks, then we at least need to defend ourselves against them. And the only way to do that is to go to Lough Bealach and get a whole bunch of demonglass."

Sighing, Dad sank into one of the chairs next to the table. "It's a fool's errand," he said.

"Do you have any other ideas?" Aislinn asked.

Dad tipped his head back, like an answer might suddenly appear on the ceiling. Then he looked back at me. "This is honestly what you want to do?"

"Maybe Cal will be able to get in. Maybe not. Either way, we're not going to get anything accomplished sitting out here in the boondocks. No offense," I added to Aislinn, who waved it off.

Dad held my gaze for a long time before finally

112

giving a weary nod and saying, "You're right. But how will we get there? The Itineris is too dangerous for you and could be deadly to humans," he said, gesturing to Mom.

"I'll deal with the airline again," Cal said.

To Finley's and Aislinn's questioning looks, Dad clarified, "Cal was able to conjure up tickets and falsify paperwork for us to get out of England. It's not the most glamorous use of magic, but it is certainly useful."

"Fair enough," Aislinn said. "In that case, girls, go grab your things. And Finley, go ahead and gas up the truck. We've got a long drive to the nearest airport."

As I looked around the room at all these people—my family—excitement thrummed through me. Yes, this might go down in history as the stupidest thing I'd ever done, but it felt so good to have a plan that I didn't care if it was a bad one. And looking at everyone's faces, I think they were all feeling the same thing. Well, except for Torin, who was just staring at all of us with a bored expression.

I followed Finley and Izzy out of the room and up the stairs. I was nearly at the landing when a light suddenly burned my eyes. At first I thought it was just the glare from the window at the top of the stairs, and I moved my hand to shade my face. That's when I realized that the light was *coming* from my hand. I watched as a bright golden glow encased my arm, then spread down to cover my torso. Izzy turned around, and I saw her mouth drop open. She reached for my sleeve, but as we watched, her fingers passed through me and my arm vanished.

The golden tendrils moved faster now, winding their way around my body like snakes. I watched as my legs became translucent and then disappeared altogether.

It all happened so fast that I didn't even have time to panic. All I could do was look down at Mom, who was running up the stairs toward me and shouting my name.

"Mom!" I felt my lips move, but no sound came out. Someone else was running into the hallway, and I thought it might be Dad. But then the glow covered my eyes, blinding me. There was the weirdest sensation of being bent and pulled, like someone was trying to fold my body in on itself, and I was moving so fast that every bone in my body rattled. It was like being yanked through a tornado.

And then, just as abruptly, everything stopped.

I was standing up, which seemed like a miracle, considering how badly I was trembling. My breath sawed in and out of my lungs painfully hard, and I studied my feet and tried to remember how to breathe without sounding like a hyperventilating walrus. Eventually, the wheezes became more like gasps, but there was still something wrong with my eyes. I'd been wearing dingy white sneakers, but now, my feet looked black. And was I wearing *knee socks*?

I blinked again. At the Brannicks', I had on jeans. Now from my knees up, I saw a swirl of blue, black, and green plaid.

And then I looked up, and suddenly, I wasn't gasping anymore. I wasn't even breathing.

The house was even more decrepit, and the ferns that bracketed the front door were dead. What had once been a "sag" in the front porch was now more like a crater, and even though it was August, there were no leaves on any of the oak trees that had once shaded the place.

I didn't know how, or why, but there was no denying it.

I was back at Hex Hall.

# PART II

"But I don't want to go among mad people," Alice remarked.

"Oh, you can't help that," said the Cat: "we're all mad here."

*—Alice's Adventures in Wonderland*

# CHAPTER 13

I wasn't alone on the front lawn of Hex Hall. There was a crowd of kids milling around, maybe a hundred altogether, all looking as shocked and rattled as I felt. I spotted Taylor, a dark-haired shapeshifter I'd kind of been friends with, standing a few feet away. Her eyes met mine. "Sophie?" she said, confused. "Where did you come from?" She glanced down and seemed startled to realize she was wearing her Hecate uniform. "Where did *I* come from?" she added, more to herself than to me.

I shook my head. "I don't know."

A buzz began to rise from the group of students, and I could feel confusion turning to panic. Nearby, two faeries—I thought they were Nausicaa and Siobhan—embraced, brightly colored tears dripping from their wings.

As I moved through the crowd, I could only make out snatches of conversation, but I heard words like, "golden light" and "getting grabbed out of thin air." So whatever had happened to me had happened to the rest of them, too.

I'd been through a lot in the past few months, but this left me feeling paralyzed. I stood there on the lawn of Hex Hall, wearing my uniform, surrounded by my former classmates, and having no idea what to do. We'd finally made plans at the Brannicks'. Getting to Ireland, getting to Lough Bealach. Amassing a bunch of demon-glass.

My being magically transported back to Graymalkin Island—a place that had *freaking disappeared*—had not been in any of those plans.

Spinning around, I looked for more familiar faces. The whole area was surrounded by fog, obscuring anything past the oak trees lining the drive. Overhead the sun was a hot white disk behind gray clouds.

Still confused, I started to walk toward the house. And then I heard, "Sophie."

I turned around. Her pink hair faded and her face pale, Jenna gave a shaky smile. "There you are," she said, like we'd just been separated for a few minutes and not for weeks.

It's a miracle I didn't send her sprawling on the gravel

as I ran at her and threw my arms around her. I could feel her tears on my collarbone, and I was doing my best not to get snot all over the top of her head, but we were both laughing.

"Oh, Tiny Pink Jenna," I half sobbed, half giggled. "I have never been so happy to see a vampire in my life."

She squeezed me tighter. "I've never been so happy to be squished by a demon!"

In that moment, I didn't care that I'd been pulled back to Hex Hall by some kind of scary, dark magic, or that I was probably going to get killed one way or another. Jenna was here, and she was alive, and we were together. Everything else was fixable.

When we pulled apart, I noticed a new bloodstone hanging around her neck, this one larger and more ornate than the one she used to wear. Jenna followed my gaze and gave a watery laugh as she slid the stone on its chain. "Yeah, I upgraded," she said. "I got it from Byron. Swore it was one-hundred-percent shatterproof."

I raised an eyebrow, taking in the elaborate silver-and-amethyst setting. "It's also one-hundred-percent tacky, but if it will keep you safe, then I'm all for it."

"I'm going to get you a matching one that says 'BFFs' in like, runes or something."

I laughed at that, probably harder than the joke deserved, but I was so relieved to see her that I felt downright giddy. "So you really were with Byron this whole time?"

She nodded. "Yeah. That night, after you got back with Cal and Archer, the other Council members came to my room. They took me to this insanely creepy place." Jenna shuddered at the memory, and I had a feeling I knew exactly where she'd ended up: the dungeonlike chamber underneath Thorne Abbey that served as a kind of magical courtroom.

"Lara Casnoff wanted me staked," Jenna said, and my hands reflexively squeezed hers. "She said it was stupid to ever allow vampires to cohabitate with Prodigium, so I had to be executed. Mrs. Casnoff asked to be the one to do it."

Now my grip on Jenna's hand was so tight, it must have hurt her. I imagined Jenna, terrified and shaking, being led upstairs by someone she'd once trusted, knowing death was coming.

I would kill Mrs. Casnoff. I would blast that stupid hairdo right off her head, once I had my powers back.

"Thank God for her," Jenna said, and I blinked.

"What?"

"It was Mrs. Casnoff who contacted Byron. She took my bloodstone from me because she said she'd need some kind of proof I was dead. Apparently when you stake vamps, their bloodstones explode. Then she snuck me out of the house using this passage behind—"

"Behind a painting," I finished. I'd escaped Thorne Abbey the same way.

Nodding, Jenna said, "Right. Byron met me at the edge of the property and gave me this." She lifted the clunky pendant from her neck. "He took me back to his nest in London, and let me tell you, this place has nothing on Lord Freaking Byron's nest for weirdness. But Vix was there," she said, smiling a little. Vix was Jenna's girlfriend and another vampire.

But then all the amusement faded from her face. "I heard about Thorne. All Byron learned was that your body wasn't found. For like, a month, there was no news, and I thought . . ."

I wrapped my arms around her again. "I know," I murmured. "I thought the same thing about you for a long time, too."

She sniffled and pulled away, rubbing her nose with her hand. "Anyway, then he started hearing these strange stories that you were with the *Brannicks*."

"I was," I said, and when Jenna widened her eyes at me, I raised a hand and said, "It is a very long story, and I promise I'll spill all later. Condensed version: my mom is a Brannick, I am the unholy love child of a Brannick and a demon, and the bar for family dysfunction is now set super high."

Jenna, to her credit, knew when to just roll with it. "Okay, then."

"The more pressing question right now is, why are we back at Hex Hall?"

Jenna looked around, taking in the unnatural fog, the dilapidated (well, *more* dilapidated) feel of the house. "Something tells me it's not for a class reunion."

"Did you get pulled through some kind of magic tornado, too?" I asked her.

"No, I flew in here as a bat. It's a new thing I learned from Byron."

"Ha ha," I said, swatting at her arm.

She smiled back and said, "Yeah, same thing, actually. Like being yanked through the air at nine bajillion miles an hour." Her face grew serious. "What kind of magic could do that? Look around, Soph. There's like, at least a hundred of us here. All pulled from God knows where at the same time. That's not just hard-core, it's—"

"Scary," I finished.

The rest of the group was starting to coalesce around the front of the house, and I had the unsettling feeling that we were all waiting for someone—or something—to come out the front door. Like at any second, Mrs. Casnoff was going to step out, and it was just going to be another school year. Jenna and I stayed close together, and we hung to the back of the crowd.

Someone on my other side nudged my shoulder, and I shifted closer to Jenna to make room. And then a hand closed over mine.

Before I even turned my head, I knew.

"Mercer." Archer smiled down at me. "Fancy meeting you here."

As much as I wanted to, I couldn't just throw my arms around his neck and kiss the heck out of him. And I really wanted to. So I settled for lacing my fingers with his and pulling him slightly closer.

Archer here, safe, his hand in mine. And Jenna, pressed tight to my other side. My heart was so full, I could hardly breathe, and even though I tried to keep it light, my voice was strained when I said, "Of course. Everything going to hell, and you turn up. I should've known."

He shrugged, even though his eyes were burning with the same emotion currently racing through my veins. "Eh, Italy was getting boring. Figured I might as well see what you ladies were up to. Jenna," he said, nodding across me.

I could feel Jenna stiffen slightly; The Eye had killed Jenna's first girlfriend, who'd also been the vamp that made Jenna. Needless to say, she wasn't exactly Archer's biggest fan. Still, she gave a curt nod. "Archer."

"So, were you covered in golden light and sucked

through some kind of vortex to get here, too?" I asked Archer, trying to keep my mind on the task at hand and not the way his fingers were softly stroking my palm.

"Hmm? Oh, yeah, golden light, then it was like someone was using my body to do origami. And then, bam, back at Hex Hall. Any idea what's going on?"

It was Jenna who answered. "None. Do you see anybody you remember?"

"I ran into Evan, the warlock I used to room with, while I was looking for you. He, uh, wasn't too happy to see me."

Archer winced a little as he raised a hand to his cheekbone. It looked a little swollen, and a bruise was already forming. "Oh, right," I said. I'd nearly forgotten the various rumors about Archer after he left the school. "People think you killed Elodie. And tried to kill me, so maybe we should stop with the hand-holding."

I wasn't sure if Archer was confused or pissed or some combination of the two, but he dropped my hand, and said, "Why do—"

But whatever he was going to say was cut off as the front door of Hecate Hall slowly creaked open. All heads swiveled toward it, and I swore I could hear footsteps coming from inside. I held my breath and wished I hadn't told Archer to let go of me.

Mrs. Casnoff stepped out into the dim light, wearing

the same suit she'd worn the day I'd met her. That was the only thing that was the same.

She looked a good ten years older than she had the last time I'd seen her, and her hands, as she spread them wide in welcome, were shaking. Her royal blue skirt and jacket seemed to hang on her bony frame, and there was some kind of dark stain on her silk blouse.

But most disturbing of all, her dark blond hair, that hair that she always teased, threatened, or enchanted into ridiculously ornate updos, was now completely white and streaming down her back. It fluttered around her head like spiderwebs.

"Students of Hecate Hall," she said, her voice wavering like an old lady's. "Welcome to a new semester."

# CHAPTER 14

"Oh my God," Jenna murmured, just as I said, "Holy hell weasel," under my breath. I won't repeat what Archer said.

Someone in the crowd—I think it was Taylor—shouted, "But the school is closed. Everyone was saying . . ."

Her voice trailed off, and one of the faeries piped up, her voice high and clear. "You have no right to bring us here. The Fae are no longer in alliance with the rest of Prodigium. On behalf of the Seelie court, I demand you send us home." Ah. That was Nausicaa. She was the only one of the faeries that talked like she was rehearsing a play.

Next to me, Jenna leaned in closer and said, "The Fae broke their alliance? Did you know that?"

I shook my head just as Mrs. Casnoff pinned Nausicaa with a glare. No matter how feeble she seemed, she could still throw one heck of a dirty look. "Alliances and treaties have no meaning here at Hecate Hall. Once you've been a student here, your allegiance is to the school. Always." She gave a smile that was more like a grimace. "It was in the code of conduct you signed when you were sentenced here."

I remembered that, a thick pamphlet I'd barely read before scrawling my name on the dotted line. I suddenly wished I had of power of time travel so that I could go smack Sophie From A Year Ago around, and tell her to read things first.

"Now, I'm sure there are many questions," Mrs. Casnoff continued in what had to be the understatement of the year. "But for now, report to your rooms. All will be explained at tonight's assembly."

"This is crap!" someone shouted. I rose up on tiptoes and saw a tall boy with reddish hair.

"Evan," Archer murmured.

The crowd sort of scooted away from the boy as he and Mrs. Casnoff faced each other down.

"I beg your pardon, Mr. Butler?" Mrs. Casnoff asked, and this time, she sounded a lot more like her old self and less like a frail old lady.

"The Eye and the Brannicks have been killing us off, and the school freaking disappeared. And now, what, we're all just supposed to start a new school year?"

No one was whispering now. In fact, everything had gone unnaturally quiet, I realized. The wind had died, and there were no birds, no distant sound of the ocean. It was like the island was holding its breath.

"Enough," Mrs. Casnoff said. "As I said, the assembly this evening will answer all—"

"No!" Evan shouted, his voice echoing in the still air. "I'm not setting foot in that place until you tell us what the hell is going on. How did you get us here? Why is *he* here?" Evan jerked his thumb at Archer, and several people glanced in our direction. Archer was wearing a bored expression, but the bruise on his cheek was darker against his suddenly paler skin.

"Mr. Butler," Mrs. Casnoff snapped, drawing herself up taller. "Stop it. Now."

Evan snorted. "Screw this." The girl next to Evan, a witch whose name I thought was Michaela, put a hand on his arm and said something to him, but he shook her off. "There's no way I'm spending another year in some rotting mansion, hidden away from the whole damn world. Not when a war is coming." With that, he shoved his way through the crowd, his feet kicking up a cloud of dust down the gravel driveway.

"Evan." Mrs. Casnoff's voice rang out, and this time, there was more in it than anger or irritation. It almost sounded like a warning.

But Evan didn't even turn around.

"What the heck is he gonna do, swim to the mainland?" I muttered under my breath.

By now, Evan had reached the thick wall of fog circling the house. He hesitated, and I saw his shoulders go up and his hands clenched into fists at his side, like he was trying to psych himself up. He raised a hand, and I saw a couple of sparks shoot from his fingertips. They died almost immediately with a faint popping sound, like a wet firecracker.

Next to me, Archer wiggled his own fingers, and the same thing happened to his magic. "No powers allowed, apparently," he murmured.

I looked back at Evan and thought that he'd probably come back now. Instead, he moved one foot into the fog.

For a moment, he stood there frozen, half in, half out of the gray haze. "What's happening?" Jenna asked. "Why isn't he moving?"

"I don't know," I said, and Archer slipped his hand back into mine.

That's when Evan started to scream. As we watched, the mist seemed to grow tentacles that wrapped around the rest of Evan's body. One shot out and grabbed his arms, swallowing them, as a second curled around his torso. A third wound its way sinuously around his head, and Evan's cry suddenly stopped. And then he was gone.

No one moved. I think that was the weirdest part, how there was no screaming or fainting. This was real. Evan was . . . well, if not dead, then gone.

Almost as one, the crowd of students turned back to face Mrs. Casnoff. I don't know what I expected her to say or do. Cackle, maybe. Or look down her nose at all of us and smugly declare, "I told him not to go."

But she was leaning against the porch rail, and she didn't look smug, or satisfied, or even grimly pleased. Just old and tired and maybe a little sad.

"Go inside," she told us listlessly. "Your room assignments are the same as they were the previous semester."

There was another pause, and then, slowly, the students nearest the house began to shuffle up the steps.

"What do we do?" Jenna asked.

"I guess we go inside," I said. "It's either that or get eaten by fog. I think I'd rather take my chances with the house."

We followed the crowd, making our way onto the porch. As we passed Mrs. Casnoff, I stopped. I wasn't sure what I wanted to say to her, or what I wanted her to say to *me*. I just felt like we should acknowledge each other in some way. But even though I stood just three feet from her, Mrs. Casnoff didn't even glance in my direction. She stayed by the railing, taking shaky breaths, staring out at where Evan had disappeared. Finally, I turned away and walked through the front door.

From inside the house, I could hear gasps and muffled sobbing, so I braced myself for Hex Hall to be every bit as screwed up as the island.

I hadn't braced hard enough.

The first thing that hit me was the heat. Graymalkin Island was off the coast of Georgia, and it was mid-August, so it had already been crazy humid outside. But the house had always been cool and comfortable. Now it was stifling, and the air was almost too thick to breathe. I could smell mildew and damp, and the wallpaper was peeling in places. The first time I'd been in Hex Hall, I'd thought it had looked gross and dirty. Then, it had been a spell making me see it that way. I didn't think that was the case now.

There was also something weird going on with the light. I remembered the main hallway as being well lit, but now it was so dim that parts of the room disappeared in the shadows.

I took a step forward, and something crunched under-foot. Glancing down, I saw that it was brightly colored glass. And then I realized why everything looked so different. The huge stained-glass window that had dominated the space was broken. It had depicted the ori-gin of Prodigium, a huge sword-wielding angel kicking the three angels who would go on to become witches, shape-shifters, and Fae out of heaven. But now the avenging angel was missing its head and most of the sword, and there was a huge, jagged hole right in the middle of the other three figures. It looked like they'd been cut in half by something with giant claws.

For some reason, it was that shattered window that got to me. Apparently, I wasn't alone in that. A few feet in front of me, a group of four witches stared up at the headless angel, their arms wrapped around each other. "What is going on?" one of them wailed plaintively. No one had an answer.

Archer, Jenna, and I weren't exactly clutching each other and sobbing, but we were pretty shaken as we formed a little huddle. "Okay," I finally said. "Can we all agree that this is maybe the most screwed-up situation we've ever found ourselves in?"

"Agreed," they said in unison.

"Awesome." I gave a little nod. "And do either of you have any idea what we should do about it?"

"Well, we can't use magic," Archer said.

"And if we try to leave, we get eaten by Monster Fog," Jenna added.

"Right. So no plans at all, then?"

Jenna frowned. "Other than rocking in the fetal position for a while?"

"Yeah, I was thinking about taking one of those showers where you huddle in the corner fully clothed and cry," Archer offered.

I couldn't help but snort with laughter. "Great. So we'll all go have our mental breakdowns, and *then* we'll somehow get ourselves out of this mess."

"I think our best bet is to lie low for a while," Archer said. "Let Mrs. Casnoff think we're all too shocked and awed to do anything. Maybe this assembly tonight will give us some answers."

"Answers," I practically sighed. "About freaking time."

Jenna gave me a funny look. "Soph, are you . . . grinning?"

I could feel my cheeks aching, so I knew that I was. "Look, you two have to admit: if we want to figure out just what the Casnoffs are plotting, this is pretty much the perfect place."

"My girl has a point," Archer said, smiling at me. Now my cheeks didn't just ache, they burned.

Clearing her throat, Jenna said, "Okay, so we all go up to our rooms, then after the assembly tonight we can regroup and decide what to do next."

"Deal," I said as Archer nodded.

"Are we all going to high-five now?" Jenna asked after a pause.

"No, but I can make up some kind of secret hand-shake if you want," Archer said, and for a second, they smiled at each other.

But just as quickly, the smile disappeared from Jenna's face, and she said to me, "Let's go. I want to see if our room is as freakified as the rest of this place."

"Good idea," I said. Archer reached out and brushed his fingers over mine.

"See you later, then?" he asked. His voice was casual, but my skin was hot where he touched me.

"Definitely," I answered, figuring that even a girl who has to stop evil witches from taking over the world could make time for kissage in there *somewhere*.

He turned and walked away. As I watched him go, I could feel Jenna staring at me. "Fine," she acknowledged with a dramatic roll of her eyes. "He's a *little* dreamy."

I elbowed her gently in the side. "Thanks."

Jenna started to walk to the stairs. "You coming?"

"Yeah," I said. "I'll be right up. I just want to take a quick look around down here."

"Why, so you can be even more depressed?"

Actually, I wanted to stay downstairs just a little longer to see if anyone else showed up. So far, I'd seen nearly everyone I remembered from last year at Hex Hall. Had Cal been dragged here, too? Technically he hadn't been a student, but Mrs. Casnoff had used his powers a lot last year. Would she still want him here?

To Jenna, I just said, "Yeah, you know me. I like poking bruises."

"Okay. Get your Nancy Drew on."

She jogged up the stairs. I waited in the foyer for about fifteen minutes, but there was no sign of Cal, or either of the Casnoffs. Curious, I wandered in the direction of the cellar. It was down a narrow hallway just off the foyer, and while the corridor had always been dim, now it was completely covered in shadows. I could barely make out the wooden door and had to move my hands over it for a while before I found the iron doorknob. I twisted it, but it was locked. Of course.

"I already tried it," Archer said from behind me.

I was glad it was dark, so that he couldn't see me blush yet again. "I told you, Cross. It's all kissing in castles and Applebee's from now on." I turned so that my back was to the door.

He walked forward. "Ah, but this is technically *outside* the cellar," he murmured as he pulled me into his arms.

# CHAPTER 15

As soon as our lips met, I was glad I had my back against the door. My knees were in *definite* danger of failing me. Archer wrapped his arms around my waist and held me tighter as I clutched the front of his shirt and poured all that I'd been feeling for the past few weeks into that kiss—the despair I'd felt when I'd thought he was dead, the relief I felt now, pressed between him and the cellar door.

When we finally parted, I rested my forehead on his collarbone and took deep breaths. It was a few moments before I was capable of speech. "I thought you said we'd do this 'later.'"

He kissed my temple. "It's been like, twenty minutes. That counts as later."

Chuckling, I raised my head to look at him. "I kind of missed you."

Even though it was dark, I could see him smile. "I kind of missed you, too."

"I should probably get upstairs now."

"You probably should," he murmured, lowering his mouth to mine.

By the time I finally made it up to Jenna's and my room, I was practically skipping. But as soon as I walked through the door, my happy feelings evaporated so quickly, I practically heard the pop.

"Oh, man," I said softly. "Why do I keep being surprised when everything turns out gross and depressing?"

Jenna was sitting in the middle of her bed. "I thought the window was the worst," she said quietly. "Or, you know. Evan getting eaten. But now I really feel like crying."

Our room had never been what anyone would call luxurious, but thanks to Jenna's obsessive love for pink, it had been . . . okay, I was going to say "comfortable" but "bright" and "maybe a little insane" were probably better descriptions. Still, it had been ours, and I'd never really realized how much Jenna's lights, scarves, and Electric Raspberry comforter had made that tiny dorm room feel like home.

There were no lights now. Just two beds, shoved to opposite walls; one battered desk; and a dresser that listed heavily to one side. The mirror above the dresser was weathered and cracked, distorting our reflections. Maybe it was that gray light from all the fog, or maybe it was just that this room, like the rest of the house, seemed to have had all the color bled out of it. Whatever it was, this dorm room was not home anymore. In fact, it felt an awful lot like a cell.

I started to say that to Jenna as I moved out of the doorway. But the second I did, the door slammed behind me, hard enough to make me jump. Down the hallway, I could hear other doors slamming, too, and a few muffled shouts.

"Locked?" Jenna guessed.

I jiggled the handle. "Yup."

"Do you think Archer is right about everyone here being de-magicked? Or maybe the fog, like, made his and Evan's magic . . . de-magic."

Crossing over to the closet, I sighed and said, "I'm betting the kids here are de-magicked, but it doesn't really matter." I flung open the closet. Just as I'd thought, the only things hung up inside were Hex Hall uniforms. "I'm pretty much de-magicked myself these days," I said to Jenna over my shoulder. "Also, maybe we should stop saying de-magicked. It's starting to sound weird."

She sat up straighter. "What?"

"You know, when you say things too much, and—"

"Sophie," Jenna said, tilting her head and frowning at me.

Sighing, I sat down on my own bed, facing her. "Thanks to some mojo from the Council, I'm currently powerless."

Her expression softening, Jenna breathed, "Oh, Soph. I'm so sorry."

"It's not as bad as it sounds," I told her. "My powers aren't *gone* gone. They're still bumping around in here, but I can't use them unless I touch this particular—whoa."

"What?"

I crossed the room to grip the footboard of Jenna's bed. "There's this spell in the Thorne family grimoire. If I touch it, my powers will be restored. And Dad was sure the Casnoffs had the grimoire. It might be *here*, Jenna." I let go of her bed to pace as my magic pounded inside me. "If we find it, I could be demoning up the place by dinnertime." And possibly using my powers for the Casnoffs. Fear, oily and hot, slid over me at the idea, and I suddenly felt sick.

"Or Lara could have it."

"What?" I asked. "Oh. Lara. Damn it, I didn't think of that." I felt my magic slide back down to settle in the pit of my stomach, almost like it was disappointed, too.

"We can still look for it," Jenna said quickly. "Or Lara

might show up. We'll find some way to get your powers back, Soph."

I smiled at her. "Jenna, once again, *your* powers of Awesome amaze me."

"It's a skill," she agreed, nodding somberly.

Giggling, I tossed a pillow at her, and for a moment it was like nothing had changed; we were just Sophie and Jenna, hanging out in our dorm room, getting ready to go to Methods of Magical Execution 1500–Present, or some other boring class. For the next hour or so, we sat on our beds and filled each other in on everything we'd been through the past month. She told me what life had been like at Byron's (no surprise, there had been lots of crushed velvet, and drinking blood out of skulls, and "Byron's version of open mic night," Jenna had said with a shudder).

"I wonder what Vix thinks happened to me," Jenna said. "I was standing right next to her when I whooshed back here."

"You'll get back to her, Jenna. Promise."

I wasn't sure how much Jenna believed that, but she nodded. "I know. Okay, so now tell me all about the Brannicks."

So I did, including Finley and Izzy and the reappearance of my dad and Cal. I even fessed up about Cal's and my betrothal, the kiss, and everything that had happened with Archer back at Thorne Abbey. Until I started spilling them, I hadn't realized just how many secrets I'd been keeping from Jenna.

I think even she was a little bit shocked, because she raised her eyebrows and said, "Wow. You were busier than I thought this summer."

"Are you mad?"

She considered it, and then said, "No. I feel like I should be, but . . ." She sighed. "I get why it wasn't easy to talk to me about the Archer stuff. Besides, I went through nearly a month thinking you were dead, so it's hard to feel anything but *Yay, Sophie,* you know?"

Relief surged through me. "Well, good. Because if I'm gonna get to the bottom of whatever is going on here, I'm definitely going to need my vampire side-kick."

Jenna snorted and tossed her hair. "Whatever. You're obviously the sidekick. With that hair, and all the sarcastic remarks?"

"Hmmm," I said, pretending to think it over. "And you do have a way more angsty backstory."

Jenna waved her hand. "Exactly. Vampire for the win!"

We laughed again. Then I glanced out the window. The gray sky was already darkening, and the fog that surrounded the house seemed to slither.

Jenna had gotten quiet. "What do you think is going to happen to us?"

The first thing that came to mind was "Nothing good," but instead I wrapped an arm around her shoulders and said, "We're going to be fine. Think of all the stuff we've already been through. You think a little killer fog is gonna get in our way? Ha!"

Jenna didn't look convinced, but she did say, "I'm not sure if you're confident or delusional, but thanks anyway."

The sky was nearly black by the time our door finally creaked open. Mrs. Casnoff's voice, as thin and reedy as before, drifted through the school. "Students, at this time, please report to the ballroom."

Jenna and I joined the groups of kids headed down the stairs. No one was crying now, so I guess that was an improvement. "Sophie," Taylor said, appearing at my elbow. Her voice was kind of garbled because her fangs were out. "So, what's all this about?"

"How would I know? I'm every bit as clueless as everyone else."

She frowned, which had the effect of shoving her incisors even farther out. It had been a while since I'd been around shapeshifters; I'd forgotten how unsettling they could be. Caught in between humans and animals, they could definitely cause the heebie-jeebies.

"But your dad was Head of the Council," she said. "And you were with the Council all summer. You must know something."

"And why is Archer Cross here?" That was from Justin. His voice had apparently changed over the summer, since he actually said the words instead of squeaking them. "He's an Eye."

"Didn't he try to kill you?" Nausicaa had drifted up, and she narrowed her eyes at me. "And if so, why exactly were you holding his hand earlier?"

Conversations like this usually ended in pitchforks and torches, so I held my hands out in what I hoped was an "everyone just calm the heck down" gesture. But then Jenna spoke up. "Sophie doesn't know anything," she said, nudging me behind her. That might've been more effective if Jenna weren't so short. "And whatever reason we're here, the Council had nothing to do with it." Jenna didn't add that that was because the entire Council, with the exception of Lara Casnoff and my dad, was dead. "She's just as freaked out as the rest of us, so back. Off." From the expressions on the other kids' faces, I guessed Jenna had bared her fangs, and maybe even given a flash of red eyes.

"What's going on here?" a familiar voice brayed. Great. Like this night didn't suck out loud enough already. The Vandy—who had been a cross between

145

school matron and prison guard at Hex Hall—shoved her way through the crowd, breathing hard. Her purple tattoos, marks of the Removal, were nearly black against her red face. "Downstairs, now!" As the group began moving again, she glared at Jenna and me. "Show your fangs again, Miss Talbot, and I'll wear them as earrings. Is that understood?"

Jenna may have muttered, "Yes, ma'am," but her tone said something totally different. We jogged down the stairs to join the rest of the students lining up to go into the ballroom. "At least one thing at Hex Hall hasn't changed," Jenna said.

"Yeah, apparently the Vandy's powers of bitchery are a constant. I find that comforting."

Less comforting was the creeptasticness of the school at night. During the day, it had just been depressing. Now that it was dark, it was full-on sinister. The old-fashioned gas lamps on the walls had once burned with a cozy, golden light. Now, a noxious green glow sputtered inside the milky glass, throwing crazy shadows all over the place.

As we moved down the hall, I stopped by one of the parlors. The big window that had looked out over the pond (and Cal's cabin) was broken. More of that terrifying fog spilled inside through the jagged window frame, swirling around the floor. I noticed that several of the photographs that lined the walls were now lying on the carpet.

"I know 'What's Going On?' has practically become a catchphrase around here," I said to Jenna, "but seriously. What *is* going on?"

Jenna studied the fog and shook her head. "It's like the house is sick," she said. "Or poisoned. The island, too."

"Maybe. I mean, the Casnoffs have a giant pit they use for raising demons." Archer and I had found that pit over the summer, and I still had nightmares about the ghouls who had guarded it. "Magic that dark— that *evil* . . . Do you think it could actually infect a place?"

Her expression troubled, Jenna murmured, "Wouldn't surprise me."

"Are broken windows a new decorating theme around here?" Archer asked, coming up behind Jenna and me and poking his head into the parlor.

"So it would seem," I said. I was still looking outside when a faint light appeared in the gloom. It took me a minute to realize that it was from Cal's cabin. Was someone out there? Was *Cal* out there?

But just as quickly as it had appeared, the light went out again. Frowning, I turned from the doorway, and I went to slip my arm through Archer's. Then I remembered what Nausicaa had said earlier. Now wasn't exactly the best time for PDA, probably.

The three of us trailed behind everyone else into the ballroom. Here, at least, things looked more or less the same. Of course, the ballroom had always been one of the more bizarre rooms at Hex Hall, so that didn't say much. Still. I was relieved to see the familiar jumble of tables and chairs and not, like, tree stumps or whatever.

But then I looked at the front of the room, and any relief I might've been feeling evaporated. Mrs. Casnoff was slumping in her usual chair, staring off into the distance. Her hair was up now, but it was still unkempt. The Vandy was also sitting at the table, but the other three teachers we'd had at Hex Hall—Ms. East, Mr. Ferguson, and Byron, of course—were missing.

And sitting at the other end of the table, dressed in a bright blue suit, smiling like she was at a freaking tea party, was Lara Casnoff.

# CHAPTER 16

Somehow, I got through dinner. Well, I pushed food around on my plate. Jenna and Archer did the same. In fact, as I looked around, all I saw were full plates. Maybe it was fear or nervousness keeping everyone else from eating, but for me, it was this weird mixture of rage and elation. Lara Casnoff had taken so much away from me, and my powers ached to do some serious smiting. But at the same time, the fact that she was here meant that it was very likely the grimoire was here, too. I was lost in thoughts of where the book could be when Lara stood up, clapped her hands, and announced, "If you're all finished eating, we can get on with the presentation."

"Do you think there's going to be a dance number?" Jenna muttered as we shifted our chairs to face the front of the room. I always appreciated a good dance number joke, but it was hard to chuckle as I stared at the woman who had tried to kill me more than once. I willed her to meet my eyes, for some kind of acknowledgment of what had happened this summer. But she never did.

I felt an almost overpowering sense of déjà vu as I sat in my chair, Archer next to me, and watched Lara Casnoff stand in front of the room. Had it really been only a year ago that Archer and I had sat in this same room, practically strangers? Back when I'd thought I was just a regular witch. Back when Hex Hall had been a school and not some kind of prison.

Lara raised her hands in welcome. "I'm sure you're all wondering why you're here," she said, her voice ringing out loud and clear in the silent room. All of the students were very still. There was none of the unrest and anger that had filled us earlier today. Maybe it's because we all wanted answers. Or maybe we were just afraid we'd get eaten, too.

"First of all, let me apologize for your current accommodations," Lara continued, pacing the front of the room. Her heels reverberated as loudly as gunshots. "We're funneling a great deal of magic into your protection here at Hecate Hall, and I'm afraid that's affected the house itself. But then, this school was never meant to be a five-star hotel, was it?" She was still smiling, but there was hardness in her eyes now. "In any case, I'm Lara

Casnoff, and I will be working with Anastasia Casnoff as headmistress for this year. Now, I'm sure you have many questions. But first, I think it's time we tell you the truth about events that occurred this summer."

A glimmering speck appeared beside her hip, and I knew what was coming next. Sure enough, the speck grew until it was a huge, shimmering screen. And then we were all shading our eyes as fire raced across the screen. "This is Council Headquarters in London," Lara said over the sound of the flames. "Several months ago, L'Occhio di Dio, along with a large group of Brannicks, attacked. Over half of the Council was killed, and this was the result." She gestured to the burning building.

Lara's voice rang out again. "And then, only a few months later, The Eye attacked our secondary head-quarters at Thorne Abbey." On the screen, the house loomed up, as immense and impressive as it had been the first day I'd seen it. Looking at it, I felt a wave of sadness wash over me. I'd been happy there. I'd also been freaked out and nearly killed more than once, but still. It was where I'd gotten to know more about my history. It's where I'd gotten to know Dad.

Once again, bright orange light nearly blinded me as Thorne Abbey was also engulfed in flames. "Thorne Abbey was destroyed. Anastasia and I were lucky to escape with our lives. Unfortunately, the Head of the Council, James Atherton, was not so lucky."

Several heads swiveled in my direction, and I worked to keep my face impassive. When I looked from the screen over to Lara, I saw that she was staring right at me.

"There can be no doubt now that we're at war with our enemies," Lara said. "The Eye and the Brannicks will not be happy until all Prodigium have been wiped from the face of the earth." She clapped once, and the screen shrunk back down to a tiny dot, and then vanished altogether. "And that is why all of you are here."

I realized I was sitting on the edge of my seat.

"Why were all of you sent to Hecate Hall originally?" Lara asked. At first, I thought she didn't want an actual answer, but then she nodded at one of the younger witches.

The girl looked around before answering, "Because we did something wrong. Exposed our powers to the human world."

Lara shook her head. "It isn't that your magic was wrong," she said. "It's that your magic was strong. Powerful. That's nothing to be ashamed of. And it's certainly not something for which you should be punished. You"—she spread her arms out wide—"all of you, are the most valuable people in Prodigium society. You feel as though your powers are out of control, but they're not. They're simply too much for you to handle at times."

It was close to something Cal had said to me back at Thorne Abbey, that my spells weren't destructive so much as "too big."

"So are you going to teach us to control them?" I heard someone call out.

Lara's smile spread across her face, so big and bright that it was actually terrifying. "Better than that. You've all been brought here for a very special purpose."

"This isn't going to be good, is it?" Jenna whispered.

"Maybe the special purpose involves us eating brownies?" I suggested. "Or, like, wrangling unicorns? That may actually be possible."

Jenna studied me. "You must be *really* freaked out."

I was. And it turned out, I was right to be, because the next thing Lara said was, "For hundreds of years, Prodigium have been looking for a way to make themselves stronger. More powerful. Invincible, even." Once again, her eyes met mine. "And now we've found a way. Clarice?"

The Vandy got up from the table, a small velvet bag in her hand. She reached inside it and pulled out a crumpled and ragged sheet of paper, holding it over her head so that everyone could see. My magic started slam-dancing inside my chest.

"What is it?" Archer asked me.

I didn't get a chance to answer. "This piece of paper

is the key to our salvation," Lara continued. "On it is the most powerful spell ever created. It can imbue each and every one of you with the most powerful magic in the universe. And not only will this spell keep you safe from our enemies, it will allow you to obliterate them once and for all."

Suddenly, both Archer's and Jenna's hands clamped down on my wrists.

"What?" I whispered, looking back and forth between them.

"You were about to get up," Archer replied through clenched teeth, never taking his eyes of Lara.

"And then you were probably going to start yelling about how she's going to turn us into demons," Jenna added, so low I could barely hear her. "And we're lying low, remember?"

They were right. And Lara was already watching me, that same creepy smile curving her lips. She wanted me to jump up and start shouting about demons and mind control. Then I'd look like a nutjob, and that would be that. So even though it was killing me to just sit there, I did it.

Lara's grin slipped a little as I held her gaze, saying nothing. "So that's why you've all been brought here," she said, turning her attention back to the other students. "To train. To prepare. And to participate in a ritual that will make you all more powerful than you'd ever thought possible."

"If we're so 'valuable,' why are we being held here against our will?" asked Siobhan, one of the faeries.

"The spells guarding this island are for your protection," the Vandy barked, and even though that hardly answered the question, it was apparently all the answer we were going to get, because Lara just nodded and said, "Exactly. Now, we'll start preparing you for the ritual tomorrow morning, first thing. So I suggest you all head back to your rooms and get some rest."

If it was a "suggestion," I wondered why it sounded so much like a threat. But slowly, kids started getting up and moving for the door. Heads were together, and there was whispering, but no one protested or tried to ask any more questions. Maybe everyone else had decided to lie low, too.

But me? I was kind of over that.

Even as Jenna hissed for me to come back, I walked to the front of the room and stood directly in front of Lara Casnoff, the woman who had tried to kill me. The woman who'd tried to kill Archer, and Jenna, and had put my dad through a ritual that had nearly killed him.

"You're going to turn them all into demons?" I demanded. "Did you forget the part where your last demon went rogue and started killing people?"

She didn't answer my question. "You certainly are a resilient little thing, Sophie."

"And you're evil and super condescending."

"Is this the part where you tell me that you're going to stop me? That I won't get away with it?" she asked, raising an eyebrow. "Because if it is, let me give you some advice: grow up."

With that, she handed the spell back to the Vandy, who replaced it in the bag.

I watched the two of them walk out of the ballroom, Mrs. Casnoff trailing behind, as Archer and Jenna came to stand next to me.

"Well, we know the plan now," Jenna said. "Any counter plans?"

"Stop the Casnoffs from raising a demon army, save everybody, and get the heck off this island. Then maybe we'll have a party or something. You know, to celebrate how awesome we are."

"Sounds solid enough," Archer said, bumping my shoulder with his. "Any idea how exactly we're supposed to do any of that?"

The greenish lights in the ballroom winked out, and I sighed. "None."

# CHAPTER 17

The next morning, I was blasted out of bed by Hex Hall's version of an alarm clock—this sonorous howling sound that was half bell, half growl. The room was still dark, and when I glanced out the window, all I could see was that damn fog.

Jenna was already at the closet, pulling out a uniform. Last night, we'd discovered the dresser was filled with white T-shirts and blue pajama pants. They were all the same size, but when you put them on, the clothes shifted and slid until they fit. The uniforms were apparently the same, because as Jenna slipped into the skirt, the hem brushed her shins, only to slither back up her body until the skirt fell just below her knees.

"I don't know if that's convenient or creepy," she said, inspecting her legs.

Shoving off the covers, I got out of bed and went to get my own uniform. "Let's go with creepy, shall we?"

Jenna pulled on her blazer, and I noticed she was chewing her lower lip, obviously thinking something over.

"You know, that's a dangerous habit for a vampire," I told her, nodding at her mouth.

"Huh? Oh, right," she said. "Sorry, I was just . . . Soph, if their big plot is to make everyone a demon, why bring you here? Or me, for that matter? Lara wanted me killed just a few months ago. What changed her mind?"

The same thought had kept me up last night. Over and over, I'd replayed Torin's words: me, at the head of the Casnoffs' demon force, using my powers for them. Was that why I was here?

But all I said to Jenna was, "They're evil and twisted. Who knows why they do anything?"

I could tell that answer didn't satisfy her, so I added, "But that's what we're going to find out, right? Operation Nancy Drew Goes To Hex Hall starts today!"

Jenna opened her mouth to say something, but then there was a sudden flash of light in the middle of the room. She shrieked, and I threw my hand up to shade my eyes as the glowing ball morphed into a familiar shape— the greenhouse where we used to have Defense classes. The three-dimensional image rotated slowly as Lara's voice filled the room. "At this time, all students are to report to the greenhouse."

Scowling, I waved my arm through the spell. It swirled like smoke before dissolving. "Freaking drama queen," I muttered. "How hard would it have been to announce that last night? Or to just do the voice thing?"

Jenna was still staring at the spot where the spell had been. "What do you think they're going to do to us there?"

"I—"

Before I got any further than that, I saw another flash of light, and the next thing I knew, I heard myself saying, "Look, they're not going to kill you, so maybe you should chill out for a sec."

Jenna shook her head slightly, like I'd just slapped her. "What?"

*Tell her you're me! Or I'm you. Whatever!* I demanded.

I didn't actually expect Elodie to respond. It wasn't like she usually listened to my mental commands. But this time, thankfully, she did.

"It's Elodie," she told Jenna. She breezed through the explanation of just why she could use me as her personal puppet so quickly that Jenna could only blink in response.

"If Sophie hadn't used *my* magic in *her* body," Elodie summed up, "she would've been dead like, ten times by now."

*Okay, it was only twice,* I grumbled inside.

Elodie ignored me. "And no," she said, raising my hand to cut off Jenna's next question. "I can't possess anyone else. Trust me, I've been trying to get inside Lara Casnoff ever since we got here. Which . . . sounds really wrong."

I felt my shoulders shrug. "Anyway, you looked like you were about to eat your own lip, and that's totally gross, so I figured I oughta swoop in and put your mind at ease. Last night, when I was trying my hardest to possess anyone who's not *this* freak, I overheard the Casnoffs talking. Apparently, turning a vampire into a demon seems like an awesome idea, so that's why you're here. No staking on the agenda."

Using Elodie as a spy hadn't even occurred to me. *Oh my God, this is perfect!* I shouted. Well, mentally shouted. *Of course! They can't see you unless you want them to; you can go anywhere in the school, and—*

*Jeez, not so loud,* she interrupted. *I'm in your head, so use your* inside *inside voice.*

Elodie went to brush my hair out of my eyes, muttering, "God, how does she live like this?"

*If you promise to stop taking over whenever you feel like it, I promise to get a hot oil treatment,* I replied, and she snorted.

Jenna folded her arms tightly across her chest. "So, what—you're like, helping us now?"

My eyes rolled. "No, I'm on Team Take Over The World With A Demon Army. Of course I'm helping you. Mostly so that whenever this is over, Sophie can get back to important stuff. Like how to unbind me from her."

Jenna nodded, distracted. "You've done magic through Sophie, you said. Can you try to do some now? Like, something simple?"

"This place has some kind of magic blocker on it," Elodie said, even as the same thought went through my brain. "No unauthorized persons can do spells."

"Right, but the Casnoffs don't even know you're here," Jenna said, a slow grin spreading on her face. "A ghost using a powerless demon to do magic? Bet they didn't think of that."

*Worth a shot*, I said to Elodie. Apparently she agreed, because my fingers came up, and there was a brief surge of power in my veins. Sparks flew, and within seconds, Jenna's pink stripe was the same white-blond as the rest of her hair.

"Holy crap," Jenna said, pulling her hair in front of her eyes. "It worked!"

Relief flooded through me, and I wasn't sure if it was mine or Elodie's.

There was a sudden banging on our door. Jenna jumped, and Elodie flicked my hand out toward her.

Bright fuchsia snaked down Jenna's hair again, and then, with that same awful, disorienting sensation I'd felt the night with the werewolf, Elodie was gone.

I sat down on my bed, trying to catch my breath, as Jenna opened the door. The Vandy stood there, glaring at us, and my heart plummeted. They knew. They'd sensed magic happening in here, and now they'd sent the Vandy to come collect us.

I sat there, trying not to pant in terror, while Jenna openly trembled.

"You were told to report to the greenhouse," the Vandy said, her eyes going back and forth between us. "Now, get your skinny butts down there."

You know when you have the most inappropriate reaction to something ever? I was so happy that we weren't being hauled off to be murdered that I burst out laughing. I mean, big, loud, honking laughter. Jenna shot me a panicked look as the Vandy's scowl got even darker. "What's so funny, Miss Mercer?"

I stood up on wobbly legs and did my best to stop cracking up. "Sorry, it's just, um . . ."

"You said 'butts,'" Jenna blurted out. "And Sophie's got a really immature sense of humor."

"Right," I said, seizing on that. "Butts. Ha ha!"

I think if the Vandy *could* have murdered us right then and there, she probably would have. Instead she just thrust one finger toward the staircase and said, "Move it."

We scrambled from the room.

Outside, the sky was every bit as gloomy and gray as it had been the day before. The fog seemed to have moved out a little bit, so we could make our way down to the greenhouse without fear of getting absorbed. Still, the ground felt mushy underfoot, and the grass, once bright emerald green, was now a sickly whitish-brown, like the underside of a mushroom. As we passed a huge oak tree, one of its blackened branches gave an ominous crack.

Once we were sure the Vandy was far enough behind us to make eavesdropping impossible, I lowered my head close to Jenna's and said, "Okay, so we have a ghost-spy."

"A ghost-spy who can do magic," Jenna added.

I nodded. "Even better. Which means that maybe the playing field is leveled after all."

Jenna squeezed my hand, and I was actually feeling kind of optimistic as we approached the greenhouse. I mean, I wasn't going to start *skipping* or anything (mostly because I was afraid I'd slip in all the muck), but all in all, I felt worlds better.

Through the glass walls of the greenhouse, I could see most of the other students standing in a circle, and I was in a good enough mood to joke to Jenna, "Ooh, wonder if we're gonna play Duck, Duck, Demon."

She laughed, but the sound died in her throat almost immediately as the crowd inside the greenhouse parted enough for us to see what they were all circling around.

There, shimmering chains of magic wrapped around his wrists, was Archer.

# CHAPTER 18

Jenna and I slid through the door as inconspicuously as we could. My heart was hammering, and all I wanted to do was rush to Archer, but Lara was standing right next to him, a smirk on her face. "This whole 'lying low' thing sucks so hard," I whispered to Jenna as we fell to the back of the crowd.

She gave me a sympathetic look, and then we turned our attention to Lara. "Students," Lara said. "As many of you have heard, Mr. Cross here is a member of L'Occhio di Dio." She walked closer to Archer and unbuttoned the top several buttons of his shirt, pulling the fabric away to reveal the gold-and-black tattoo just over his heart. I heard several gasps from the crowd. Of course, everyone had heard Archer was an Eye, but hearing about it and actually seeing proof were two different things. "And The

Eye are our enemies," Lara continued, circling Archer. I met his gaze, and he tried to smile at me, but I could see he was shaking.

My hands curled into fists, nails biting into my palms. My magic was like a tsunami inside me, pounding against its prison.

"But Mr. Cross is far and away the worst of L'Occhio di Dio. Would anyone care to tell me why?" Her gaze locked on mine. "Miss Mercer? Since you're the one he tried to assassinate last year, why don't you inform your classmates of the danger Mr. Cross represents?"

"He wasn't sent here to as—assassinate me," I insisted. I probably would have sounded more confident if I hadn't stumbled over the word "assassinate."

I cleared my throat, and kept going. "He was sent here to watch me, nothing more."

"And was he also sent to watch Elodie Parris? Why exactly, Miss Mercer, would The Eye have such an interest in you?"

I was standing on shaky ground, and Lara and me both knew it. It was like she had woven chains around me, too, only with words instead of magic. I didn't want to own up to my demon-ness in front of the entire student body—after all, everyone at Hex Hall still thought I was a regular witch—and I was afraid that anything else I said was just going to get Archer in more trouble. So even though I felt sick, I lowered my eyes and pressed my lips together.

"I can tell you what The Eye wanted with Sophie," Archer spoke up. He was grinning, but his voice was tight with pain. "We heard she was particularly skilled at Chutes and Ladders, and since The Eye holds a Chutes and Ladders tournament every summer—" His voice broke on a cry of pain as Lara twisted her fingers, and the glowing threads of magic around him burned white hot for a moment. I had to bite the inside of my cheek to keep from screaming.

"Archer Cross is not only a member of L'Occhio di Dio, but he's also a traitor to his people," Lara said, moving to stand closer to him. "He represents the greatest threat any of us can ever face. Which is why he'll be so very useful to us."

Jenna slipped her hand in mine and squeezed my fingers as Lara said, "Today, we'll be using Mr. Cross for practice. The ritual I discussed last night will increase your powers, but first I need to see what we're working with." And then, like she was getting us ready for a game of Red Rover, she clapped her hands and said, "All right, everyone, line up. You will each get one chance to use your most powerful attack spell on Mr. Cross. I do ask that you don't do anything that will kill him. Mr. Callahan is on hand to heal him, but even his powers only go so far."

Mouth dry, I looked up. I'd been so focused on Archer in the middle of the room that I hadn't noticed Cal, standing at the very back of the room, leaning against the gallows. His arms were folded over his chest. He was watching me, the expression on his face a weird mix of relief, anger, and tension. I lifted my fingers in a kind of wave, and he nodded in return. Jenna followed my gaze, and her grip on my hand got tighter. "Cal," she murmured. "That's at least one more thing in our favor."

And it was. Too bad it was impossible to feel happy about anything as I spent the next few hours watching my classmates torture Archer. Because I didn't have magic, I was allowed to sit the exercise out and watch. And Lara ensured that I watched. The first time I tried to shut my eyes, I realized they were frozen open. I couldn't move my neck either, so turning my head away was out of the question.

Michaela was the first witch to go. She hesitated, and her attack spell, when she finally cast it, was weak. It bounced off Archer's chest and barely made him rock back on his heels.

I thought maybe they'd all do that. I mean, sure, Archer was the "enemy," but it wasn't like these kids were killers. And if it hadn't been for Lara, maybe they would've gone easy on Archer.

But when Michaela went to stand at the back of the

line, Lara sent a bolt of magic crashing into her back that brought her to her knees.

"The next person to purposely hold back will get far worse than that," Lara declared, and I wondered how I could have ever thought that she was nice. Or sane.

So I sat there, tears streaming down my face, and watched Archer take one attack spell after another from the witches and warlocks. The faeries froze him with ice, or burned him with heat. One conjured a vine out of thin air that wrapped itself around Archer's throat until he passed out.

I don't want to talk about what the shapeshifters did.

After every attack, Cal walked forward and laid his hands on Archer's body until Archer regained consciousness, or stopped bleeding, or started breathing again. Each time Archer stood up to face yet another kid, he looked a little paler, a little more broken, and the closer Jenna got to the front of the line, the more my stomach twisted itself into knots. The idea of watching my best friend bite and drink from the boy I loved was so wrong, so nauseating, that I couldn't let myself even contemplate it. Thank God, in the end, I didn't have to.

Taylor went right before Jenna, and when Cal knelt next to Archer to heal him, he looked up at Lara and said, "That's enough. Any more, and I won't be able to bring him back."

Lara frowned, but waved her hand and said, "Fine. You'll get your shot tomorrow, Miss Talbot." She turned her attention back to the rest of the group, all of whom looked . . . I don't even know what the right word is. Shattered. Depleted. There's no worse feeling than being forced to use your powers to hurt someone.

"Good work today," Lara said, and you would've thought we'd all just aced a math test or something, not tortured a classmate. "Now that I have a better idea of your various strengths, we can work on honing your powers. Everyone back to the house."

No one spoke a word as they shuffled through the doors. Jenna came back to sit by me, and as soon as Lara left, I could move again. Blindly, I ran to Archer, who was sitting on one of the thick mats we'd used in Defense. His elbows rested on his raised knees, and he had his head in his hands. I knelt in front of him, awkwardly wrapping my arms around his neck. He uncurled himself, pulling me to him. For a long time, we held each other, my hands fisted in his hair; his, stroking my back.

"I'm okay," he said at last. "I know that's hard to believe, but nothing hurts. I mean, except for my mind and soul, but those were always a little broken." Gently, we disentangled ourselves and rose to our feet. "Your magic is awesome, man," he said to Cal, who I just realized was standing at the edge of the mat, next to

Jenna. "Although I have to say, now that you've brought me back from the edge of death—what, like, hundreds of times?—I'm starting to feel like our relationship is a little unbalanced."

"You can buy me a burger when we get out of here," Cal said, and as usual, I had no idea if he was joking or not.

I stepped away from Archer and reached out to give Cal one of those uncomfortable side hugs. "It's good to see you," I told him. "And not just because of, um . . ." I gestured to Archer, who raised an eyebrow at me but didn't say anything. Willing my face not to go red, I asked Cal, "Did you get here yesterday like the rest of us?"

Sighing, Cal shoved his hands in his pockets. "Yeah. One minute, I was heading out to the tent to grab some stuff; the next, there was all this light, and here I was. Back in my cabin, actually."

"Why are we just now seeing you?" Jenna asked.

"The cabin was locked," he replied. "Windows sealed shut, everything. Then this morning, I got the order to come here. Lara said they needed my 'special skills.' Gotta admit, I didn't think it was going to be anything this intense."

Now that he mentioned it, Cal did look awfully gray and exhausted. Healing magic is hard, and just one spell took a lot of Cal. To repeatedly bring someone back from the brink of death? No wonder he looked ready to keel over.

Still, Cal was tough, and he shook off his obvious weariness to ask, "So they're turning everyone into demons, huh?"

"That seems to be the plan," I said. Briefly, I filled him in on the assembly last night, adding, "And from what Elodie said, it's like they want to do some kind of experiment on all of us, see what happens when you put a demon in a vampire."

"What do you mean, 'Elodie said'?" Archer asked, furrowing his brow.

"Oh. Um, Elodie haunts me. And now, uh, she can possess me and stuff. Which"—I hastened to add since Archer's expression had gone dangerously dark—"is actually a *good* thing, because she can do magic through me."

Jenna and I stood there, letting the boys take that in.

"Okay," Archer said slowly. "Well, that's incredibly disturbing, but I'm all for anything that helps us get out of here faster. Especially if I'm going to be used as some kind of guinea pig for torture." I moved closer to him, wrapping my arm around his waist, and pretended not to see the way Cal suddenly looked away.

"So what do we do now?" Jenna asked.

I sighed. "Honestly, I want to say run. Spend some

time researching spells that will get us through that killer fog, and then maybe find another spell that can make a magical boat or something."

Cal made a sound that might have been a laugh, and Jenna smiled at me. Archer's arm tightened around my waist. "But?" he prompted.

"*But,*" I added, "that's like putting a Band-Aid on Marie Antoinette's neck. I think our best bet is to try to talk to Mrs. Casnoff."

"Why?" Archer asked.

"I don't know. It's just . . . she could've staked Jenna, but she didn't."

"Because she wants to put a demon in her," Cal pointed out.

I shook my head. "Maybe, but I'm not so sure. Look, Lara is completely evil, but Mrs. Casnoff was . . . Okay, nice isn't exactly the right word, but you guys have seen how awful she looks. Something is bothering her. It's worth a shot to try to get her alone."

"Maybe she knows where the grimoire is," Jenna said, reaching out to grab my arm.

"She might," I said, shooting for "enthusiastic" rather than "ambivalent and maybe a little scared." As badly as I wanted my powers back, Torin's second prophecy sat lodged like a stone in my chest. Just thinking about it made my head hurt.

So I turned to Archer, running my fingers over the front of his shirt. It was still stained with blood. "We'll deal with Mrs. Casnoff. But first, there's someone else we need to talk to."

# CHAPTER 19

"I don't like this," Archer said later that afternoon, as we sat across from each other on the floor of my room.

"I don't either, but you have to admit it's better than being tortured every day."

Archer muttered something under his breath that sounded like, "Not so sure about that."

Back at Thorne Abbey, I'd been able to summon Elodie. Well, I wasn't sure if it was technically summoning, or if she just showed up when she felt like it. So I felt kind of stupid as I said, "Um, Elodie? You around? I need to talk to you."

There was a stir of movement out of the corner of my eye, and suddenly Elodie was floating near the closet. "What—" she mouthed at me. And then she saw Archer.

For a long moment, they just stared at each other. Then, as nicely as I could, I said, "Look, Elodie, I know you and Archer have . . . issues, but I need your help. The Casnoffs are using him for target practice, and if that keeps up, he'll probably die."

Elodie made a gesture that was pretty easy to interpret.

"I told you this was pointless," Archer said, moving to stand up. I caught his sleeve and pulled him back down.

"Wait. Elodie, please."

She floated over toward us, that same unreadable expression on her face. "What do you want me to do?"

Relieved, I let go of Archer's sleeve and said, "Anything you can. Some kind of protection spell, or invisibility spell . . . something."

Folding her arms over her chest, Elodie glared at Archer. Then, with a wave of her hand and an, "Oh, fine," she swooped into me.

It was so weird to have Archer looking at me but seeing Elodie. His expression was stony and cold, something I'd never seen on his face before. Even weirder was watching him with Elodie's thoughts in my head. She was angry; I could feel that pumping through my veins, thumping inside my stomach. But it was more than that. She was . . . sad. Hurt.

"Give me your hands," I heard my voice say. He hesitated for a moment and then laid his palms over mine.

As soon as he did, I had an image of those hands cupping my face as he kissed me. No. Not me.

Elodie.

*Stop thinking about that!*

*You think I want to have that memory?* she snapped in reply.

"Okay," she told Archer, who was looking somewhere over my shoulder. "I can't make you invisible or anything, but this spell will keep you from feeling the pain and limit any real damage that can be done to you. It won't last forever, though, so I suggest you and Sophie find some way out of here ASAP."

"Oh, great, because that hadn't occurred to us."

"Do you want the spell or not?"

Scowling, Archer nodded and gripped my hands tighter. After a moment, I felt Elodie's magic rain down from the top of my head, spreading down my fingers and into Archer's. As soon as the magic faded away, Elodie dropped his hands, wiping mine on my thighs.

"There," she said.

Archer flexed his fingers, looking at them as he said, "Thanks."

"Whatever" was Elodie's only reply, and then she was gone, leaving me sprawling on the floor.

I'm sure it was very attractive.

I felt firm hands on my shoulders, and the next thing

I knew, I was sitting up and leaning against Archer's chest.

"That was weirder than I thought it would be," he said against my temple.

I tried to snort. "You're telling me. How do you feel?"

"Better," he said. "But if this protection is only going to last so long, I think the sooner you talk to Mrs. Casnoff, the better."

Unfortunately, that ended up being easier said than done. For the next few days, I only saw Mrs. Casnoff at dinner, where she'd sit in her seat, staring blankly at the wall, and I wondered just how the heck I was ever going to get her alone.

That wasn't the only thing that proved difficult. Jenna and I were determined to search for the grimoire, but between all the "training sessions" Lara forced on us (which were still unbearable to watch, even though I knew Archer was faking pain), and the fact that our doors were locked as soon as the sun went down, we hadn't really had a chance. I'd tried calling Elodie again, but after the spell with Archer, she seemed to be keeping her distance.

By our fifth day back at Hex Hall, I was beginning to go crazy. "We have to do something," I told Jenna that morning as we made our way from the greenhouse.

"We've been here nearly a week and we're nowhere closer to finding the grimoire, we haven't got the first clue how to stop the Casnoffs from turning all the kids here into demons, and I haven't seen Mrs. Casnoff alone since—"

I glanced behind me to see that Jenna was frozen in place. She pointed to the pond. "Um, she's alone now."

There was a little stone bench by the water's edge. Mrs. Casnoff was sitting on it, her back to us, white hair fluttering around her shoulders.

"Holy crap," I said softly. I'd been wanting to get her alone for so long that I was actually shocked that it had finally happened.

"Go," Jenna said, nudging me with her elbow. "Talk to her. I'll meet you back at the house."

I watched the back of Mrs. Casnoff's head and wondered where to even start. I had so many things I needed to say that they all seemed jumbled up.

When I sat down next to her, she didn't even turn her face toward me. "Hello, Sophie," she said, her gaze still trained on the water.

"Hi," was all I could say at first.

"She was so quiet," Mrs. Casnoff said, and for a second, I was confused. Then she said, "When we were little. Father was afraid she might never speak," and then

I realized she meant Lara. "But I knew. Her mind was always working. Working, working, working. She was more like our father than I was.

"'The ends justify the means'—he said that all the time," she whispered. "The ends justify the means."

Impulsively, I reached over and covered one of her hands with mine. Her skin was ice cold and felt as fragile as paper. "You don't believe that," I said. "Hex Hall . . . Look, it wasn't my favorite place, but it wasn't a *bad* place. I know *this*"— I gestured to the fog, the school, the whole poisoned island—"isn't what you want."

But Mrs. Casnoff didn't look at me. She just kept shaking her head, and murmured, "It's what he wanted. It's what he gave up everything for."

"Who?" I asked, my throat tight. "Your dad?" Then I shook my head. This might be my only chance to talk to her, and I needed to stay focused. "Why did you bring me here?"

Mrs. Casnoff turned to me, her face tear-streaked and tired. "Sophie Mercer," she said. "A fourth-generation demon. The only one. All the others, too new, too fresh, too . . . unpredictable. But you." She reached forward and grabbed my face between her hands and I instinctively reached up to pull her off me. "You're our best hope."

"Best hope for what?" I asked.

"It's in the blood," she said softly. "In the blood. Yours, and mine, and my father's, and Alice's . . ." Mrs. Casnoff trailed off, looking at me but not seeing me.

"What does that mean?" I demanded, but she let me go, her eyes going hazy again. "Mrs. Casnoff?" I reached out and shook her shoulders, but it was like she didn't even feel it. Despair slammed into me, and I fought the urge to shake her until her teeth rattled. What was in the blood? How could I be her hope for anything?

"Sophie," I heard someone say, and I turned to see Cal standing behind the bench. "Come on," he said softly, holding his hand out.

I looked at Mrs. Casnoff again, at her white hair and ravaged face. And then I put my hand in Cal's and let him lead me away from her.

"I thought she could help," I said to Cal, once Mrs. Casnoff was far behind us. "That's stupid, I know, but . . . she cared about us, Cal. She cared about this place."

We walked side by side, and Cal eventually dropped my hand. His bent elbows kept brushing mine as we made our way to the house. "She's sick, Sophie," he answered as we crested the slight rise near his cabin. Hex Hall stood before us, looking more forlorn than ever. "Just like everything else here," he said, and sighed. I thought of how much Cal had loved this place, the pride he'd taken in it.

"I'm sorry," I said turning to him. His clear hazel eyes met mine, and a tiny bit of humor flickered there.

"You say that a lot."

Tugging at my Defense uniform (which was even uglier than I'd remembered; bright blue stretchy cotton was not a good look on anyone), I gave a little laugh. "Yeah, well, I feel it a lot." *Especially where you're concerned*, I wanted to add.

Cal didn't say anything to that, and after a moment, started walking toward the house. I waited a few seconds before following. There was so much I wanted to say to him, but I didn't even know where to start. *Cal, I think I love you, but I'm maybe not* in *love with you, even though kissing you was pretty boss* was maybe one approach.

Or: *Cal, I love Archer, but my feelings for you are all confused because you are both awesome and smoking hot, and we're already technically engaged to be married, which adds to the giant pot of boiling emotions and hormones I've become.*

Okay, maybe don't say *boiling*. . . .

"You okay?"

"Huh?" I blinked, surprised to see we'd come to the front of the house. Cal was standing with one foot on the bottom porch step, staring at me.

"You have this weird look on your face," he said.

"Like you're doing really complicated math in your head."

I couldn't help a little snort of laughter. "I was, in a manner of speaking." As I moved past him and into the house, I resolved to talk to Cal like a mature grown-up person.

Eventually.

For now, I gave him a little wave and ran away to my room.

Jenna was sitting on her bed when I got there, practically vibrating with excitement. "Well?"

I just shook my head. "A bust. Mrs. Casnoff is too screwed up to be any help."

To my surprise, Jenna didn't seem to take the news particularly hard. Instead, she leaned forward and said, "Okay, well, that sucks. But, Soph, guess what I saw today."

I flopped across my mattress, toeing my sneakers off. "We're on a cursed island surrounded by killer fog, and ruled by two crazy-ass witches. I really can't begin to guess, Jen."

"Lara, coming out of the cellar," she said, blowing her pink stripe off her forehead. "And looking super secretive and suspicious. Well, I mean, more super secretive and suspicious than usual."

Ah, the cellar. A dank, creepy place full of magical

artifacts that had a tendency to move around. Archer and I had spent an awful lot of quality time down there last year.

"Anyway, I mentioned it to Taylor, and she said she's seen Lara go down there every day since we got here. Which makes me think—"

"There's something important down there. Like maybe the grimoire," I said, and I could swear my magic did a leap of excitement inside my chest.

Jenna gave a nod, but before I could say anything else, a familiar presence took over. "I was just coming to tell you two the same thing," I heard myself say. "She's definitely hiding something down there because the door is magicked like crazy."

*Long time no see,* I told her.

*I've been busy.*

Jenna blinked rapidly. It was always a shock for me to suddenly become Elodie. I couldn't imagine how weird it must feel for the people watching it happen. But Jenna went with it. "Could you open the door using your magic?"

"Of course," Elodie scoffed. Sitting up, she went to toss my hair, but my fingers just got hopelessly ensnarled. "Oh, for the love of God," she muttered, trying to untwist the strands from a ring I wore.

There was a knock at the door, and I could feel Elodie

about to swoosh on out, when Archer said, "Mercer? You in there?"

*Go on*, I told Elodie, but she didn't budge. Thankfully, Jenna opened the door and immediately said, "Sophie's here, but Elodie's possessing her right now."

"In that case, I'll wait out here," he said.

I could feel . . . *some* kind of emotion building up in Elodie. But before I had time to even identify what she was feeling, she was gone.

While I came back to myself, Archer was sitting next to me on my bed, an arm wrapped around my shoulders. Jenna filled him in, both on my pointless talk with Mrs. Casnoff and what we'd learned about the cellar. "Elodie thinks she can do a spell on the door that will let Sophie in," she finished.

Archer shifted on the bed so that he could look at my face. "I'll go with you," he said.

I raised both eyebrows at him. "Cross, you're the Casnoffs' personal torture guinea pig. It's a miracle they're letting you stay in your room and not, like, chaining you in a dungeon. If they catch you wandering around in the cellar—"

"If the Casnoffs were going to lock me up, they would've done it already."

"Why haven't they?" Jenna wondered out loud, and Archer shrugged.

"Maybe it's because they know I can't escape? Or maybe having to look at the dude they've been flaying alive every day is punishment for the other students. Either way, I'll take it."

Archer turned back to me, and that familiar grin flashed over his face. "Come on, Mercer. Me, you, the cellar. What could go wrong?"

# CHAPTER 20

A few days later, I found myself back in the cellar. But this time, I was involved in an activity way more fun than cataloging magic junk.

"What happened to the promise of making out in castles?" I asked as Archer and I pulled back for a breather. I was leaning back against one of the shelves, my hands clutching Archer's waist. Over his shoulder, there was a jar of eyeballs staring at me, and I nodded toward it. "Because, see, things like that? Kind of a mood killer."

He glanced at the jar and then turned back to me, waggling his eyebrows. "Really? I find it has the opposite effect."

Giggling, I elbowed him in the stomach and pushed myself off the shelf. "You're sick."

He smiled and ducked his head to kiss me again, but

I skirted around him. "Come on, Cross, we came down here for a reason, and it wasn't fooling around."

Smirking, Archer folded his arms over his chest. "May not have been your reason, but—"

I cut him off. "No. Don't distract me with your sexy talk. We need to search this place, and that spell Elodie did will only last so long." Elodie had swooped into my body at the cellar door, doing a quick spell to unlock it. She hadn't even looked at Archer, much less said anything. And the second the lock clicked open, she'd vanished.

The smirk disappeared from Archer's face, and he actually looked kind of sullen.

"Are you honestly that bummed about not hooking up right now?" I teased.

But he was deadly serious when he shook his head and said, "It's not that. It's Elodie."

"What about her?"

Archer rolled his eyes. "I don't know, Mercer. Maybe it's that I'm not completely crazy about the ghost of my ex-girlfriend occasionally inhabiting the body of my current girlfriend."

I backed up another step and ran into another shelf. Something fell off and thunked against the dirt floor. "Whoa, I'm your girlfriend now?"

Archer shrugged. "We've tried to kill each other,

fought ghouls, and kissed a lot. I'm pretty sure we're married in some cultures."

Now it was my turn to roll my eyes. "Whatever. Look, the fact of the matter is, I don't have any magic right now. Elodie does. If her occasionally using me as her puppet means that I have powers again, then I'm fine with it. And you should be, too. My body, my ghost, and all that."

There was obviously more Archer wanted to say, but in the end, he just nodded and said, "Fine. I'll deal."

Something about the way he said that irritated me, but I let it slide. "Okay, so where should we start?"

Archer unbuttoned his cuffs and began rolling up his sleeves. "Well, Jenna said Lara's been down here, what? At least three times this week?"

I nodded. "Yup. Never brings anything down here with her, never has anything when she comes back up."

"Okay," he said, blowing out a long breath. "So whatever she's doing, she must be using one or more of the artifacts already down here."

I glanced around at the jam-packed shelves. "So let me get this straight: She's doing . . . something. With some stuff. That's somewhere."

"That pretty much covers it, yeah," Archer replied.

"Yay for vague," I muttered, shrugging off my blazer. I tossed it on the nearest shelf and grimaced as a puff of dust and grime rose in the air. "Ugh, gross. Would it kill the Casnoffs to do the occasional cleaning spell? I swear to God, everything in here is covered with a least an inch of . . ." My words trailed off as a thought occurred to me. From Archer's sudden grin, he'd apparently had the same idea.

"Bet if you've been using an artifact at least three times a week, it's pretty dust-free," he said.

"So we look for the least disgusting shelf. Easy enough."

Or at least that's what I thought. For about twenty minutes, Archer and I walked around each and every case, looking at every slot. I saw a few items I recognized from cellar duty (a red piece of fabric, some vampire fangs in a jar), and some things I was pretty sure I'd only ever seen in nightmares. What I didn't see was a clean shelf. Even the artifacts themselves were covered in dust, which was weird. Because they were magic, the items in the cellar moved around by themselves all the time. They usually didn't have time to gather . . . A thought suddenly occurred to me.

I stood on my tiptoes to look over the bookcase. "Cross."

His head popped up a few shelves over. "What?"

"Check out the magic crap."

He shot me a look. "Oh, is that what we're supposed

to be doing? Because I've just been drawing hearts and our initials in the dirt."

"Hilarious," I deadpanned. "What I mean is, why are all the jars and boxes and stuff covered in dust, too? I mean, they move around all the freaking time, right? They shouldn't be in one place long enough to get dusty."

"Good point." Archer's eyes scanned the shelf in front of him for a moment before he said, "Here we go," and pulled out a large glass jar. Inside, I could just make out a pair of white gloves. I remembered them; they flew, and Archer and I had once spent nearly half an hour chasing them around the cellar. It had taken both of us to force the gloves into that jar.

Now Archer unscrewed the lid and dumped the gloves on top of the shelf. They lay there, completely still, and I couldn't shake the feeling that they'd died.

Archer moved to another shelf, and after some rummaging around, pulled out an old drum, its skin mildewed and ripped. "There's no magic left in this either," he said, holding it up for me to see.

Turning in a circle, I took in all the magical knick-knacks, feeling their . . . well, quietness. "There's no magic in any of them," I told Archer. "Can magic just . . . drain out?"

He came around to stand next to me. "I've never

heard of that happening, but who knows? It's weird though, that's for sure."

"Weird stuff happening at Hex Hall. Who'da thunk it?" I said lightly, but my heart sank with disappointment. I'd been so sure we'd find something down here that might stop whatever the Casnoffs were up to. I don't know why I'd thought it would be so easy.

Archer hooked an arm around my neck, pulling me in so that he could brush his lips against the top of my head. "We'll figure it out, Mercer," he murmured, and I pressed my cheek closer to his chest.

We stood there for a long moment before he said, "You know, we still have like, half an hour down here. Seems a shame to waste it."

I poked him in the ribs, and he gave an exaggerated wince. "No way, dude. My days of cellar, mill, and dungeon lovin' are over. Go castle or go home."

"Fair enough," he said as we interlaced our fingers and headed for the stairs. "But does it have to be a *real* castle, or would one of those inflatable bouncy things work?"

I laughed. "Oh, inflatable castles are totally out of—"

I skidded to a stop on the first step, causing Archer to bump into me.

"What the heck is that?" I asked, pointing to a dark stain in the nearest corner.

"Okay, number one question you *don't* want to hear in a creepy cellar," Archer said, but I ignored him and stepped off the staircase. The stain bled out from underneath the stone wall, covering maybe a foot of the dirt floor. It looked black and vaguely. . . sticky. I swallowed my disgust as I knelt down and gingerly touched the blob with one finger.

Archer crouched down next to me and reached into his pocket. He pulled out a lighter, and after a few tries, a wavering flame sprung up.

We studied my fingertip in the dim glow.

"So that's—"

"It's blood, yeah," I said, not taking my eyes off my hand.

"Scary."

"I was gonna go with *vile*, but scary works."

Archer fished in his pockets again, and this time he produced a paper napkin. I took it from him and gave Lady Macbeth a run for her money in the hand-scrubbing department. But even as I attempted to remove a layer of skin from my finger, something was bugging me. I mean, something *other* than the fact that I'd just touched a puddle of blood.

"Check the other corners," I told Archer.

He stood up and moved across the room. I stayed where I was, trying to remember that afternoon Dad and

I had sat with the Thorne family grimoire. We'd looked at dozens of spells, but there had been one—

"There's blood in every corner," Archer called from the other side of the cellar. "Or at least that's what I'm guessing it is. Unlike some people, I don't have the urge to go sticking my fingers in it."

I lowered my head and screwed my eyes shut. "I know what this is. I read about a spell that used blood in the four corners of a room." I pictured the grimoire, saw my fingers turning the pages. "It was a holding spell," I finally said. "The blood turned the room into a cage, but it took a crazy amount of magic. One witch couldn't do it alone, because it would drain all her power." I looked up, and Archer met my eyes. "Unless the witch could drain magic from something else," I said.

Archer glanced around the cellar. "Or a lot of some-things."

"Well, that's one mystery solved," I said, rising to my feet. "Of course, now the question is, what is Mrs. Casnoff holding down here?"

"And where?" Archer added, but I shook my head.

"I know the where," I told him. "At least I think I do. The holding spell works like a kind of magical net. The blood in the corners grounds it, and the spell itself arches over the room."

We both glanced up, like we were expecting to see

shimmery threads arcing across the ceiling. But there was nothing except the usual dusty beams.

"The spell is at its strongest in the center of the room," I added. "So whatever you want to hold, you wanna put it as close to dead center as you can."

"You must've been awesome at Memory as a kid," Archer mused.

I shrugged. "When you're perusing a book full of the most powerful dark magic ever, you pay attention."

Our gazes fell to the center of the room, where there was nothing but one of the cellar's bazillion shelves. And under that shelf, drag marks in the dirt.

We both moved to either end of the shelf. It took a minute (and a couple of impolite words from both of us), but we managed to move it several feet over. Then we stood there, breathing hard and sweating a little, and stared at the trap door in the floor.

"Whatever's down there," Archer said after a moment, "it's hard-core enough that Casnoff went to all this trouble to hold it. Are you sure you want to do this, Mercer?"

"Of course I don't," I said, grabbing the iron ring affixed to the trap door. "But I'm gonna."

I yanked at the ring, and the door came up easily. Cool air, smelling faintly of dirt and decay, wafted up. A metal ladder was bolted to the side of the opening, and I counted ten rungs before it disappeared into the blackness below.

Archer made a move to step into the hole, but I stopped him. "I'll go down first. You'll just look up my skirt if I go after you."

"Sophie—"

But it was too late. Trying to shake the feeling that I was stepping into a grave, I grabbed the ladder and started to climb down.

# CHAPTER 21

There are probably a few things worse than climbing into a hole that is actually *underneath* a creepy basement, but at that moment, it was hard to think of any of them.

I was only a few steps down the ladder before I was plunged into darkness. The dim light in the cellar wasn't strong enough to penetrate the gloom. I was also pretty sure that the tunnel was narrower now, and as I took another step down, both my shoulders brushed the walls.

The metallic taste of fear flooded my mouth as my suddenly sweaty hands slid on the iron rungs.

"Mercer?" Archer called from above me. "You okay?"

I rested my forehead on the back of my hands, and tried to keep the panic out of my voice as I replied, "Yeah, fine. Why do you ask?"

"Because you're gasping."

Oh. Now that he mentioned it, my breath was heaving in and out of my lungs pretty quickly. I made an effort to slow it down as he asked, "Is it the dark, or—" He grunted a little and shifted. Dirt rained down on me, and I shut my eyes.

"Both," I choked out. "Apparently I'm claustrophobic now. That's, uh, new. Probably a side effect of fleeing a burning building through an underground tunnel." I took another shaky breath. "Yay for psychological trauma."

"Come back up," Archer said automatically, and I kind of loved him for that.

"No," I said, willing my feet to keep moving. "We're trying to save the world here, Cross. No time for panic attacks."

I kept going, one rung at a time, and eventually, Archer started moving, too. I wasn't sure how long it took us to make our way down. It felt like hours, and my heart was in my mouth the whole time as the earth itself seemed to press down on me.

Finally, the tunnel began to widen, and a dim glow penetrated the gloom. When my feet finally hit the dirt floor, I turned and found myself facing another, shorter tunnel. This one was at least six feet high and about four feet wide. Whatever the light was, it was coming from something at the end of this bigger tunnel. I turned to see

Archer standing behind me, a wary expression on his face. "In my experience, nothing good *glows*," he said.

"That's not true," I answered, slipping my hand in his. We began walking toward the light. "Lots of good things glow. Glow sticks. Glowworms. Awesome glow-in-the-dark shirts . . ."

He snorted with laughter, but his fingers tightened on mine. We kept walking, and something cold and wet dripped on my neck. I shivered but kept moving. The light grew brighter. Archer and I turned a corner, and as soon as we did, a low moan filled the air. It took me a second to realize that it had come from me.

We were facing a large, brick-lined room. The glow we'd seen came from a single bare bulb on a cord, just like the one upstairs in the cellar. Standing in the chamber, shoulder-to-shoulder, were about a dozen kids. Or at least, they'd once been kids.

They gazed sightlessly ahead, arms rigid at their sides, like mechanical dolls waiting for someone to turn them on. Behind me, Archer muttered something, but I couldn't really hear him. A wave of nausea swept over me as I moved in front of Nick, staring into his blank eyes. Daisy stood next to him, her dark hair messy, lips slightly open, as if she'd been in the middle of saying something when she was frozen. Behind them, I saw Anna and Chaston. The glamour they'd used to make themselves as beautiful as Elodie was gone now, so they looked a lot plainer than I remembered. They also looked younger, and pain shot through my chest.

I remembered joking with Nick in the garden at Thorne, using magic to dress each other in stupid clothes. And how he used to look at Daisy. The way she'd unconsciously curl into him whenever they were sitting together.

"She's keeping people down here in storage," I said, my voice echoing. "Like they're *things*. Archer. This is . . . Look, I knew whatever was down here would be bad. It's not like Lara Casnoff would use a powerful blood spell to guard her chocolate chip cookie recipe. But this?"

"Yeah," Archer said softly. "This goes beyond bad, and straight into nightmarish." He rested his hand on the back of my neck. "This is the guy who attacked me in the mill, right?" He nodded at Nick.

"Yeah. They must've caught him somehow." I reached out and touched Nick's hand. It was cold and waxy.

"What do you think happened to all of them?"

"I don't know. It might be the holding spell. Or it might be some other kind of magic on top of that." There was so much dark power coming off these kids that I knew they were all demons. Every single one of them. Between that and my own powers so frantic inside of me,

I couldn't get a sense of just how much magic was actually going on in this horrible little cavern.

Archer blew out a long breath. "I never thought I'd feel sorry for someone who tried to disembowel me."

"It wasn't him. I mean, it was, but it wasn't. The Casnoffs made him into a monster. Since they raised him, they . . . I don't know, sicced him on you. They made all of them into monsters." I waved my hand at the other kids standing there in this little holding cell. "And if the Casnoffs have their way, we'll all end up down here."

Pulling me closer, Archer murmured, "We're not going to let that happen."

"How?" I cried out, the word bouncing around the room. "Look at what we're up against, Cross. We can't use magic. We can't leave this place." I flung my hand out. "We don't even know what's going on in the rest of the world. All we can do is—is play Scooby-Doo in the cellar."

"That's not all we can do, Sophie," Archer said.

Whenever Archer used my first name, I knew he was serious. "What do you mean?"

He backed up a few steps. "Look, you want the Casnoffs gone and these kids saved, or at least.. . . . well, put out of their misery, I guess. You don't want anyone to raise demons ever again. There are other people who want those things, too."

"Please tell me you are not talking about The Eye."

He looked away and shoved his hands in his pockets. "I'm just saying that you and The Eye have a common goal here."

I wasn't sure if I was stunned, or angry, or disgusted. It was kind of a mixture of all three. "Okay, is there a gas leak down here? Or did you hit your head on the tunnel? Because that's really the only excuse for you saying something so freaking stupid."

"Oh, you're right, Mercer," he said. "The idea of trying to fight an army of demons with a bunch of trained soldiers is beyond ridiculous. Maybe we can go get Nausicaa and see if she'll give us some faerie dust to make the problem go away."

"Don't be a jackass," I snapped.

"Then don't be naïve," he retorted. "This is too big for us to handle, Sophie. This is too big for Prodigium to deal with on their own. But if we could all work together, there's a chance that—"

"What do you think, Cross? That we'll ask The Eye to help us, and they'll be all, 'Sure, no problem! And once we're done wiping out the demons, we certainly won't kill the rest of you, even though that's like, our mission in life!'"

Glaring at me, Archer said, "And a few months ago, you thought that's all that the Brannicks were, too.

Prodigium killers. But you certainly weren't opposed to getting their help to deal with this."

I blinked at him, faltering. "Th—that's different," I sputtered. "They're my—"

"Your family?" he asked quietly. "Because The Eye is mine."

"But you're not one of them. Not really."

"Yeah, Mercer, I am," he said. "And if you don't get that by now . . ." He heaved a sigh as he rubbed the back of his neck, looking at some point over my shoulder. "Whatever," he finally summed up.

He turned away and started walking back toward the ladder. I stared at his back for a few seconds before following him. It was hard to believe that just a little while ago, we'd been joking and kissing; and thinking about that, I had a sudden urge to burst into tears. Couldn't our relationship be easy and happy for more than a couple of hours at a time?

We made our way back up the ladder, and this time, I was too miserable and angry to feel claustrophobic. At the top, he leaned back in to give me a hand up, but I batted it away and heaved myself out of the tunnel.

I shut the trap door behind me, and without saying anything, we maneuvered the shelf back over it. Then I walked past him, heading for the cellar steps. I was on the first one when I felt his fingers encircle my wrist. "Sophie, come on. I don't want to fight with you."

Turning, I opened my mouth to say I didn't want to fight with him either. But before I could, I saw the telltale flash out of the corner of my eye, and the next thing I knew, my arm was jerking out of his grasp. "If you don't want to fight with her, maybe you shouldn't suggest she team up with people who want to kill her," my voice snarled.

Archer backed up so fast he nearly stumbled, and I wasn't sure I'd ever seen him look so freaked out. But he recovered quickly. "Elodie, if I wanted to talk to you, I'd do a séance or something. Maybe go on an episode of *Ghost Hunters*. But right now, I want to talk to Sophie. So clear out."

Elodie had no intention of doing that. "You always were a crappy boyfriend," she said. "Once you left, I chalked that up to you, you know, not actually liking me. But unless I'm blind as well as dead, you really like Sophie. In fact, hard as it is for me to fathom, I think you love her."

*Shut up, shut up, shut up!*

*Screw that,* she retorted. *You two spend all your time making stupid jokes and being all witty. Someone has to get real.*

"What's your point?" Archer asked, narrowing his eyes at me. Her. Whatever. God, this was getting confusing.

"Cal loves her, too, you know. And the last time I checked, he wasn't part of a cult of monster killers. I'm just saying that if you're going have loyalties *that* divided, maybe it's time to bow out gracefully."

You couldn't say Elodie didn't know how to make a dramatic exit. The next thing I knew, I was pitching forward into Archer's arms, my head swimming.

Archer clutched my waist and then abruptly shoved me at arm's length. "Sophie?" he asked, looking intently into my eyes.

"Yeah," I said, my voice shaking. "I'm back."

His fingers loosened, becoming more of a caress than a grip. "So you can't control when she swoops in like that? She can just take you over . . . whenever?"

I tried to laugh, but it came out more of a cough. "You know Elodie. I don't think anyone has ever controlled her."

Frowning, Archer pulled his hands back and shoved them in his pockets. "Well, that's awesome."

I grabbed the railing to steady myself. "Archer . . . that stuff she said. You know it's not true."

He shrugged and moved past me onto the steps. "Saying the most hateful thing possible is like Elodie's superpower. Don't worry about it." He paused and looked over his shoulder. "We should probably go tell Jenna what we found down there."

Oh, right. We'd just unearthed a whole bunch of demons. That probably trumped our relationship issues. Another few seconds passed. "Come on, Mercer," Archer said, holding his hand out to me.

This time, I took it.

# CHAPTER 22

"See, this is so much better," Elodie said, as we studied my reflection in the mirror over my dresser. Even though the image was warped and distorted, I had to admit that I did look nice. Elodie had smoothed a hand over my hair, and the next thing I knew, it was falling in soft waves to my shoulders.

*That's awesome,* I told her, *but I'm letting you use my body so that we can break into Lara's office, not so that you can give me a makeover. Besides, if I wander around looking like* this, *people will either know I'm doing magic somehow or wonder how I managed to sneak a flatiron into Hex Hall.*

It was an odd thing, watching my face crumple into a scowl at . . . myself.

"You're supremely irritating when you're right," she

said, waving her hand. Once again, my hair sprung out in a messy halo of curls.

After we'd gotten back from the cellar, Archer and I had told Jenna and Cal about the kids down there. All of us had decided that getting into Lara's office was the next plan of attack. "There's bound to be something in there," Jenna said. "Either the spell that makes kids into demons, or the grimoire. . . ."

"Maybe she'll have a file folder labeled, My Evil Plan," I suggested. "That would be super helpful."

It had taken us three days to come up with a strategy to get into the office. Cal was distracting Lara with questions about his own powers and how they might be useful to "the cause," while Jenna and Archer kept an eye on Mrs. Casnoff. Since she'd taken to just wandering in circles around the pond, that wasn't particularly challenging.

Which left the most important part to me and Elodie: using Elodie's magic to get into the office and search it for anything that might help us stop the Casnoffs. As far as plans went, it wasn't exactly D-day, but it was the best next step.

Now Elodie looked at my reflection and said, "It's weird. Looking in a mirror and seeing you."

*Yes, I think we've established this is kind of awful for everyone involved. Can we go now? We don't have much time.*

Heaving a sigh, she turned away from the dresser. As she did, I thought I saw the mirror . . . I don't know, ripple for a second.

*Did you see that? In the mirror?*

Elodie glanced back. "All I see is you. Me." She waved her hand. "You know."

I studied the glass, but Elodie was right. Nothing there. *Probably just a trick of the light,* I told her. *Sorry.*

"It wouldn't surprise me," she muttered, opening the door. "That mirror is super jacked."

We made our way onto the landing. I noticed a few of the younger witches huddled on one of the sofas, their heads close together. It wasn't the first time I'd come across one of these whispering pods of kids, and I wondered if maybe we weren't the only ones coming up with plans.

*I don't swing my hips like that when I walk,* I said to Elodie as we passed them. *Cut it out.*

She gave no sign of hearing me.

The house was nearly silent. Dinner had ended an hour or so before, and it was getting close to sundown. Everyone would be locked in their rooms then, which meant we had to hurry.

I could feel my heart pounding as we stepped into the main hallway. More glass had fallen from the stained-glass window. Now the angel who had created witches and warlocks was missing half her face, and a little shudder went through me as we tiptoed around the glass. I wasn't sure if it was me who was creeped out or Elodie. Probably both of us.

When we reached Lara's office, Elodie laid my hand on the doorknob. I could feel the magic sizzle up my arm, and gave a mental gasp.

"Why do you think Lara is Lara Casnoff, and Mrs. Casnoff is Mrs. Casnoff?" Elodie whispered as she worked her magic on the enchanted door. "It's her family name, right? So shouldn't she be Miss Casnoff? Or Ms.?"

*Of all the things to wonder about, that's what you're focused on? Her marital status?*

"It's weird, that's all I'm saying," she hissed in reply.

*You know you can talk to me in my head, right? You don't have to talk out loud and make everyone think I'm a crazy person. Just FYI.*

"The only time I can talk is when I'm in your body, so sue me, I'm taking advantage of that."

Before we could snipe at each other anymore, the door suddenly gave way. Pushing it open, Elodie dashed inside, closing the door behind her. Lara Casnoff's office was the total opposite of Mrs. Casnoff's, complete with soaring bookcases and a heavy wooden desk so brightly polished that I could see myself in it.

"Any idea on where we should start?" Elodie whispered.

*The desk*, I finally said. *It'll be locked, and if it's anything like Mrs. Casnoff's desk, magic won't work on it. There's a nail in my pocket. Get it out, and I'll talk you through jimmying the lock.*

Elodie's disdain flooded over me, but she got the nail and went to work on the lock. "Were you a burglar in the real world?" she muttered as she worked.

*No. My mom and I lived in a particularly bad apartment once. The lock never worked right, and we always had to break in. Have to admit, I never thought the skill would come in handy again.*

She gave a little chuckle. "What did you break in Mrs. Casnoff's desk for?"

*Information on Archer. After he left.*

"Ah. You're welcome, by the way?"

*For what?*

She jiggled the nail harder. "For putting him in his place the other night. Working with The Eye," she scoffed. "Yeah, that's a brilliant plan."

*He's just trying to think of something*, I said automatically. I wasn't sure why I was defending him when I'd basically said that idea was the stupidest thing ever to have stupided, but I didn't like the scorn in her voice. Well, *my* voice, her words.

211

Elodie paused in trying to open the desk drawer and shoved my hair back with both hands. "What's it going to take for you to realize that Archer Cross is bad news? He's an Eye. He's a liar and a jerk, and he's not nearly as funny as he thinks he is. And you're betrothed to Cal. Boys who can heal all wounds and are super hot, to boot? Don't exactly come around every day."

*I don't think about Cal like that.*

Pressing the point of the nail back into the lock, Elodie snorted. "Um, hi, I've been in your head. You totally think about him like that."

*Look, this isn't a slumber party*, I snapped. *Can you please get back to work?*

"Fine," she muttered. "Don't listen to me. But I'm telling you, Cal is the way to go. Heck, if *I* had a body, I wouldn't mind—"

*I'm going to need you to stop right there.*

I'm ninety-nine percent sure she wasn't going to stop right there, but before she could say anything else, the lock on the drawer gave way.

"Aha!" Elodie whispered. "Success!"

Here's the thing. When she slid open that drawer, I didn't expect to find anything. Not really. I mean, maybe a cryptic note or two, or a stupid riddle written on parchment that we had to decipher.

So when I saw the book sitting right on top of a pile

of papers, I didn't realize what I was looking at. It was only when Elodie said, "Um . . . is that the grimoire you were talking about?"

I looked at the cracked black-leather cover, felt the power coming off it in waves. *Yeah. It totally is.*

"Well, that was . . . easy."

She reached out to take it, and without thinking, I shouted *No!*

Wincing, she raised my hands to my ears. "Ow! I told you, inside voice!"

*It can't be this simple,* I told her, Torin's words ringing in my ears. *It's a trap. A trick.*

"Or maybe something is finally going our way," she suggested. "Come on, Sophie. Gift horse. Mouth. Don't look at it."

Again, she reached out to pick up the grimoire, but this time, it wasn't my mental screaming that stopped her.

It was the low creak of the door opening.

# CHAPTER 23

Before the door had moved more than an inch or so, Elodie scooped up the grimoire and shoved it awkwardly into the waistband of my skirt. As soon as the book touched the skin of my back, we both winced. The magic coming off of it felt like a low-level electric shock, and my arms and legs broke out in goose bumps.

I had to hand it to Elodie. If I'd been in control of my body, there would have been flailing and knocking things over, and I probably would have caught my clothes in the drawer. But Elodie smoothly closed the drawer without a sound, and sat down in Lara's chair like she belonged there. An excuse was already formulating in her head—or my head, it was hard to tell—when Cal stuck his head around the door.

Elodie sat down with relief. "Oh, it's you."

Frowning, Cal gave a curt nod. "I stalled Lara as long as I could. She said she was heading to the greenhouse, but I still wanted to give you a heads-up."

Elodie stood up and walked around the desk. "It's fine," she said. "I found what I was looking for."

*I? Why are you saying "I" and not "we"?*

There was no reply in my head as she smiled at Cal. "Thanks for the warning."

He scanned my face with yet another one of his inscrutable expressions. I wondered if he had trademarked them. "So, are you Sophie? Or Elodie in Sophie?"

"Just me," she said with a little shrug. "Elodie whooshed on out of here when you opened the door."

I didn't worry about inside voices now. *What are you doing?* I yelled as loudly as I could. She stiffened a little and caught Cal's arm. "Come on. We should get out of here."

As she and Cal walked back upstairs, the grimoire a buzzing weight against my back, and my fingers still nestled in the crook of his arm, I kept up a constant refrain to Elodie.

*Stop it. Right now. Either tell him you're me, or get the hell out of my body.*

We'd reached the third floor. The sitting room was empty, and Elodie steered Cal past it toward my room. *Trust me*, Elodie finally replied. *I'm doing you a favor.*

She opened the door and gestured for Cal to follow

her. I watched him hesitate, and for a second, I thought he was going to realize that I wasn't me. But then he followed her. Jenna was gone, and Elodie hopped up onto the dresser, ankles crossed. Cal softly closed the door behind him. "Did you find anything?" he asked in a low voice.

Elodie nodded. "Did I ever. I found the grimoire."

Cal blinked at her. "The grimoire? What, just sitting out in the open?"

"In Lara's locked desk. Hey, do you know why Mrs. Casnoff, is, well, Mrs. Casnoff? I mean, that was her dad's name, so why the Mrs.?"

*Seriously?* I asked.

Rubbing the back of his neck, Cal said, "Huh? Oh, uh, she was married a long time ago, but all the Casnoffs keep the name. It's a tradition or something. But about the grimoire—"

"Did she have an arranged marriage? Like us?" Elodie asked, sliding off the dresser. She moved to stand in front of Cal, so close that I could see my reflection in his eyes. As stupid as it sounds, I was surprised by how *me* I looked. I was so sure some sign of Elodie would show up in my face. But there was nothing.

Still, Cal gave her an odd glance as she sidled in closer. *Come on*, I begged silently. *See it. See* me.

But the moment passed, and after giving a little shake

of his head, Cal said, "Yeah, I guess. Sophie, did you see the spell? The one that could give you back your powers?"

Elodie was taken aback by that, and my hand strayed to the book, still pressing against my back. "Oh, right, that. Yeah, I was just about to find that spell, actually."

*No!* I howled yet again, but thankfully, Cal had the same thought. "Don't," he snapped, grabbing my wrist as my fingers reached for the grimoire. Since my hand was still behind my back, that basically meant he was holding me against him. *Result,* Elodie exulted in my head.

Cal's breath was warm on my face as he said, "Maybe she made the book so easy to find on purpose. If you touch that page and get your powers back, you'll be a demon again. Maybe that's what the Casnoffs want."

Now the twisting in my stomach had nothing to do with whatever Elodie was up to, and everything to do with what Torin had told me. For the first time, I let myself think that there was a chance he hadn't just been screwing with me. The thought was almost too terrifying to bear.

"I didn't think about that," Elodie said, and I'd never heard my voice sound like that. It was husky. Almost sexy.

For the first time ever, I saw Cal falter. "I just don't

think you should touch that spell. Not now, at least."

"I won't."

"Good."

"So why are you still holding on to me?"

I felt like I was watching a car crash in slow motion, only I was actually *in* the car. *Stop it*, I said again, and this time I wasn't shouting. I was pleading. *Not for me, but for Cal. You're screwing with him, and he doesn't deserve it.*

*No*, she replied as she curled my fingers around the back of Cal's neck. *But Archer does.*

Cal's lips were tentative on mine, and there was a part of me that wondered if he suspected. But then Elodie pulled him tighter, and I think that even if he did suspect, he didn't care anymore. The kiss in the tent had been intense, but this was . . . well, it was hot. Probably because Elodie was practically coiling my body around Cal's, kissing him with way more fervor than I'd ever shown.

So many feelings were rushing through my system, I couldn't figure out which were mine, and which were Elodie's. Anger, lust, sadness, triumph. They all pounded inside my skin, and between that and the magic thudding like a second heartbeat in my chest, and the electric shock of the grimoire against my spine, I felt like I might actually explode into a million pieces of blue plaid.

But before that could happen, the door opened, and

even as I shrieked for Elodie to let go of Cal, I knew it was too late.

"Whoa," I heard Jenna say, and then Archer asking, "What?"

Suddenly, my eyes were open, and I could see both of them standing in the doorway. Jenna just seemed confused more than anything else. But Archer . . .

If I'd had any doubts about how Archer felt about me, they were eradicated when I saw the look on his face. I'd never had my spleen ripped out, but if I had, I figured I'd make the same face Archer wore now.

I felt my lips twist in a smirk, and inside my head, Elodie was practically dancing. "Not such a great feeling watching someone you're in love with hook up with someone else, is it?" she said to Archer.

Cal, who still hadn't let go of my wrist, suddenly stepped back. "Elodie," he said. It wasn't a question.

*I will never forgive you for this,* I told her. *I don't care if I can't do magic for the rest of my life, you will never get into my body again.*

*This wasn't about you,* was her only reply.

And then she was gone.

I hit the floor, one of my knees scraping painfully on the hardwood. Cal and Jenna both rushed forward to help me to my feet. The instant I felt steady, Cal dropped his hand and moved away from me. Jenna kept a tight grip on my elbow, and as I looked up, I realized why Archer hadn't helped me.

He was gone.

I turned to Cal, miserable. "I'm so sorry. Again. Some more. I . . . I never would have—"

He cut me off with a brisk shake of his head. "It wasn't you," he said, but his voice was gruff, and he still wouldn't look at me.

Unsure of what else to say, I fumbled for the grimoire, handing it to Jenna. "We found this in Lara's desk. Cal thinks it might be some kind of trap. I mean, why would they make it so easy to find?" I remembered what Mrs. Casnoff had said the other day about me being their best hope, about something "in the blood." If the Casnoffs wanted me to have my powers back, it couldn't be a good thing.

Jenna took the book from me but didn't open it. "Okay," she said. "Go deal with Archer."

"He's upset, but this is more important," I said, nodding at the grimoire. Let Cal and Jenna think I was brave and self-sacrificing. That was better than telling them that I was too chicken to talk to Archer right now. How exactly does one say, "Sorry the ghost of your ex-girlfriend used me to make out with my fiancé"?

But Jenna was my best friend. "Soph," she said softly. "Go talk to him. Now."

I sighed. "You know, bossiness is my least favorite of your personality traits. Right up there with your unerring ability to be right all the time."

She smiled. "You love me."

Before I left the room, I noticed Cal's guarded expression, the tightness of his shoulders. I would have given anything for mind-reading powers.

It didn't take long to find Archer. He was in the green drawing room, the one where I'd first met Elodie, Chaston, and Anna. Sitting on the floor, his back against the sofa, long legs stretched out in front of him, he was studying the one photograph that remained on the wall.

I sat down next to him, even though the carpet was unpleasantly damp. Sickly pale light from the one lamp in the room kept a lot of his face in shadow.

"So, that sucked," I said, trying to sound as jovial as possible. "Side effect of dating in the magical world, I guess."

He made a sound of amusement, his shoulders jerking slightly. But he still didn't look at me. "You think those guys ever had these kinds of problems?" he asked, nodding toward the picture. It was the one depicting the very first class at Hecate Hall, back in 1903. There had only been a few students that year, back when the school hadn't been used for punishment but as a kind of safe house.

"Probably," I said. "That chick in the straw hat seems kind of skanky."

He laughed for real then and finally turned his head toward me. "I know it was her," he said, reaching out to take my hand. Our fingers curled together. "But still. It was seeing the girl I . . . it was seeing you kiss Cal. And even though I knew it was her as soon as I saw the two of you—"

"It was still bad," I finished softly. "I get that, I do. It used to kill me watching you kiss Elodie."

"It killed me to kiss her," he said, and once again, his eyes drifted to the picture. "But it wasn't just that it sucks to see your girlfriend with her tongue down some other dude's throat."

I winced at that, remembering just how heated things had been when Archer and Jenna had walked in. Archer either didn't notice or pretended not to. "It's that Elodie's right. Cal cares about you. And he's a really good guy. And even though I want to hate him for being betrothed to you . . ." He gave a helpless shrug. "I can't. Which must mean he's extra-special dreamy."

"Stop it," I said, jerking our joined hands. "Cal's my friend. That's it. You're the guy I—"

*Love*, I wanted to say. But the word froze on my tongue, and I ended up just saying, "Want. Chose. Whatever."

He held my gaze, and his dark eyes were as serious as I'd ever seen them. "Maybe I shouldn't be."

Shocked, I leaned away from him. "What does that mean?"

"It's just . . . If you were with him, you'd be happier. Better off."

Okay, now I was getting angry. "That's really not for you to decide. And if you feel that way, maybe you should just go ahead and give me the 'It's Not You, It's Me' speech right now."

To my surprise, Archer smiled. "That's the thing, though," he said. "I can't. I could stand it if you left me, but I don't think there's any way I could leave *you.*"

I blinked at him. "You are so screwed up."

"That's what I've been trying to tell you."

Wrapping my hand around the back of his neck, I pulled his face to mine. "I happen to like screwed up," I whispered, our lips nearly touching. "So don't ever say crap like that again, okay?"

I could tell there was more he wanted to say. Instead he just sighed, "Okay."

"Well, this is a lovely moment."

I whipped my head around. Lara stood just inside the room, smiling beatifically at us. "So glad to have found you, Miss Mercer," she said to me. "I think it's time we two had a little chat."

# CHAPTER 24

For the second time that day, I found myself in Lara's office.

The room faced the trees at the back of the house, and I watched the fog curling around the blackened trunks. I focused on that so that I didn't have to focus on the little chaise longue in front of the window, where Mrs. Casnoff sat, her hands in her lap, her face empty.

Sinking into the leather chair on the other side of the desk, Lara studied me. She didn't seem angry. Just curious. Almost amused.

"I trust I didn't interrupt anything too important between you and Mr. Cross."

I clenched my fingers tightly together so that she couldn't see them shaking. "No, just the usual. You know—how to bring you and this whole twisted plan of yours to ruin, and escape this crazy island."

She laughed. "Even now, your sense of humor doesn't desert you. If it weren't so annoying, I'd respect that." She leaned forward on the desk, palms together, and there was something about her that reminded me of all the guidance counselors I'd met (and trust me, back when I went to regular school, I'd met plenty). "Is that why you've been trying to talk to my sister? Why you broke into my office today?"

I flinched, and Lara settled back into her chair, lips curling into a satisfied smile. "Didn't think I knew about that, did you?"

I wanted to be quippy. I wanted to say something that would show she hadn't just scared the heck out of me. We'd had the edge for what, maybe ten minutes? And if she knew we'd been in her office, did she know we'd taken the grimoire?

At least I still had sarcasm on my side. "I'm disappointed that you know about it," I told Lara, taking a seat in the chair opposite her desk, "but seeing as how you're an evil witch, I'm not exactly *surprised*."

She narrowed her eyes. "Everything is a joke to you. A game. My father's lifework, the salvation of our race . . ."

"Your father's lifework was to enslave a bunch of teenagers? No wonder you two turned out so awesome,"

I said, jerking my head toward Mrs. Casnoff. She showed no sign of hearing me.

Okay, now Lara was pissed. She sat up straighter in the chair. "Do you know what my father sacrificed to create you and your line? Do you know what *we* have given up?" She pointed one long finger at Mrs. Casnoff. "To keep our kind safe. To protect us from those who would eradicate us."

"You're turning people into monsters," I said. "Kids. What your father did destroyed Alice. And then he destroyed her daughter, and if you two had had your way, you would've done the same thing to me and my dad."

"The ends—"

"Justify the means. That's what *she* said. What is that, your family motto or something?"

Lara stilled, her knuckles white. "Would you like to know about my family, Sophie?"

Pressing myself back against my chair, I shook my head. "I think I know enough about your family, thanks."

"You don't know anything," Lara said, and then she flicked her fingers in my direction.

At first, nothing happened, and I wondered if all she'd done was give me the witch version of her middle finger.

And then my vision started to go black. Shaking, I tried to grip the armrests of the chair, but the chair wasn't there anymore. *I* wasn't there anymore. Surrounded by darkness, I almost felt like I was back in the Itineris. That feeling of claustrophobia threatened to choke me.

A spark unfurled in the darkness, a shining speck that slowly unfurled itself into a picture. I was staring at a painting of a snowy village, and then, as I watched, the painting began to move. Men and women trudged down a white-covered lane, their heads bowed against the cold and the wind. No one told me what I was looking at, but the knowledge filled my head, like I'd always known it. This was Alexei Casnoff's hometown, and the small house in the dead center of the picture was his house.

Then I saw him, a dark-haired boy, his face pressed against a window. He was waiting on his father, and I could feel his impatience and worry like they were my own emotions. Behind him, a pretty woman with dark blond hair stroked his head and murmured to him in Russian. Even though I couldn't speak a word of that language, I could still understand what she was saying. "It's going to be all right, Alexei. Your father and the others will keep us safe, I promise."

I understood then that the entire village was made up of Prodigium, and something important was being decided today. Something about moving, safety. Hiding. But before I could work out just what it was, the painting shifted again.

There were no snow-covered streets now, no quaint

little cottages. Now there was just chaos, fire, and smoke. The flames were so bright, I wanted to cover my eyes, but I didn't have hands. Or eyes for that matter. I saw Alexei, running down the street, pursued by villagers.

*They know what we are*, Alexei was thinking. *They found us, they found us, they found us. . . .*

Behind him, figures lay very still in the street, and I knew that they were his parents. I could see his mother's blond hair fanning around her head, some of it still smoldering. And the tiny shape next to them was his baby sister, and he was so *scared*. His terror and grief flooded through me, almost unbearable. The flames faded, and the picture began to bleed into another scene. Alexei was older now, maybe in his early twenties. He was handsome, less severe than he'd looked in the few photographs I'd seen of him.

He was riding in the back of a car past rolling hills and bright green grass that seemed very familiar. He was excited, and his fingers kept drumming nervously on the book he held on his lap.

The grimoire.

The car rattled over a stone bridge, and Thorne Abbey suddenly loomed into view.

Alexei could see the girls on the lawn, all students from a women's college in London. They were boarding at Thorne because it wasn't safe for them in the city anymore. Alexei watched them, and a tight smile crossed his face. *At last*, he was thinking. *At last.*

And then the scene abruptly went black, and the next thing I knew, I was back in Lara's office, panting in my chair.

"I think that gives you the gist of it," Lara said, calmly shuffling some papers.

I was still shaking, trying to remind myself that it wasn't my whole family who had just been murdered in the streets. When I felt like I could talk again, I said, "Humans murdered his family. And he was scared, and wanted a way to protect other Prodigium and maybe score a little revenge in the process. But that . . . that still doesn't make what he did right." I swallowed revulsion as I remembered the anticipation that had shot through Alexei as he'd watched a bunch of innocent girls run on Thorne Abbey's lawn. Alice, my great-grandmother, had been one of them. "Besides, I know this isn't about protection. Maybe that's how it started out, but what did your dad really want to use Alice for? Because you know what I think? I think a pet demon would be pretty handy if you wanted to keep every Prodigium on the planet under your control."

Lara didn't even attempt to deny it. "Possibly. Of course, a whole squad of 'pet demons' would be even handier." She set the papers down and carefully opened a drawer. She pulled out the grimoire, and my heart plummeted to my toes.

"Where did—"

"Oh, Miss Talbot was very quick to hand it over. If you wanted the book, all you had to do was ask," she continued, and I stared at her, confused.

"What?"

"We were going to give it to you eventually, anyway. You're not much use to us without your powers intact." She flipped through the pages until she reached the spell that would restore my magic. Just seeing the words on the page made me feel like I was about to jump out of my skin.

Lara held the book out to me. "Go on. Touch it." Then she chuckled. "Oh yes, Sophie, I knew that your father had made you touch this spell. I knew all about the hours you two spent going over this book."

My magic was only inches away. Everything inside me screamed for that spell. But I met Lara's eyes and asked, "Why would you want me to restore my powers? Because the second I do, I'm blasting my way out of here."

But Lara just smiled at me. "Sophie, when your father taught you about demons, did he tell you how they're controlled?"

"The witch or warlock who raised the demon can

control it. But since no one technically raised me, no one controls me."

"That's what we thought, too," Lara acknowledged with a little nod. "But then we did some research. You know, your father's collection at Thorne was very useful. And imagine our surprise when we discovered that the ability to control a demon is passed down through blood."

*In the blood,* Mrs. Casnoff had said. *In the blood. Yours, and mine, and my father's, and Alice's . . .*

And now I suddenly realized what she'd meant.

"Our father performed the ritual that turned your great-grandmother into a demon," Lara said. "Our bloodline created yours. That means that once you're re-powered, you'll be under our control."

I couldn't take my eyes off the spell, even as I started to shake. "That's impossible," I said, like saying it might make it true. "If you could've controlled me, you would've done it before."

"We didn't know we could, so we never tried," Mrs. Casnoff said, speaking for the first time.

"But why? Why would you want to control me when you can raise as many demons as you want?"

"New demons can be . . . unpredictable," Lara said. "But you? A fourth-generation demon? The chance of you . . . losing control, let's say, is very, very low. Which

231

makes you better suited for a leadership role." Lara grinned at me then, and there was nothing sane in her eyes. "Every army needs a general, after all."

Stomach lurching, I shot to my feet, backing away from the desk. "No. No, I'll stay powerless forever before I'd put myself under your control."

Lara tossed the open book onto her desk, and my magic howled.

"You say that," she said, leaning back in her chair. "But your powers want to be released. Being a demon is who you are, and now that you've seen that spell, the magic inside of you won't rest until it's been restored."

All I wanted to do was press my hands against that page.

"Why don't you just make me?" I asked Lara. If all I had to do was touch the page, she could walk around the desk and grab me. Terrified, I realized that I wished she would do just that, and I backed away.

"Spells like this are delicate," she told me. "You can't force something this powerful on someone. So it has to be your choice. And the grimoire will sit here," Lara called after me as I bolted for the door, "open to that spell, every day, Sophie. Calling to you. You could save yourself a lot of pain if you gave in now."

I fumbled with the doorknob, my skin suddenly drenched in cold sweat. When the door finally swung open, I ran, my magic screaming so loudly that I wanted to cover my ears against it.

Jenna was waiting for me in our room, and when I opened the door, she leaped to her feet. "Oh my God, are you okay? When Lara came up here and asked for the grimoire, I nearly died, and—Soph?"

Up here, the longing for the grimoire wasn't as intense, but I was still trembling as I let Jenna lead me to my bed. She curled up next to me. "What happened?" she asked softly.

By the time I was done telling Jenna about Lara's office, I had stopped shaking, but I *had* started crying. "I want my powers back so badly," I told Jenna as she stroked my hair, "but I can't risk being some . . . thing they can control. I was just so sure that if I could get my magic back, everything would be okay. But this? God, Jenna, this is so much worse."

"Shhh," she murmured. "We'll figure it out. We'll figure it out."

But her voice was wavering, and we fell asleep on her bed, clutching each other like little kids.

I thought it was thunder that woke me up. I sat up in bed, blinking, as a low rumble filled the house. The windows rattled, and I when I put my feet on the floor, I could feel a slight vibration.

"Wazzit?" Jenna murmured sleepily.

I walked over to the window, trying to make sense of what I saw. Lights were playing in the fog, flickering and dim at first, but then growing so brightly that I could see the dark shapes of the trees the mist usually concealed. I could hear doors opening out in the hall, the sound of bare feet on wooden floors.

More light blazed into our room, and there was another rumble, this one so strong that I felt my teeth rattle. Fully awake now, Jenna leaped out of the bed and opened our door. The other girls were all gathered on the landing, looking out the broken stained-glass window. I could still feel the grimoire, and I dug my fingernails into my palms, hoping the pain would keep me from rushing downstairs. Lights continued to flash, and the rumbling got louder and stronger. Several of the younger girls covered their ears.

Someone nudged my elbow, and I glanced back to see Nausicaa standing there, her wings beating softly in the thick air. "Lara came by our room to get Taylor tonight," she said. "Do you think . . ." She nodded at the lights. "Did they do something to her?"

My magic was nearly choking me as the vibrations got stronger, shaking more shards of glass out of the window. I couldn't hear them crash to the floor. The light flared one last time, so bright that we all shut our eyes and twisted our heads away.

And then everything was still.

We all stood there shivering, as a sudden cold wind blew through the broken window.

Somewhere in the distance, I heard an inhuman howl.

"Yeah," I said to Nausicaa. "I think they did."

# CHAPTER 25

The second I woke up the next morning, I could feel the grimoire like an ache in my bones. It was well after noon before I felt like I could get out of bed. Going downstairs was agony, but I had to see what was happening.

It ended up being much worse than I thought, and trust me, I'd prepared for all kinds of awful. The stained-glass window was completely shattered now, just a few shards still clinging to the wooden frame. Sometime in the night, it had started raining, and now water poured through the jagged opening. Jenna and I stood in the main foyer and watched the rain run down the wallpaper, soaking into the carpet.

"Do you think Taylor was the only student taken last night?" Jenna asked.

I was so busy trying not to shove her down and

bolt for Lara's office and the grimoire that it took me a moment to answer her. "I don't know. I don't know if they can change more than one at a time. But it doesn't matter. Either way, they've started now." A shudder racked my body, and my powers pushed against my skin, begging to be released.

"What are you two doing down here?" a voice snapped.

The Vandy stood behind us, hands on her hips. Even though she was scowling, her eyes were tired, the creases around them more pronounced.

"We were just—" Jenna said, but the Vandy raised her hand.

"I don't care what you were doing. Get back up to your room. Now."

Jenna moved toward the stairs, but I stayed where I was. "Is this what you want, too?" I asked the Vandy. "All the kids here turned into demons? Because I know you're kind of a jerk, but I didn't think you were evil."

Her scowl twisted into something uglier. Something almost pained. "That's enough!" she snapped, pointing toward the stairs. "Go."

Leaning heavily on Jenna, I made my way back up to our room. As soon as the door closed behind us, I heard the click of the lock. While I collapsed on the bed, shivering with pain and need, Jenna paced. "They're just going to keep coming for all of us. Every night, we're going to lie in our beds and listen to that—that nightmare, and wonder if we're next."

She sat down heavily on her bed. "Sophie, what are we going to do?"

*Get the grimoire. Restore my powers.* The thought was so strong, I groaned and covered my ears with my hands. "I don't know," I told Jenna, and tears clogged my throat. Was there any feeling in the world worse than hopelessness?

I rolled onto my side, and the need for the grimoire pounded alongside my pulse. I was so wrapped up in my own agony that when I saw something moving in the mirror, I thought I was just hallucinating. But then Jenna said, "What the heck was that?"

Forcing myself to focus, I sat up and squinted at the glass. Another flicker, almost like a shadow, was moving inside the mirror. And then the picture came in clearer.

Torin.

He was only there a second before disappearing again, but I jumped off the bed, ignoring the shrieking in my head. "You saw that, right?" I asked Jenna.

She was still on her bed, her eyes wide. "Yeah. There was a dude in the mirror. What—"

But I was already pressing my palms against the glass. "Torin? Are you in there?" I had no idea how he'd managed to move from the mirror at the Brannicks' to this one, but I wasn't complaining. His image wavered in front of me again, almost like a TV that was getting bad reception. I caught the flash of irritation on his face as he faded back out. But just before he did, he mouthed two words: "Your parents."

"What?" I cried out, slapping the glass with one hand. "What about my parents? Torin? TORIN!"

When he didn't reappear, I wanted to scream with frustration.

Jenna appeared at my side. "Elodie. See if Elodie's magic can . . . I don't know, pull him through."

After what she'd done, I hated the idea of Elodie back in my body. But desperate times . . .

"El—" was all I got out before she whooshed in.

*Pull him through,* I told her, my voice cold.

She didn't answer, but I could feel her magic rain down over me and through my fingertips. But as hard as she tried, as much as I kept saying, *Come on, come on, come on,* there was no sign of Torin. Finally, my hands dropped away from the glass, and Elodie said, "I can't. Whatever he's trying to do, my magic isn't strong enough to help."

Sighing, she turned and leaned against the dresser. Jenna was still standing in front of me, her arms folded tightly across her chest.

"Sophie's magic could do it," Elodie told her.

Jenna stepped closer, and I knew she was searching Elodie's eyes for me. "She can't get her powers back. If she does, the Casnoffs could—"

"Control her? Yeah, I know. But don't you think it's worth the risk?"

*Um, no?* I said, even as Jenna chewed her lip and didn't answer.

"All I'm saying," Elodie continued, "is that in a contest of wills between Sophie and Lara Casnoff? I'd put my money on Sophie. Maybe they would be able to control her. Or maybe, just *maybe,* she could fight it."

*I can't. It's too big of a risk. What would happen to Jenna if I was under Lara's control?*

*What will happen to her if you go on like this? I can feel you, Sophie. You're going to be in agony until you touch that damn spell. So I say go touch it and see what happens.*

Jenna lifted her hands to frame my face, tilting my head down. "Soph," she said. "I can't believe I'm about to say this, but . . . I think Elodie is right. With your powers, there's a chance you might be giving yourself over to the Casnoffs, yeah. But without your powers? There's *no* chance we'll get out of this."

Elodie turned and opened the top dresser drawer. There, on top of a pile of clothes, was the grimoire.

*How did that get in here?* I asked, suddenly understanding why its pull had been so strong this morning.

*I brought it here to do this.* My hand picked up the book, flipping to the spell, and Elodie brought my palm over the page.

*NO,* I screamed, and Elodie hesitated.

*You have to,* she finally said, her voice firm. *I thought it would be easier if I did it for you.*

*No,* I said again, but even inside my own head, I sounded weak.

*Do it,* Elodie replied. *End this.*

I felt her leave, and stumbled back against the dresser. After getting my breath back, I raised my head and stared at the open door. My magic was rioting inside of me.

Jenna took my hand. "You can do this," she said. "I know you can. You're stronger than they are."

I wasn't so sure about that.

But I was sure about what I had to do.

I didn't let myself think about it. I just snatched the grimoire off the floor where I'd dropped it when Elodie had left. My fingers unerringly turned to the spell that was screaming for me. And then, without letting myself so much as take a deep breath, I pressed my hand against the page.

It was like something exploded inside my chest. I stood, frozen, as my powers uncurled, magic spilling into my veins. The hardwood floor around my feet cracked, and Jenna leaped back with a shriek.

Breathing so heavily I was nearly panting, I flung the grimoire to the floor and slammed both my hands against the mirror. *Torin*, I thought, and yanked.

He appeared so suddenly in the glass that I jumped.

"What in the bloody hell was that?" he cried, blinking furiously before his gaze finally landed on me. When it did, he grinned. "Oh, well done, Sophia."

I didn't have much time. I could feel something, like an itch at the back of my mind, and I knew Lara, somewhere on Graymalkin Island, was suddenly becoming aware of what had happened. "Why were you trying to reach me? Where are my parents?"

"Hmm? Oh, right, my glorious mission. After you left—"

"Save it!" I barked. "What do you want and where are they?"

He frowned. "All right, all right. They're in Ireland. At Lough Bealach. I was supposed to get through and see if you were harmed in any way, but—"

I was already moving, scooping up the grimoire, shoving it once again into my waistband.

It was easy work to blast the lock off the door. It was even easier to use my magic to call for Cal and Archer. Cal was in his cabin, Archer in his room, and I spoke in both their heads at the same time. *Meet Jenna and me outside. Get ready to run.* And then, because I realized I'd just basically screamed inside their brains, I added, *Please. And sorry about the yelling.*

Jenna followed me out onto the landing. I was maybe three steps down the stairs when it happened.

With a sudden jerk, I came to a stop. I couldn't run. I couldn't leave the island. How foolish of me. No, what I needed to do now was go to Lara. Lara needed me, and she would—

"Sophie?" Jenna asked, touching my elbow.

I turned and looked at Jenna. She was in my way. She would try to stop me from getting to Lara, from fulfilling my destiny. So there was only one thing to do, really.

I had to kill her.

# CHAPTER 26

I clutched Jenna with one hand, wrenching her toward me, and there was no regret or sadness in my heart. If anything, I felt a little disgusted, like I was killing a bug. This . . . *thing* was in my way. I had to dispose of it.

Magic surged from the soles of my feet, making me feel giddy and whole.

I saw her realize what was about to happen, saw the fear and despair that crashed over her. But once again, I didn't feel anything. Not pity or even satisfaction. I just wanted her gone so that I could get to Lara.

But before the spell could make its way to my fingertips, Jenna grabbed my face. "Sophie," she said quietly. Urgently. "Look at me. You're better than they are. You can fight them." Tears filled her eyes, and there was a twinge in my chest. Her fingers dug into my cheeks. "Please," she begged. "Soph, you're my best friend. I love you, and I know you. I know you can fight this."

I screwed my eyes shut, even as everything within me ached to kill her. To destroy her, to destroy everything. Gripping the banister, I felt the wood crack and bend under my hands.

"Sophie," Jenna said again, and suddenly I could see her, sitting on her bed, laughing the first night I'd met her. I could feel her arms around me last night as I'd cried about the grimoire.

*Jenna*, I thought. *I can't hurt Jenna.*

Something inside me gave way, almost like a chain had snapped. Inside my head, I could hear Lara's howl of rage, and then I was crying and hugging Jenna so tight I was surprised she didn't snap in half.

"Oh my God, I'm sorry, I'm so sorry," I told her.

She laughed, but it was a watery sound. "I told you you were better than them."

In the distance, something rumbled, and I pulled back from Jenna to look at the broken stained-glass window. The day had gone even gloomier, and tendrils of fog were starting to curl around the window frame. "Let's hope so," I said.

"Mercer!" I turned to see Archer standing at the top

of the stairs. At the same moment, Cal burst through the front door.

I looked back and forth between them before saying, "Okay, I promise I'll explain more fully when we're not dead. But for now, I have my powers back, I know where my parents are, and we're going to the Itineris to get off this island. So let's go!"

I don't know if it was my tone or the fact that the rumbling had gotten louder, but both guys leaped into action.

The four of us ran out of Hex Hall and into the pelting rain. The fog was rolling forward, and I stopped, raising one hand. Sparks shot from my fingers, and the fog rolled back, churning in on itself. A feeling of contentment flooded through me as I felt magic surging up from my feet. I flung another hand out, and the fog seemed to flinch in its rush to pull back. "Okay," Jenna said, tugging at my arm. "You're back to being a badass. Now, *run*."

From behind I could hear the front door of the house opening. I didn't look back. Cal, Jenna, Archer, and I sprinted out across the now-clear lawn, heading for the woods. I only dared one quick glance over my shoulder. Someone stood framed in the doorway. From his height, I thought it might be Nick. And then the figure leaped off the porch and began running toward us, and I *knew* it was Nick. Nothing could move that fast, not even a shapeshifter. As he got closer, I could see his face, those terrifying, blank red eyes. I'd been strong enough to throw off Lara's control, but it was obvious Nick was still very much her plaything. I threw out an attack spell, but he countered it with a simple wave of his hand.

I stopped, bracing myself, but he wasn't coming for me. Hands out, claws extended, he reached for Jenna. "No!" I screamed. And then everything happened at once. Jenna stopped to look behind her, Nick lunged, and suddenly Archer was between them, grabbing Nick's outstretched arm and wrenching it away from Jenna, just as Nick's other claw raked across Archer's chest. I saw both of them grimace in pain before sending another bolt of magic at Nick. This one hit him hard enough to blast him away from Archer, and he crumpled to the ground.

Archer's blood splattered the grass. Cal moved toward him, but Archer shook him off. "We don't have time. Come on."

I reached Jenna, who was pale and shaky, but unhurt. "Th-thank you," she said to Archer, who just repeated, "We don't have time."

And he was right. Something was moving toward us from the house. I could feel dark magic rolling off it, and I knew it was another demon. We plunged into the woods.

I stopped long enough to tell Archer, "Lead them to the Itineris." Archer had used the Itineris on Graymalkin to escape before. "I'll bring up the rear."

He didn't reply, just jerked his arm toward Jenna and Cal, who dashed after him. I jogged behind, my shoulder near my ears in anticipation of an attack spell. But even though I could hear shouts and cries from behind us, no magic came.

We emerged from the woods onto a stretch of beach.

And then I remembered something. Holy crap, I'd obviously been without magic for way too long to have forgotten one of the coolest spells I could do.

"Stop!" I yelled. Archer, Cal, and Jenna all skidded to a halt on the sand. I waved my hands at them to come closer. "Okay, everybody hold hands," I said.

Archer stared at me, one hand pressed to his bleeding chest. "Sophie, this really isn't the time for a friendship circle."

"It's not that," I said. "It's this."

I closed my eyes and channeled all my magic into a transportation spell. There was a rush of icy air, and then we were standing in the grove of trees that housed Hex Hall's very own Itineris.

"Wow," Jenna breathed. "It is *awesome* to have you back."

Magic and satisfaction rushed through me. "You said it," I agreed. "Now come on."

And with that, the four of us dove into the Itineris.

# PART III

Thus slowly, one by one,
Its quaint events were hammered out—
And now the tale is done,
And home we steer, a merry crew,
Beneath the setting sun.

—"A Preface,"
*Alice's Adventures
in Wonderland*

# CHAPTER 27

You know what would be great? If I had one instance of magical travel that didn't leave me feeling like someone had just tried to rip my spine out through my nose. I lay on cool, stony ground, my inner organs trying to rearrange themselves. Next to me, I heard someone gasping and gagging, and a familiar voice saying, "It's okay. Just give yourself a few minutes."

Mom.

I rolled my head to the side to see her kneeling over Jenna, who was curled on her side, shivering. Itineris travel was especially hard on vampires. I clambered to my hands and knees, looking around. It was evening, and we were by some large body of water. I could hear it lapping against the shore, and the air felt damp. Behind me was a big boulder, a shallow alcove carved in its center.

I was guessing that was the Itineris. Just past Jenna and Mom, Archer was sitting up, looking around him in confusion. Cal was standing next to . . . I squinted, trying to get a better look. Finley. I recognized her long red braid.

Panicked, I suddenly remembered the grimoire, my hands flying to my lower back. To my shock and relief, it was still there, wedged securely against my skin.

I stood up, but my knees felt watery, and the ground suddenly wobbled in front of me.

A hand supported my elbow. "Easy," my dad said. He was smiling at me, the dark markings on his face black in the moonlight. With a little cry of relief, I threw my arms around his neck, burying my face in his jacket. When I finally felt like I could speak, I pulled back and croaked out, "How? How did you get Torin to Hex Hall?"

Dad blinked rapidly, and at first, I thought he was surprised by my question. Then I realized that, no, he was fighting tears. Seeing my father, who practically had a PhD in Stiff Upper Lip, on the verge of crying because he was so happy to see me made my own eyes sting. Then he cleared his throat, straightened his shoulders, and said, "It was exceedingly difficult."

I laughed through my tears. "I bet."

"It was Torin's idea," someone said behind me, and I turned to see Izzy standing there. Like my parents and her sister, she was dressed in jeans and a black jacket, although she also had a black cap pulled over her bright hair. "We had tons of old spell books, and after you and Cal disappeared, he started looking through them. Found a spell that would let him travel to a different mirror."

"Of course, the problem was finding *your* mirror," Aislinn said, coming out of the darkness.

"Aren't you afraid that he'll permanently peace out from *his* mirror and start hanging out in girls' locker rooms or something?"

Aislinn's eyes slid to Izzy. "Torin has his reasons for wanting to stay with us," she said, and even in the dim light, I saw red creep up Izzy's cheeks. Maybe one day, I'd get to the bottom of whatever was going on there. Preferably once I was done getting to the bottom of the thousand *other* things on my agenda.

Jenna had started breathing normally again, her fingers wrapped tight around her bloodstone. Satisfied, Mom patted her shoulder and said, "Just stay down for a little bit. Rest."

Closing her eyes, Jenna nodded. Only then did Mom come over and wrap her arms around me. "I think we've met our quota for tearful reunions," she chuckled against the top of my head.

"When this is done, I promise I'm never going to leave the house ever again. We'll just stay in and order pizza and watch bad television."

Mom pulled away and looked over my shoulder. "Oh, I think you might want to get out every now and then," she said.

I felt the warm weight of Archer's hand on my waist. "Hey, I like pizza and bad TV."

I turned to him, surprised. "Your chest—"

"Cal," he said by way of explanation. "I owe that guy, like, a mountain of burgers. It's getting embarrassing."

Mom flashed me a little smile before saying, "You know, this isn't how I imagined meeting Sophie's first real boyfriend."

"Mom."

Archer gave me a little squeeze. "You mean I'm the first guy your parents have rescued from an enchanted island via use of a magic mirror? I feel so special."

I rolled my eyes and turned to face the water. "So I'm guessing that's Lough Bealach."

"It is," Aislinn said. "We've been busy since you vanished." Finley and Izzy were right behind her. Mom stepped back slightly so that she was beside her sister.

"So have we," Cal said, and I suddenly realized he was standing on the other side of me.

"Come on, honey," Mom said to me. "Let's go inside."

"Inside what?" I asked.

"Over here," Finley said, pointing to a small stone building covered in moss. I followed everyone into the hut. Maybe once upon a time, this had been a cozy little spot. And hey, maybe the lack of windows had been great at keeping the house warm from the cold wind off the lake. But with nine people crammed inside it, and a peat fire smoking in the tiny hearth, it was uncomfortably close and warm. It didn't help that I found myself jammed between Cal and Archer, both of them pressed tightly against my side.

An ancient-looking card table sat in the middle of the room, covered in maps and books. Man, give the Brannicks any space, and they'll turn it into a War Room.

Aislinn took her customary position on one side of the table. "Okay," she said. "Tell us everything that's happened."

Cal, Archer, Jenna, and I managed to achieve something truly impressive: the *four-way* glance. "It's really complicated," Jenna said at last.

"We used a sixteenth-century warlock trapped in a mirror to tell you where we were," Dad said dryly. "I think it's safe to say we're well-versed in 'complicated' by this point."

Archer gave a little laugh. "I like your dad," he whispered in my ear.

257

"You would," I muttered back.

"The Casnoffs are using the school as a breeding ground for demons," Cal said, getting right to the point in his usual way. For the first time, I noticed the line around his mouth, the tight way he was holding his shoulders. Cal kept so much inside of him, I sometimes forgot that what the Casnoffs were doing was as nightmarish for him as it was for me. I went to take his hand, but as soon as my fingers brushed his sleeve, I changed my mind. After what Elodie had done, touching Cal was now out of the question.

Clearing my throat, I turned my attention back to Dad. "What Cal said. But it's more than that." I reached out to Dad, and even though he was technically across the room, it was easy for him to grasp my fingers. Once he had, I sent a low pulse of magic to him, and his eyes widened.

"Your powers," he breathed.

I nodded. "Fully functional." I pulled out the grimoire and tossed it on the table. "Thanks to that."

As briefly as I could, I explained about the Cansoffs and how their bloodline should've let them control me.

"Lara did a spell that showed me their family history," I continued. "It's dark stuff. Humans basically wiped out Alexei Casnoff's entire village. Weird as it sounds, this all started with a little boy trying to feel safe. He was so sure demons would keep all Prodigium protected, and he passed that belief down to his kids." I glanced around the tiny, smoky room. "That's what you guys maybe don't get. We're not dealing with people who are all, 'Mwahaha—yay, evil!' The Casnoffs think they're in the right."

"Which is what makes them so terrifying," Dad said, nodding. "People are so rarely villains in their own minds."

I thought of Mrs. Casnoff muttering, *The ends justify the means,* and would've shivered if the room hadn't been so darn hot.

"Okay, so that's their plans," Archer said with a sigh. "What are yours?"

"We're going to the Underworld," Izzy said. She bounced a little as she said it, her eyes bright and her tone implying that "the Underworld" was akin to "Candy Land."

"Slow down, Iz," Finley said, laying a hand on her sister's shoulder. "It's not quite that simple."

"Go figure," Jenna said weakly.

"First off, Sophie is the only one who will be going," Finley said; Aislinn breaking in to add, "She's the only one who *can* go."

"Okay, but you guys didn't know I had my powers back when you came here," I said, working my hand out from between Archer and me to wipe a drop of sweat from my forehead. "So how did you know I'd be able to go?"

"We didn't," Mom said, propping a hip on the card table. "We'd thought about sending your father, hoping maybe his DNA would be enough to get him through." She sighed and rubbed her eyes, looking older and more tired than I'd ever seen her. "We had to try something."

"But now that you have your powers, you should be able to access the Underworld with no problems," Dad said. "You'll venture down there—alone—to collect as much demonglass as you can."

"Why does everyone keep talking like this is a walk in the park?" Archer asked. He tried to raise his hand, probably to push it through his hair, leaving me to dodge his elbow. "'Oh, Sophie will just go skip down to the Underworld to put some demonglass in a basket!'"

"No one takes Sophie's safety more seriously than her father and I do," Mom said. Her voice was low and even, but her eyes were steely. I wasn't sure if it was the Brannick in her, or just the mom.

"I know that," said Archer, backing down. "And I know . . . Look, I know Sophie is a demon. She could wipe the floor with any of us, magically speaking. But what exactly does going to the Underworld entail? I mean, are there other demons down there? Monsters? What could happen to her?"

My parents exchanged a glance, and then Aislinn cleared her throat. "We don't really know. No one has ever attempted this before."

"So, what?" Archer asked, clearly angry now. "You're just sending her and hoping for the best? That's insane! There has to be some other way to fight the Casnoffs."

Afraid that he was going to bring up The Eye again, I tugged at his shirtsleeve. "Hey," I said softly, wishing we weren't having this conversation in front of my entire family. "No one is making me do anything I don't want to do." I looked at Aislinn. "The demons that Lara has raised . . . Is demonglass the only way to defend ourselves against them?"

"It is."

I paused to take a deep breath, hoping my voice wouldn't shake as I said, "Then I'll go into the Underworld."

"Thank you, Sophie," Dad said, and Aislinn gave a brisk nod. "So it's decided. Tomorrow morning at dawn, Sophie goes to the island in the middle of the lake, and from there, through the portal."

My stomach in knots, I stared at all the people I cared about most in the world, and quietly agreed. "Tomorrow."

# CHAPTER 28

The next morning, I paced along the rocky shore of Lough Bealach and tried to figure out the best way to get across.

The barest hint of pinkish-gray was just starting to appear over the horizon. I had no idea what time it was, but my body told me it was roughly "Ouch, This Is Way Too Early" o'clock. I'd only gotten a few hours of sleep. After Dad's announcement that I'd be heading to the freaking Underworld the next day, no one had really been in the sleeping mood. Aislinn, Finley, Izzy, and Mom had spread out sleeping bags in the hut while I'd conjured up tents for Dad, Archer, Cal, me, and Jenna. They weren't anything to write home about (and the one Jenna and I shared was kind of saggy in the middle), but they were still the first things I'd magicked up in a while.

When I was done, Dad had said, "You created something out of nothing. You realize that, don't you?"

I let that sink in. Creating something out of nothing was nearly impossible for regular witches and wizards to do. Under Alice's teaching, Elodie had mastered it, but the spell had always been tricky for me. And Dad was right: I'd just done it, almost without thinking.

"It's so good to see you using your powers again," he said softly. I looked at the purple marks on his face, and just wrapped my arms around him in response.

Now, as I stood by the water, I felt my powers swirling peacefully inside me. When I'd wanted to go through the Removal, Dad had told me that taking away my magic was akin to trying to rip out the color of my eyes. He'd been right. Without my powers, I had felt like a huge piece of me was missing.

I rubbed my arms, even though I'd used my magic to transform my Hex Hall uniform into a thick black sweater and jeans. Ireland in September was a lot chillier than Georgia had been. Of course, the cold wasn't the only thing making me shiver. Rising up out of the water was a big freaking rock.

I rubbed my arms even harder and sat down next to Aislinn on one of the boulders ringing the shore. I'd gotten up before dawn in the hope of avoiding any more tearful farewells, but Aislinn had already been awake and waiting for me at the edge of the lake.

"I told Grace to let me see you off," she had said. "I was afraid it would upset both of you too much if she did it herself. Same for your father, and you need to be focused right now." Her voice was gruff, but I was still grateful to have her there.

"So should I just conjure a boat?" I asked her now.

She shrugged. "I'm not the one with magic. Just get over however you think is best."

"I could swim," I suggested. "Ooh! Or maybe magic up like, a sweet Jet Ski?" I held my hands out in from of me as if I were clutching the handlebars of said sweet Jet Ski. Aislinn watched me for a moment before saying, "Is this what you always do when you're nervous?"

My hands fell back to my sides. "Pretty much."

I turned back to the water. "See, the thing is, I'm pretty sure I could make a boat. But then if I do, do I give it a motor? Or a sail? Or am I expected to row myself all the way—"

"Please be quiet until you think of something." The words themselves weren't particularly threatening, but Aislinn had a way of looking at you that made you feel like she was mere seconds away from kicking you in the face.

The only sound was the lapping of the waves against the shore, and the chattering of my teeth. I peeked over my shoulder at the ring of tents. Jenna had been sound asleep when I'd crawled out just before dawn. I hadn't woken her up, partly because I thought she could use the rest. But the main reason was that waking her would've meant telling her good-bye, and telling someone good-bye when you're planning on walking into hell would've felt kind of . . . final.

It was the same reason I hadn't gone into the hut to find Mom, and why I'd skirted around Archer's tent. I'd been nearly to the shore when I'd heard him softly call, "Mercer."

Kneeling in the doorway of his tent, his hair a mess, his Hex Hall uniform ridiculously wrinkled, he'd nearly broken my heart. And when I ran to him as soundlessly as I could and practically dove on top of him, I'd told myself that our kiss was just your normal boyfriend/ girlfriend saying good morning thing. Even when he pulled me inside, the tent warm and cozy and smelling like him, I hadn't let myself think that might be the last time I'd see him.

And when he'd pulled me closer and murmured, "Mercer, I love—" I had covered his mouth with my hand.

"Don't say that. Not now. Say it sometime when there is absolutely no chance of death on the horizon, okay?"

He mumbled something beneath my palm, and I rolled my eyes as I pulled it away from his mouth. He dropped a kiss on the tip of my nose. "All I was going to say was that I love this tent you made for me. But I guess I can tell you again later. When you get back."

Curling my hand around the back of his neck, I'd pulled him down to me. "You better."

A blush creeping up my neck from the memory, I swung my gaze away from his tent and back toward the lake. I was coming back. I was going to be fine, and getting down into the Underworld to collect demonglass wouldn't be hard at all. Maybe I'd make it back before lunch.

Of course, I couldn't make it back if I never left.

And just like that, the simplest way to get across the lake occurred to me.

Standing up, I pointed a finger at the water. The surface of the lake began to ripple, and then, with a great whooshing sound, the water in front of us slid back, leaving a narrow, silver muddy trail along the lake's bottom. The path wove all the way to the base of the rocky island.

"What it lacks in pizzazz, it makes up for in practicality," I said, hoping Aislinn couldn't hear how terrified I was. But she put her hand on my shoulder—the first time she'd ever touched me—and said, "You'll be fine. If there's one thing I've learned about you, Sophie Brannick, it's that you are one tough little thing."

I almost said, "Sophie Mercer." Instead I just said, "Thanks, um, Aunt Aislinn."

She pulled her hand back. "Let's not get carried away."

"Right, sorry."

I turned back to the watery path and tried to remind myself that I had done all kinds of terrifying things. Escaped a burning building. Faced off against a werewolf. Fought creepy demon mind control. Walking through some water shouldn't be that scary. Still, my feet refused to move.

"You ready to go?" a voice said from behind me.

Cal.

He stood just at the edge of the water, hands in his pockets.

I stared at him in confusion. "You can't."

"I can't go into the Underworld with you, but there's nothing in the rule against having an escort out there."

Aislinn looked back and forth between us, finally saying, "You can try it."

Experimentally, Cal put one foot on the path. I tensed, waiting for the water to rush back in over him. When it didn't, I let out the breath I'd been holding.

"Seems safe enough," Cal said, and Aislinn shrugged.

"Well, there you go," she said.

Without so much as a "Hey, try not to get killed," she turned back for the stone hut. I wouldn't let my eyes follow Aislinn. If I looked back, I was afraid I'd go running after her.

Instead I walked out to stand next to Cal. Underfoot, the surface gave slightly. Gingerly, we made our way down the watery road. "Brannicks and magic and hell, oh my," I joked, and Cal gave a snort of what might have been laughter.

I hit a particularly slippery spot and wobbled for a second before Cal grabbed my elbow. I didn't want it to be awkward, and I really didn't want my entire face to go red, but that's exactly what happened. I glanced up. Our eyes met, and Cal jerked back his hand so fast that he overbalanced. As he started to fall, I went to grab him, and the next thing I knew, we both went down. I hit the wall of water to my right, just as Cal slid to the left. I fell into the water, completely immersed, only to have it spit me back out onto the path.

I sat there, arms and legs akimbo, hair dripping water into my eyes. Cal sat opposite me, every bit as drenched, looking totally bewildered. Once again, we locked eyes.

And this time, we both burst out laughing.

"Oh God," I spluttered. "Your face!"

"My face?" he said, his laughter dwindling to a chuckle. "You should see your hair."

He rose to his feet, leaning down to offer me a hand. I took it gratefully. Once I was upright again, I ran my hand in front of my body, magic fluttering out of my fingertips to dry my hair and clothes. Cal did the same to himself, and then we studied each other.

"All right, now that the weirdness between us has caused actual physical damage, I think it's time we talked it out, don't you?"

He gave a half smile and then turned back to the path. "We don't need to be weird," he said. "These past few days, since the thing with Elodie, I've been thinking." He took a deep breath, and I knew that this was one of those rare occasions when Cal was about to say a lot of words at once. "I like you, Sophie. A lot. For a while, I thought it might be more than that. But you love Cross."

He said it matter-of-factly, but I still caught the way his ears reddened. "I know I've said some pretty awful stuff about him, but . . . I was wrong. He's a good guy. So, I guess what I'm saying is that as the guy who's betrothed to you, I wish we could be more than friends." He stopped, turning around to face me. "But as your friend, I want you to be happy. And if Cross is who you want, then I'm not gonna stand in the way of that."

"I'm the worst fiancée ever, aren't I?"

Cal lifted one shoulder. "Nah. This one warlock I knew, his betrothed set him on fire."

Laughing so I wouldn't cry, I tentatively lifted my arms to hug him. He folded me against his chest, and there was no awkwardness between us, and I knew the warmth in the pit of my stomach *was* love. Just a different kind.

Sniffling, I pulled back and rubbed at my nose. "Okay, now that the hard part's over, let's go tackle the Underworld."

"Got room for two more?"

Startled, I turned to see Jenna and Archer standing on the path, Jenna's hand clutching Archer's sleeve as she tried to stay on her feet. "What?" was all I could say.

Archer took a few careful steps forward. "Hey, this has been a group effort so far. No reason to stop now."

"You guys can't go into the Underworld with me," I told them. "You heard Dad, I'm the only one with—"

"With powers strong enough. Yeah, we got that," Jenna said. "But how are you supposed to carry a whole bunch of demonglass out of that place? It'll burn you. And hey, maybe your powers will be strong enough to get all of us in, too." She gestured to herself and the boys. "Plus it's not like we don't have powers of our own."

I knew I should tell them to go back. But having

the three of them there made me feel a whole lot better and whole lot less terrified. So in the end, I gave an exaggerated sigh and said, "Okay, fine. But just so you know, following me into hell means you're all *definitely* the sidekicks."

"Darn, I was hoping to be the rakishly charming love interest," Archer said, taking my hand.

"Cal, any role you were after?" I asked him, and he looked ruefully at the craggy rock looming over us. As he did, there was the grinding sound of stone against stone. We all stared at the opening that appeared.

"I'm just hoping to be the Not Dead Guy," Cal muttered.

We faced the entrance. "Between the four of us, we fought ghouls, survived attacks by demons and L'Occhio di Dio, and practically raised the dead," I said. "We can do this."

"See, inspiring speeches like that are why you get to be the leader," Archer said, and he squeezed my hand.

And then, moving almost as one, we stepped into the rock.

# CHAPTER 29

As soon as we were in, the opening closed behind us. "Of course," I heard Archer say under his breath. I lifted my fingers, and an orb of light sprang from them. Not that it was particularly helpful. All I saw was a bunch of dark, slick granite, and not much else.

"So . . . is this it?" Jenna asked. "Are we in the Underworld? Because to be honest, I thought it would be hotter."

I looked around in the gloom. "I . . . don't know," I finally said. "Anyone see a sign that says, Underworld This Way? Preferably with an arrow?"

"Unfortunately, no," Archer said. "But something feels weird. Is it just me?"

Now that he mentioned it, I could feel something, too. It was like the cavern held a subtle charge. When I looked down, I saw that the hairs on my arms were all standing up. Inside me, my magic churned and thumped. "No, I definitely think we're in the right place. Which means I should probably do this." Facing the three of them, I concentrated as hard as I could. *Be safe*, was all I could think of as far as protection spells went, but I felt power surge up and then flow gently from my hands. The spell was a milky white, and it curled around Archer, Jenna, and Cal like smoke, before settling in.

"Okay, do you guys feel protected?"

"I do," Archer said. "Also, a little violated, but that's neither here nor there."

I rolled my eyes. "You two?"

"Yeah," Cal said. "Whatever you did, I think it worked."

"Same," Jenna added.

"Awesome." I started walking forward, the others following. "Archer, any helpful factoids about demon-glass you'd like to offer up?"

"Um, okay. Well, after the war in heaven, the angels who fought on the wrong side were stripped down to just their most basic level."

"Right," I nodded. "Dad told me that. Demons are just pure dark magic, nothing more. Until they're put in a body, obviously."

"I don't know, there are times when you seem

like you're just pure dark—ow." Archer broke off as I poked him in the ribs. "Anyway, the demons were forced into another dimension. What people call hell, or the Underworld, or whatever. Supposedly—and for us, hopefully—that's where you find demonglass. Which, really, is nothing more than rock that's been permeated with all that dark magic. Demon Kryptonite, basically."

"So we're going into another dimension?" Jenna asked, her voice wavering a little. "Like what the Itineris does?"

"That's the idea," Archer replied.

Seeing as how the Itineris almost always left Jenna trying not to cough out her inner organs, I understood why she sounded a little freaked out.

"This doesn't feel like another dimension, though," I said. "It just feels like—"

"A cave," Cal said.

"Yeah, a cave." As soon as I said that, my heart started to pound. Ugh, this new claustrophobia thing was *highly* annoying. "Other than the weird feeling in the air, which honestly, could be something natural, I'm not sensing anything that makes me think we're in the *actual* Underworld."

No sooner were the words out of my mouth then the orb I was carrying whooshed out. Next to me, Jenna gasped, and I did everything possible to summon the light back. When I could suddenly see everyone again,

I thought maybe I'd managed it. But then I realized the light in the cavern wasn't the soft blue I'd made. It was a harsh orange-yellow, almost like a streetlamp.

I blinked. It *was* a streetlamp. And I wasn't in a cave anymore. I was in a room. A motel room, if the cheap carpet and identical double beds were anything to go by. There were two figures in one of the beds, and from the soft, even sound of their breathing, I knew they were sleeping.

"What the hell is going on?" Archer asked, just as a low moan filled my ears. It was Jenna. She stood beside me, her eyes huge, hands pressed to her mouth.

I grabbed her arm. "What is it?" I asked. "Jenna—"

The cracking sound of wood breaking exploded through the room, and three men, all in black, rushed inside. One of them brushed against me, feeling every bit as real and solid as Cal on my other side.

The figures in the bed sat up, shrieking, and as they did, I saw the light fall on a familiar pink stripe. I watched Jenna leap out of the bed, fangs bared, as the men in black—members of L'Occhio di Dio—raised wooden stakes over their heads. There was an awful sucking sound as one of the stakes found its mark.

Amanda, Jenna's first girlfriend. The girl who had made her a vampire.

Both the Jenna in the motel room and the Jenna next

to me screamed. And then, just as abruptly, everything went dark again. The only sound was our ragged breathing and Jenna's shuddery weeping.

"It's okay," I murmured, wrapping my arms around her. "It wasn't real."

"But it was," she cried. "Th—that's exactly how it happened."

There was nothing I could say to that. I felt someone move closer to us, and then Archer's voice, very low, said, "Jenna, I'm so sorry."

Her only reply was another wrenching sob.

"Okay," Cal said. "Let's just keep moving."

At least there was no doubt that we were in hell now. I'd been prepared for fire and brimstone and all of that. But walking into a place that made you relive nightmarish moments from your own past? Swallowing, I held Jenna tighter, relit the orb, and we moved on.

We got maybe a dozen yards before my light flickered out again. This time, we were in a brightly lit, cheerful living room. Nothing in it looked familiar to me, and I glanced over at Cal and Archer. "Either of you recognize this?"

"No," they said in unison. A scream echoed through the room, sounding like it came from somewhere above us. As we watched, a dark-haired man dashed down a flight of stairs and into the living room. His shirt front was covered with blood, and his eyes darted back and forth wildly. "Elise!" he cried. Moving with supernatural speed, another man came down the stairs, leaping over the railing. I caught a brief gleam of claws, and then I slammed my eyes shut. When I opened them again, the man who'd called for Elise was lying facedown on the carpet. The other man stood over him, panting, blood dripping from his now-human hands. At his side was a woman, her eyes blood-red and her expression every bit as inhuman as the man's. She was also very pregnant, which somehow made the whole thing ten times more disturbing.

Somewhere in the house, a small child started to wail, and the man lifted his nose to sniff the air. I shook my head at the scene, confused. "They're demons." I knew they couldn't hear me, but I couldn't help whispering. "But I've never seen them before. And if she's a pregnant demon, then her baby . . ."

And then I looked at the man—mainly his dark, curly hair, the familiar shape of his eyes and nose. "Oh my God," I breathed. "Nick. These are Nick's parents. He was *born* a demon."

Jenna had stopped crying. "So why is it showing us this?"

As the demons fled through the front door, a little boy, maybe two or three, wandered into the room. There was a streak of blood on his pudgy cheek, and his dark eyes were bright with tears.

I looked at Archer. He was so pale, he'd actually gone gray. "This was my family," he said just as the scene went black. "This is what happened to them. I always wondered, but . . . God." His voice broke off with a strangled sound.

"That's it," I said. "We're getting out of here." Blue light shone from my fingers again.

"The demonglass," Archer started to say, color slowly returning to his skin.

"Screw it," I said. "We'll come up with some other way, but we can't stay here. I don't want to see anything else."

But it was too late. We were standing in moonlight, and I could feel cool air wash over my skin. The scent of lavender flooded my nostrils, and my heart sank. We were at Thorne Abbey. And in front of us, crumpled on the grass, sobbing, was Alice. She looked so young, so terrified. So unlike the powerful creature I'd known. Alexei Casnoff stood in front of her, the grimoire in his hands. There was a blond woman next to him, her hands clasped behind her back. Virginia Thorne, the dark witch who had worked with the Casnoffs to find this ritual. Alexei was already reciting the ritual, light flashing in the dark sky. I heard someone cry out, and whipped my head around to see a handsome younger guy run up to Alexei, attempting to grab the book from his hands. The wind was howling so loudly that I couldn't hear what he was saying. I could hear Alice yell out, "Henry!" As she did, her hand covered her stomach protectively, and I knew that this must be Henry Thorne, Virginia's brother.

Alice had been pregnant when she was changed, and Dad had suspected that Henry was the father. From the terror on Alice's face, I knew it was true. And so I watched as Alexei Casnoff lifted his hand, like he was swatting a bug, and sent a bolt of magic into Henry Thorne's forehead that killed him instantly.

"No!" Alice wailed, as Virginia Thorne cried out, too. With the same careless motion, Alexei killed her as easily as he had her brother. The light grew brighter, so much so that I had to turn my head away. But just before I did, Alice locked eyes with me. I knew she wasn't really looking at *me*. Just in my general direction. Still, her huge tear-filled eyes, the same shade of blue as mine, pierced right to my heart.

And then the scene evaporated.

"Please," Jenna whimpered. "*Please*, let's go."

Stumbling in the darkness, I nodded. "I am all for that," I said, reaching a hand out to steady myself. As soon as my fingers touched the cavern wall, I drew them back with a shriek of pain.

"Sophie!" Archer and Cal called out at the same time.

"I'm okay," I said, cradling my hand against my chest. "It just . . . It burned me. The wall."

I summoned another ball of light and looked at the pinkish welts raising up from my fingertips. Then I looked back to the wall. I'd thought it was just wet rock, but now I could tell that the shine I'd seen wasn't from water. "It's demonglass," I said. "The—the whole freaking place is made of demonglass."

I didn't hesitate. Lifting my uninjured hand, I said, "You guys get ready to grab as much of this stuff as you can, and then we are booking it. Understood?"

"Understood," they all echoed back.

Taking a deep breath, I closed my eyes. "Break."

Dozens of shards fell harmlessly to the ground. Jenna, Archer, and Cal rushed forward to gather them up, and then we ran back in the direction we'd come. Light flared again, followed by noises too faint to make out.

As we ran, I could hear whatever the scene was playing behind me. There were screams, one of which sounded oddly familiar. In fact, it sounded like *me*.

I froze in my tracks. Cal was already looking over his shoulder, but before I could see what he was watching, he was pushing me forward again. "Keep moving," he grunted.

Up ahead, the opening had reappeared, and we dashed

for it. As soon as my feet hit the muddy path, they slipped and slid, but I did my best to stay upright. The sooner I could get away from that place, the better. Only when we heard the grinding of stone on stone did we stop and look back. The entrance into the rock had vanished, and I nearly sagged to the ground with relief.

Then I looked at the black blades the others were holding. "Holy crap," I said breathlessly. "We did it."

I'd imagined that if we'd successfully collected the demonglass, we'd practically skip back to the shore. But the cost of getting these weapons had been awfully high, and as we trudged back down the ribbon of silt, I knew we were all thinking about what the Underworld had shown us.

Like she was reading my mind, Jenna said, "So that's what the Underworld does? Shows you the most terrible things that ever happened to you—or your family . . ." she added, glancing at me and Archer, ". . . like some kind of sick movie?"

"Seemed pretty hellish to me," Archer said, still a little shell-shocked.

"I don't think it's just things that have happened," Cal said. "Maybe it's stuff that will happen, too."

I stopped, pushing my hair away from my face. "What did you see in there, Cal?"

He shook his head. "Doesn't matter," he said. But just

as he walked past me, his gaze lingered briefly on Archer. I remembered that scream. The one that had sounded like me.

And as we made our way back to my parents and the Brannicks, I couldn't help but feel that as nightmarish as the cavern had been, the worst was still ahead of us.

# CHAPTER 30

Back at the hut, I used my magic to whip up some tomato soup and hot tea. I told Mom and Dad what had happened, downplaying the horror of it as much as I could. As I did, Mom walked around the table, draping blankets over our shoulders. "We're not in shock," I told her, even as I clutched the material tighter around my neck.

"Well, you all look awful," she said.

"Hell does wreak havoc on the skin," Archer quipped, but I could tell his heart wasn't in it. Under the table, I put my hand on his knee, and he covered my fingers with his own.

"You say the cavern showed you scenes," Dad said, poking at the fire even though it was already warm inside. "Jenna, it showed you the death of your sire."

Jenna blew on her soup and gave Dad a look. "I called her my girlfriend, or Amanda, but yeah."

Dad inclined his head. "Of course. Forgive me. Sophie, you saw Alice's transformation."

I nodded. "And the murder of my great-grandfather. Weird it showed me that when I've had so many other awful things happen directly to me," I said, beginning to tick them off on my fingers. "Elodie getting killed, having to kill Alice, escaping a burning building with the help of a ghost . . ." And then, because both my parents looked so deflated, I added, "Oh, and this really heinous pageboy haircut in sixth grade."

A few wan smiles appeared, but I think it was just to humor me.

"Yes, but that was the act that was directly responsible for all of those other horrible events," Dad said. "Well, except for the haircut. I suspect that can be laid at your mother's door."

"James!" Mom protested, but I swear I heard affection behind it. I think Dad did, too, because his lips quirked upward briefly. His expression sobered, though, when he turned to Archer. "And you saw your parents murdered by demons."

Archer clinked his spoon against the bottom of his bowl. "Just my dad. But when I—uh, baby-me came in, there was blood on my face that wasn't mine, so I'm guessing my mom was already dead."

Dad frowned, deep in thought.

"The lady demon was pregnant," I told him. "And the guy looked just like Nick. I'm thinking they were his parents."

"Of course," Dad said, his eyes going wide. "The Anderson brothers. They both disappeared, along with their wives, about fifteen years ago. Everyone thought they'd just gone underground, so to speak. Lara was close to the youngest one's wife. Very close."

"Wait. So, the demon guy and Archer's dad were brothers?" I asked. "Which makes Archer and Nick—"

"Cousins," Archer filled in, still stirring his soup. "Nearly murdered by my own relative. That has to win some kind of medal for dysfunction." Then his expression darkened. "Or maybe it's just family tradition."

An uncomfortable silence stretched out. Archer's spoon clinked on his bowl as he swirled it around and around. Finally, he said, "Anderson?"

Dad met his eyes. "Yes. If I'm right, your father was the eldest. Martin. Your mother's name was Elise."

Archer's throat moved convulsively. "That's the name the guy—my dad—said. In the vision, or whatever it was."

Dad smiled sadly. "I didn't know your parents personally, but from everything I've heard, they were good people. And they were very devoted to their only child. You."

Now the silence in the room felt like a heavy, tangible thing. Under the table, Archer's fingers were vise-tight on mine. "Do you know—"

"Daniel," Dad said, his voice soft. "Your name was Daniel Anderson."

Archer dropped his head, and I watched two tears drip soundlessly into his soup. And then he was shoving back his chair, and out the door. I stood up to follow him. But Dad touched my arm. "Give him a minute."

I bit the inside of my cheek and nodded. "Right."

Sniffing, I sat back down and curled my hands around my cup of tea. "So now what?"

"Well, now we at least have some way of defending ourselves against the demons the Casnoffs have," Aislinn said, speaking up for the first time. She, Finley, and Izzy had met us at the shore, and the three of them were currently wrapping the demonglass into cloths and putting the shards in a canvas bag. "Between the three of us," she said, gesturing to her daughters, "we could probably take them all out."

I winced. "You mean, kill them."

"No, take them all out for ice cream," Finley scoffed, but her mother said in a low, dangerous voice, "Finley, Sophie walked into hell for us today. She's as much a

Brannick as you are, and you'll talk to her with respect."

Abashed, Finley looked at me under her lashes and muttered, "Sorry."

"No problem," I answered. "But I'm serious. Is . . . is killing them the only option?"

"It's the easiest one," Mom said, coming to sit in Archer's empty chair. "Sweetie, I know some of those kids were your friends, but there's no getting them back."

"Is that true?" I asked Dad. "Are they gone for good?"

Dad shifted in his seat, uneasy. "Not necessarily. But Sophie, the risk involved in bringing them back . . . It's almost too great to fathom."

"I can fathom all kinds of things," I told him. "Try me."

I think I might have seen pride in Dad's eyes. Or maybe it was just a gleam of *Why is my offspring so insane?* Still, he answered me. "If you destroy both the ritual and the witch or warlock who used it, the spell itself can be reversed."

I shrugged. "That doesn't sound so hard."

"I wasn't finished. They must be destroyed simultaneously."

Swallowing, I tried to sound cheerful. "Again, not so bad. Get Lara to hold the piece of paper, zap them both with, um, some fire or something, and bam! Instant demon reversal."

"And they must be destroyed in the pit where the

demons were raised," Dad continued, as if I hadn't said anything. Seriously, he *had* to stop doing that. "Oh, and as the pièce de résistance, you'll need to do a spell to close the pit itself, with both the ritual and the witch inside it. And that's such an intense ritual that it could actually pull whatever's around the pit into it as well."

"Like, the person doing the spell?"

"Like, the whole damn island the pit is on."

"Oh. Okay. Well, that is definitely . . . challenging. But not impossible. And we have the grimoire, that's one bonus, right? Even if the demon-raising ritual isn't in it."

"Sophia Alice Mercer," Mom said warningly, just as Dad said, "Atherton," and Aislinn said, "Brannick."

I threw my hands up. "Look, it doesn't matter what you call me. I'll hyphenate, how about that? But listen to me. I have to try, all right? For Nick, and Daisy, and Chaston, and Anna, and all the other kids they've turned into weapons over the years. *Please.*"

"Sophie's right," Cal said, leaning forward. "If we can stop the Casnoffs and turn those kids back . . . wouldn't that be better than having to kill them?"

"I'm all for that," Jenna said.

My parents looked at each other. A moment passed between them, and then Mom turned to her sister. "Can you buy her some time? Keep her safe until she can find the ritual and hopefully destroy it?"

"We can," Finley said quickly, and Izzy nodded. "We'll stay right by her. Even if she can't destroy the witch, and the spell, *and* the pit, she can at least do one of those things, right? That has to be worth something."

Dad blew out a long breath, rubbing his hands over his face. "Yes," he finally said. "It's worth something. It would be best if we arrive at night, don't you think? Thanks to the time difference, that's still a ways off at Graymalkin Island. So, dawn?" He gave a wry smile. "Again?"

And one by one, everyone nodded. At dawn we'd take the Itineris back to Hex Hall, and we'd finish this.

"Let me go tell Archer," I said, shoving the blanket off me as I stood up. Outside, the wind had picked up, and it blew my hair in my face as I scanned the shore for him. When I didn't see him, I poked my head into his tent. He wasn't there, either. Moving around the back of the house, I shaded my eyes against the sun, looking for a familiar dark figure among all the green and rock.

I saw a movement in my peripheral vision, and turned toward it, relieved.

But it wasn't Archer. It was Elodie, wavering in the breeze. In the daylight, she was even more translucent than normal, and her red hair fluttered around her like she was underwater. "He's gone," she mouthed. "He took the Itineris."

Stomach sinking, I asked, "Where?" but I already knew.

Elodie just confirmed it when she said, "To The Eye. He told me to tell you he's sorry, but he had to."

I blinked back tears that had nothing to do with the sun or the wind. "You saw him?"

"I've been hanging around since you got here. I just wasn't making myself visible. But he must've known I was here because he called me. He said I didn't owe him anything, but I did owe you something."

She was so faint that it was hard to tell, but I thought I saw regret cross her face. "He was right. I'm sorry about the thing with Cal. It wasn't fair hurting the two of you just to hurt Archer."

"Apology accepted," I told her. I was surprised to discover I meant it. "What else did he say?"

"Just that. He's going to The Eye, and he's sorry." She screwed up her face. "Oh, some weird thing about telling you that he still feels the same way about that tent, and he promises to say it to you in person next time he sees you."

I gave a bark of laughter that was more of a sob. "That asshat," I blubbered.

Elodie nodded in sympathy. "Such an asshat."

When I'd left Thorne Abbey, I'd held Archer's sword and had a sense that somehow things would turn out all right. *Please,* I thought. *The rest of my magic is back, so let me have that power, too.*

But there was no reply except the whistling of the wind.

# CHAPTER 31

The next morning, we all gathered by the big rock that sheltered the Itineris. I was in my Hex Hall uniform, figuring that was the least conspicuous thing I could wear to sneak back into the school. Jenna was wearing the same, as were the younger Brannicks. Both of them were pretty unhappy about it, if the way they tugged at their skirts was any indication.

"You wear knee socks every day?" Izzy asked, scowling. "That's reason enough to take this place down."

Even though I was scared and worried, I chuckled. "Just wait until we get there and you experience the torture that is wool in humid weather. You'll wanna sink the whole island."

"It's not so bad," Cal said, and Jenna hooted with laughter.

"Yeah, says the guy who wears flannel in August."

"Okay," Aislinn said, fastening a holster around her waist. Three blades of demonglass dangled from it. Izzy and Finley had something similar strapped under their blazers, as did Jenna and Cal. I wasn't carrying any, for the obvious reason. I glanced down at my still-pink fingertips. At least they matched my other demonglass scar, the wide, purplish gash that cut into my palm. Thoughts like that helped make me less terrified of what was about to happen.

". . . and let Sophie get the ritual," Aislinn was saying. I had totally zoned out, and I shook my head. Now was not the time for daydreaming. Of course, we'd gone over this plan a dozen times already. We'd go to the school. Aislinn and Finley would draw the Casnoffs out. While they were doing that, Izzy, Jenna, Cal, and I would sneak back into the house and try to find the ritual. Aislinn and Finley would lead Lara and however many of her demons she released back toward the pit. I'd meet them there with the ritual, and then, using the spell in the grimoire, destroy the Casnoffs, the ritual, and the pit itself in one big destructo-blast.

It sounded totally simple. Easy even. But if I'd learned anything over the past year, it was that nothing was easy when it came to magic.

"So are we all clear?" Aislinn said.

"Crystal," I sighed.

"Okay, Finley and I will go first. Wait a few minutes, and then Sophie, Jenna, Cal, and Izzy follow."

"And we'll wait here," Dad added, nodding toward Mom. Last night, we'd all made the decision that it was too dangerous for Dad to come with us to Graymalkin. Without powers, he'd have no way of defending himself, and I'd be too distracted worrying about him.

I faced both my parents and wrapped my arms around their necks, pulling them into a group hug. "I'm going to be fine," I said, even though I think my shaking voice gave me away. "There will be Casnoff butt kicked and all sorts of names taken. And hey, maybe I'll get some cool new scars."

Both of them hugged me tighter. "We love you, Soph," Mom said.

"Quite right," Dad added, and I laughed, even as my stomach twisted itself into a balloon animal.

I pulled away before I could embarrass myself with more tears, and took Jenna's hand. Aislinn and Finley were already gone. "Ready?" I asked.

"Ready," they all said softly. I looked over my shoulder at Mom and Dad. They still had their arms around each other's waists, and I smiled.

Then I stepped forward. The blackness pushed down, and I felt that awful stillness inside of me. And then, just like that, I was back in the grove of trees on Graymalkin Island. I wasn't sure if it was my magic being stronger, or just all the adrenaline coursing through me, but the "landing" didn't seem so bad this time. Jenna didn't have it quite so easy, but as soon as Cal appeared, he laid a hand on her forehead. Her breathing immediately slowed down, and some of the color returned to her cheeks. "Thanks," she said with a grateful sigh.

From somewhere in the distance, I thought I heard a howl. "Okay, you guys ready to zap again?" I asked everyone. Izzy still looked a little shaky, but she readily put her hand in mine. Jenna took the other one, and Cal stepped close behind me, wrapping his arms around my waist.

I closed my eyes and concentrated. A breath of cold air later, we were standing on the lawn of Hex Hall. And right in the middle of what appeared it be World War III.

As soon as I opened my eyes, a bolt of magic raced toward me. I flung up my hand just in time to deflect it, but there was another right behind it. This one struck Izzy just about her left shoulder, and she cried out. Cal was at her side in seconds, already pulling her toward the cover of the trees. I tried to absorb the nightmare that was unfolding around me. There were demons. Everywhere. Demon werewolves, with blood-red eyes and purplish sparks shooting off their claws. Demon faeries, their black wings stirring the air and blazing with unearthly light. They were fighting, and at first, my eyes searched for Finley and Aislinn, thinking they must be in the middle of this. But no, the demons were only fighting each other.

I shook my head, not wanting to believe what I was seeing. I had only seen fifteen or so demons in the cellar. But there were dozens on the lawn, and Finley and Aislinn were nowhere in sight.

I tried to collect my scattered thoughts. I needed to get into the house and to find the ritual. But seeing as how a demonic faerie was currently hovering in the doorway, that was probably out of the question.

So I followed Cal and Izzy into the trees, Jenna behind me. The four of us crouched there, taking in the hellish scene in front of us. "What are they doing?" Cal wondered.

I looked at the demons as they snarled and hissed and clawed at each other. "They're fighting," I murmured. "That's the thing about demons. They're not exactly the most controllable things in the universe. God, I bet Lara doesn't even realize what she's unleashed."

I winced as one of the demon faeries flew at a familiar figure—Daisy. I thought the faerie might have been Nausicaa once, but it was hard to tell. Her formerly green wings were now a dark navy, and they appeared to have razor-sharp edges. As I watched, those wings cut into Daisy's raised arms.

Choking down my fear, I shook my head and said, "But it doesn't matter. What matters is finding that ritual and the Casnoffs, and—"

I broke off with a cry as something attempted to shove against me. Not, not against. Inside.

Elodie.

This time, my magic shoved her right back, and her ghost fluttered a few feet from me, waving her hands. "Sorry, sorry," she mouthed. "I was in a hurry. The ritual isn't in the house. It's on Lara."

"What?"

"She knew you were coming. I don't know how, but she did. Sophie, they're all demons. Every kid who was here. She's turned them."

There had been over a hundred kids at the school.

"Where is Lara?"

"She's at the pit. There are still a few she's working on."

I shuddered at that term: *working on.* "Izzy, how are you?"

She was still leaning against Cal, but her face was grim as she reached under her jacket and pulled out her shard of demonglass. "I'm fine."

I doubted that, but I reached for her hand. "We're

going to use the transportation spell. It'll take us straight to the pit. But when we get there . . ." I glanced around at everyone. "It's going to be bad. Worse than bad, probably."

"We'll manage it," Cal said.

"Yeah," Jenna said, smiling shakily. "We're kind of badass in our own right."

I gripped her hand. "Damn straight."

We huddled together, and even though I was exhausted from all the magic I'd been doing, I felt the familiar rush of air.

I knew as soon we landed that we were in the right place. My teeth and skin ached from all the magic pulsing around us. I opened my eyes to see the yawning pit Archer and I had visited back in the summer. Then, it had been nothing more than a big hole in the ground. Now it was blazing with a bright green light. Lara stood on the lip of the hole, the wrinkled piece of parchment in her hands. My heart leaped at the sight of it. The ritual. I rose to my feet. From behind me, I could hear a distant baying. We probably only had a few minutes before at least a few of Lara's demons were on us.

Across the pit, Lara saw me. Her face was lit up in the creepy green glow, turning her smile sinister as she said, "Sophie. I had a feeling we'd see you again."

If she thought I was about to do the whole "have a

conversation with the villain" thing, she was dead wrong. I raised one hand while the other reached into my waistband for the grimoire. One super magical destructo-blast coming up.

Power pooled around the soles of my feet, rising up through my ankles, filling my legs and torso until it raced down my arms and crackled at my fingertips.

"Ah, yes," Lara said, clutching the ritual tight to her chest. "Kill me. Destroy the spell. Close the pit. And then all of your little demon friends go back to normal."

I focused my powers. This had to be perfect. There wouldn't be any second chances.

"Pity about your family, of course."

I opened my eyes, confused. Then I followed Lara's gaze into the pit, and all of the magic—and blood—seemed to drain out of me.

There, unconscious at the bottom, were Finley and Aislinn.

# CHAPTER 32

Behind me, I could hear Izzy wail. I looked back as Jenna moved to her and hugged her, murmuring. But her eyes met mine over Izzy's head, and I knew what she was thinking. This was my one chance to end it. To kill Lara and destroy the ritual. To close this god-awful pit so that no one could ever be turned into a monster again. That's what Finley and Aislinn would've wanted.

The ends justify the means.

As she watched me falter, Lara laughed. "You see? This is why your family was never cut out to rule. Always putting others before the good of your own kind."

"That's what this is really about, isn't it?" I asked, and had the pleasure of watching some of the amusement drain out of her face. "You're pissed off because Daddy decided he liked his pet demons better than his own children. You keep talking about everything he sacrificed, everything you gave up for this 'cause.' What all does that include, Lara? Your mother? I've never heard anything about Mommy Casnoff."

"You shut your mouth," she hissed, flicking her fingers at me. I blocked the spell easily.

"And Mrs. Casnoff was married. What happened to her husband? Admit it. Your dad took everything from you, both of you, and then he made *my* dad Head of the Council." I shook my head. "This is nothing more than a freaking temper tantrum with a body count, and I am done with it. Nobody else is dying for this."

With that, I pointed into the pit, focusing all my magic on Finley and Aislinn. As I did, I saw a bolt of power fly from behind me, undoubtedly from Cal. But Cal's specialty was healing magic, and his attack spells were weak. It harmlessly bounced off of Lara.

She held both hands out toward Cal, Izzy, and Jenna, sending out a pulse of magic that knocked all three of them back several feet. I heard their pained "whoofs" as they landed on the ground. Then I saw Lara shoot something else into the sky, almost like a flare, and suddenly she was gone. I gritted my teeth but didn't dare break my concentration. The magic coming out of the pit was so strong and so dark that it took everything I had inside of me to fight against it. I didn't know if it was the pit itself holding them, or if Lara had done a spell.

Slowly, though, Aislinn and Finley began to move out of the pit. Only when they were several feet away from the edge did I use my powers to gently lower them to the ground.

Izzy and Cal both went to them, Izzy to fling herself on their limp bodies, Cal to try to bring them back to consciousness. I held my breath until, finally, I saw Aislinn's eyelids flutter and Finley's fingers start to move.

Jenna came up beside me and laid her hand on my arm. "You did the right thing," she said. Watching Izzy hug her mother and sister, I knew that I had. But as the crashes and howls and snarls got closer, it was hard to *feel* very right.

"Have you ever been in a demon rumble before, Jenna?" I asked.

Hoisting her own demonglass dagger, she shook her head. "Nope. I have a feeling it's going to be super violent."

"Maybe we can talk to them," I said, rubbing my nose with the back of my hand. "Have a little sit-down chat."

"With tea."

"Ooh, yeah, with the nice china, and those little sandwiches that don't have crusts."

Cal came to stand with us. Aislinn and Finley were getting to their feet, but I could tell they were far away from optimum Brannick strength. "I don't want to kill these kids," Cal said.

"Neither do I. But I don't want them to kill me, either."

"Not sure what we want is going to matter that much," Jenna said. I stared out into the trees, hearing my fate move closer.

And here's the thing: I knew I was supposed to be courageous. I was supposed to use my magic for as long as I could, and be all *Braveheart* about it. But I didn't want to. I wanted to cry. I wanted to hug my mom and dad again. I wanted to see Archer. And I wanted to know that I'd done more here than just delay Aislinn's and Finley's deaths by a few minutes.

So there was no stoic badass facing down the demon hordes. There was just a teenage girl with tears streaming down her face, her two best friends on either side of her, as all kinds of hellish creatures rushed forward.

I could see the silhouette of one of the demonic faeries heading our way. I remembered its razor-edged wings and the way they'd sliced into Daisy's arms, and my own arm trembled as I lifted it. The magic I'd used to get Aislinn and Finley out of the pit had zapped a lot of my strength, and now my powers didn't flow so much as swirl sluggishly around my feet. Still, I could hold them off for a little while.

I could hear the churning sound of the faerie's wings as it moved closer, and shot an attack spell from my fingers. But before it hit, something else snaked out and wrapped around the faerie's ankle—a silvery whip. With a shriek, the faerie fell to the ground, and my heart was suddenly racing.

"Oh, God," Jenna said. She didn't have to say any more. Jenna and I had seen that weapon before, when The Eye raided a Prodigium club in London.

"It's The Eye," I said, disbelievingly. And then, for probably the first time in Prodigium history, a demon, a warlock, and a vampire all beamed at one another as I repeated, "It's The Eye!"

And sure enough, streaming through the woods from the general direction of the Itineris were several dudes in black. "How?" Cal asked. And then one of the guys in black started running toward us. I guess it's possible that it could've been some other kind of lanky Eye with dark curly hair, but I leaped at him anyway.

Archer and I collided with enough force to knock the breath out of me, but I didn't care. I could breathe later.

"Thought you could use some assistance," he said against my temple. "There are only about twenty of us— the only guys I could get to come with me. But still. It's something, right?"

I held him tighter. "Better than something."

But as much as I would've loved to stay there, holding him forever, now wasn't the time. I pulled back and said, "Try not to kill them, okay?"

He raised an eyebrow at me, and I immediately lifted a hand. "Don't. No time for quips. Just . . . try to hold them off, okay? There's still a chance we could save them."

For once in his life, Archer didn't try to banter with me. In fact, he didn't say anything at all. He just ran off in the direction of the fighting. I spun around, planning to dash off after Lara.

But in the end, I didn't have to.

She was once again standing at the edge of the pit— only this time, she didn't look superior or amused. And she wasn't alone. Mrs. Casnoff stood next to her, her hair still snow-white, but back in its elaborate updo. She was wearing one of her Hecate Hall blue suits, and there was nothing blank in her face now. She held one hand out, and I noticed that Lara was frozen, held in some kind of spell. "This school used to be a haven for our kind," Mrs. Casnoff shouted. Her voice was hoarse and raw, but I could hear the echo of the woman I'd once known. "And you've turned it into hell on earth, Lara."

"I did this for us!" Lara shouted back. "This is what Father wanted."

But Mrs. Casnoff wasn't buying that any more than I

was. "This has to end," she said, and there were decades of sadness in her voice. She repeated, "This has to end." Across the pit, her eyes met mine, and I knew what I had to do.

Hands trembling, I pulled the grimoire out of the back of my skirt and flipped to the page detailing the ritual that would close this pit forever. I whispered the words, but they still burned inside my mouth as I said them. From within the pit, the green light began to dim.

"No," Lara said, more confused than angry. She was still frozen there at the edge, arms locked against her body.

Mrs. Casnoff wrapped her arms around her. "I'm sorry," I saw her lips say. Once again, she looked at me. "I'm sorry."

She pressed her hand against her sister's back. There was one single pulse of purple light. And then they both tumbled lifelessly into the pit.

I was openly crying now, saying the words of the spell faster and faster as the earth around us began to tremble. "Sophie!" I heard Jenna scream, but I couldn't move until this was finished. This ritual that had made my family monsters, that had killed more people than I could count, was finally ending. I was ending it.

I was so focused on that that I didn't even notice the ground under my feet giving way.

I heard someone else scream my name, maybe Izzy. And then I fell into the pit.

I landed badly and heard my ankle give with a crack. Pain, white-hot and icy cold all at once, shot through me, and I screamed as the grimoire slipped from my hands. Dirt rained down on me as the earth shook and rolled. I gave one brief stab at using my magic to float me out, but the power down here was too strong. My own depleted powers couldn't override it.

I lowered my head, shaking with fear and pain, trying to tell myself that this was okay. After all, I was dying for the greater good. Daisy, even Anna and Chaston, could go back to being regular kids—or witches and warlocks. No one would ever be turned into a demon again.

I laid down on the ground, flinching away from the sight of Mrs. Casnoff's lifeless eyes staring at me. "The ends justify the means," I murmured as the walls of the pit began to slide in.

When I felt a hand on my injured ankle, I shrieked, pulling my leg back even though that sent bolts of fire through me. I half expected to see Lara Casnoff clutching me, or one of the ghouls that had once guarded this pit. But it wasn't either of those things.

It was Cal.

As his healing magic rushed through me, and the bones of my ankle knitted themselves back together, I sat up. "What are you doing?" I yelled over the rumbling.

He just shook his head and yanked me to my feet. After that, everything happened so fast, and I was still so shell-shocked, that I hardly realized what he was doing until his hands were under my foot and I was being lifted into the air, hands from above pulling me up.

"No!" I cried, even as Aislinn and Finley hauled me to safety. The pit was collapsing faster and faster now, and I scrabbled in the dirt at the edge, reaching a hand out to Cal. I summoned up every ounce of magic I had inside me, so powerful I could hear the nearby trees creaking. "Out!" I screamed. "Get him out!"

My magic surged from me, but it was too late. The ground gave one last mighty quake, and a huge crack opened up in the mouth of the pit. Cal stumbled backward, against the far wall. In that moment, his eyes met mine. I lay there on my stomach, hand still outstretched, panting. "It's okay, Sophie," I saw his mouth say. "It's okay."

There was a blinding flash of light and a sound like a mountain giving way. Jenna pulled me back just as the pit collapsed in on itself. The entire island seemed to give a shudder, and I numbly wondered if it was from revulsion or relief.

And then everything was silent.

# CHAPTER 33

Someone was shaking me. "Sophie," a voice said in my ear. "Wake up."

Disoriented, I rolled over, strands of hair stuck to my damp cheeks. I'd been crying. Again. I sat up, and for a moment, it was easy to believe the past few weeks had never happened. I was back in my bedroom at the Brannick compound, the early morning sun spilling in the narrow window. Maybe I'd never left here, I thought woozily. Maybe I'd dreamed it all.

But no. Jenna was sitting on the edge of my bed, looking worried, and Archer hovered in the doorway. And somewhere downstairs were my mom and dad, the Brannicks, Nick and Daisy . . .

But no Cal.

"Same dream?" Archer asked, and I nodded, scrubbing

at my face with both hands. Ever since the night we'd used the Itineris to escape from Hex Hall, the whole island shaking like it was about to collapse into the ocean, I'd been having nightmares.

Dad said that was to be expected, given all I'd gone through. But it had been a month. Were they ever going to stop?

"Was I screaming again?" I asked as I tossed off the covers.

"Just crying," Jenna said, her face sympathetic. "A lot."

I tried to recall the dream, but it was already slipping away. Cal had been there again, in the pit, dirt raining down on him. And Mrs. Casnoff, her dead eyes blank. I shuddered.

Jenna went to take my hand, but I stood up and gave her my best "Everything Is Fine, No, Really, It Is" smile. "It was just a dream," I told her. Archer opened his mouth to say something, but I held up my hand. "Just a dream," I repeated. "Now, is everyone else already downstairs? Because I don't know about you two, but I'm starving."

I wasn't, actually. The thought of food made my stomach churn, and I'd already lost so much weight that I'd had to use magic to shrink my clothes. I moved past Archer, and as I did, he laid a hand between my shoulder blades. "It's going to be okay, Mercer," he said in my ear, and for just a little bit, I let myself lean against him, soaking in his warmth, his presence. Then I straightened and said, "Come on, let's get downstairs. Nick and Daisy always eat all the bacon."

Sure enough, by the time we reached the kitchen, there were only two slices left. Nick and Daisy sat at the Formica table, their plates nearly empty, while Aislinn scrambled eggs on the stove behind them. I stood in the doorway, taking that image in: a Brannick, cooking breakfast for two demons. Who could have imagined *that?*

Nick saw me and grinned. Well, tried to. Like me— heck, like all of us—he still had that haunted look in his eyes that made friendly expressions seem sad. "'Morning, Sophia. I saved you a slice of bacon. You too, Jenna," he said, glancing over my shoulder. His eyes flicked to my other side. "Sorry, cuz, you're out of luck."

Archer gave a little snort of amusement, but there was still something wary in the set of his shoulders as he moved into the kitchen. He also took the chair farthest away from Nick when he sat down. I wasn't sure Archer and Nick could ever have anything approaching a normal relationship, but that was probably to be expected. After all, Nick's parents had murdered Archer's, and Nick had tried to kill Archer not once, but twice.

That would definitely make for awkward family reunions in the future.

It also didn't help that the people who Archer considered family were now determined to kill him, too.

"Soph?" Aislinn said, snapping me out of my thoughts. "Eggs?"

"Um . . . no, thanks, I'll grab something later."

Nearly everyone in the kitchen frowned at that, so to appease them, I grabbed the slice of bacon and broke it in half. Sitting down across from Daisy, I started to chew and said, "Anything today?"

It was the same question one of us had asked every morning since we left Hex Hall. The first few days, there had been answers. "Yes, the island is still there. Yes, we found Nick and Daisy and can bring them here. Yes, The Eye has put a price on Archer's head that could buy a small island."

That last bit Archer had taken pretty hard. Apparently, his little squad of Eyes had gone back to tell their boss lady that Archer had used some kind of magical artifact to put a compulsion spell on them. That was the only reason they'd fought for Prodigium.

"Is that true?" I'd asked Archer. His eyes had slid away from mine, and he'd given an exaggerated shrug.

I took that as a yes.

But after that, there hadn't been anything. No news

of how the rest of the Prodigium world was taking what had happened at Hex Hall. Nothing about what had happened to the other kids we'd freed from being demons.

So yet again this morning, Aislinn sighed and said, "No. Nothing."

"Maybe that's a good thing," Daisy said, buttering her toast. "Maybe they've all just . . . gone away."

Now that she wasn't a demon anymore, Daisy wasn't any kind of Prodigium. She had just been a regular kid the Casnoffs had turned into a demon. I understood her desire to leave all things magical behind.

Daisy leaned over and rested her head on Nick's shoulder. Well, maybe not *all* magical things. I was glad Nick had Daisy. After everything he'd been through, he needed her. Still, I had to admit there was a hauntedness in Nick's eyes that made me wonder if, free of the Casnoffs or not, he could ever really be okay.

Outside I could hear the distant clink of metal on metal that meant Finley and Izzy were already up and training, and I thought about going to join them. Not to wield a sword or anything, but maybe to let them block some of my spells. It would be good practice for them, and it would give me something to do other than sit in my room and replay that last night at Hex Hall over and over again.

I was just about to get up when Dad rushed into the

kitchen. He was in pajamas, which was totally bizarre. Dad never came down to breakfast until he was completely dressed. Of course, his pajamas even had a little pocket and handkerchief, so maybe he felt dressed.

He had a sheet of paper in his hands and was staring at it, his eyes wide.

"James," Aislinn acknowledged. "You're up kind of late this morning. Is Grace sleeping in, too?"

Dad glanced up, and I could swear he blushed. "Hmm? Oh. Yes. Well. In any case. Um . . . to the point at hand."

"Leave Dad alone," I told Aislinn. "His Britishness is short-circuiting." Instead of being grossed out, I was weirdly happy at the thought of my parents being all . . . whatever (okay, I was a *little* grossed out). In fact, their apparent reconciliation was maybe the one good thing to come out of this whole mess. Well, that and saving the world, obviously.

Dad shook his head and held out the papers. "I didn't come down here to discuss my personal . . . relations. I came here because this arrived from the Council this morning."

I sat back in my chair. "The Council? Like, the *Council* Council? But they don't even exist anymore. Maybe you're wrong. Maybe it's the Council For What Breakfast Cereals You Should—"

"Sophia," Dad said, stopping me with a look.

"Sorry. Freaked out."

He gave a little smile. "I know that, darling. And to be perfectly honest, perhaps you should be."

He handed the papers to me, and I saw it was some kind of official letter. It was addressed to Dad, but I saw my name in the first paragraph. I laid it on the table so no one would see my hands shake. "Did this come by owl?" I muttered. "Please tell me it came—"

"Sophie!" nearly everyone in the kitchen shouted. Even Archer gave an exasperated, "Come on, Mercer."

I took a deep breath and started to read. When I got about halfway down the page, I stopped, my eyes going wide, my heart racing. I looked back at Dad. "Are they serious?"

"I believe that they are."

I read the words again. "Holy hell weasel."

# CHAPTER 34

I got out of the car, feet crunching on the shell-and-gravel driveway, and stared at the house looming up in front of me. "Well?" Dad asked, getting out of the passenger side.

Behind me, Archer and Jenna got out of the backseat and came to stand on either side of me.

Pushing my sunglasses up onto my head, I said, "It looks better. I mean, it's still creepy as hell, but it's back to its *regular* level of creepy."

Hex Hall shone under a fresh coat of paint, and the windows were repaired. The ferns bracketing the front door were back to being a lush green, and someone had fixed the sag in the porch. Still, the trees around it were black, and the grass was gray.

"It'll probably never be the same," Mom said, coming

around the car to stand with Dad and me.

Heaving a sigh, I said, "Maybe that's a good thing."

"What do you think they'll do with it?" Jenna asked, studying the house.

"I kind of wish they'd burn it down," Archer said. "Maybe sink the island while they're at it."

A breeze off the sea ruffled my hair as we made our way to the house. Inside there was no longer that sense of decay and desiccation, but I thought the house would probably always feel a little sad. Or maybe that was just me. We passed under the stained-glass window, and I looked up, pleased to see that everyone had their heads again, the colored glass glittering in the autumn light. I could already hear the murmur of voices as we approached the ballroom, and Mom took my hand. "Nervous?"

"Nah," I replied, but since I bleated it like a sheep, I doubt she was convinced.

All the mismatched tables where we used to eat were gone. They'd been replaced by a sea of black chairs, but all of them were empty. Up on the dais where the teachers had once sat were twelve chairs that probably should have been called thrones. All but one of them were occupied.

The newly formed Council all rose to their feet as I entered the room, but I immediately raised my hands. "Oh, God, please don't do that. I'm freaked out enough as it is."

One of the faeries, a huge man with emerald green wings, frowned at me. "But as heir presumptive to the Head of the Council, you're afforded a certain degree of respect."

"I can feel respected with you all sitting down. Honestly."

I thought they might argue some more, but in the end, they all sat down.

"Have you considered our offer?" a woman asked. I thought she was a witch, but it was hard to be sure.

Instead of answering that, I took a seat in one of the black chairs. "Can I ask you guys something?" No one nodded, but I kept going anyway. "Why did you pick me? I mean, sure, I'm a demon, but so is Nick. Why not ask him? Is it because of the whole 'He Once Went Crazy And Killed A Bunch Of People' thing?"

The green-winged faerie stared at me. "That is a large part of it, yes."

"But not the only reason," the woman spoke up. She linked her fingers, folding them in her lap, and I saw a few tiny purple sparks. A witch after all. "The courage, the fortitude, the . . . initiative you showed in stopping Lara Casnoff was very impressive. Especially in one so young. You didn't let fear blind you to what needed to be done." She glanced at her colleagues. "Which is perhaps something we could all stand to learn."

"Now," a tall man with white hair said, "have you made your—"

"Why did you fix up Hex Hall?"

I felt a sigh ripple through the entire Council. "Because," the witch said, "Hecate Hall has always been a useful institution to us, and we have no intention of letting these . . . unfortunate occurrences kill over a hundred years of tradition. In the next month, all students who've been sentenced to this school will return here, and life can go on as normal."

I wanted to laugh at that. Normal. Like life here had *ever* been that.

But still. She'd given me my answer.

Taking a deep breath, I stood up and said, "Okay. Yes, I accept your offer to become Head of the Council."

Relieved grins broke out on a few faces, but I held up my hand. "On two conditions."

The grins deflated.

"I will become Head of the Council, but not until I've finished school."

"Certainly," the witch said. "We can arrange for your transfer to Prentiss immediately."

Prentiss was the fancy boarding school that wealthier witches and warlocks sent their kids to. It was supposedly the opposite of Hex Hall in nearly every way. I shook my head. "No, I don't mean Prodigium schooling.

I mean real schooling. College. A normal, human college."

The green-winged faerie frowned. "But you still have another year before you can go to college, correct? Isn't that how it works? And if you won't go to Prentiss, then where? A human high school seems unfeasible."

Another deep breath. "I know. That's my other condition. I want you to reopen Hex Hall. Not as a reform school, or a place of punishment, but what it used to be. A safe place. A school for all Prodigium who want to come here. Although, have to admit after the last year, there might not be many of them. But we can try. So those are my conditions."

I stood there, hands clasped in front of me. Once again, I thought of Cal saying, "It's okay. It's okay," as the pit closed in on him. He had given his life for mine. I had to make that count. And he'd loved Hex Hall. Believed in it, taken care of it, called it his home. The least I could do was restore it.

For Cal.

So when the witch looked straight at me and said, "We accept," it wasn't fear or regret or dread that shot through me. It was satisfaction.

Mom, Dad, Jenna, and Archer were all waiting for me when I came out of the ballroom. Before any of them could say something, I took my parents' hands and said,

"We can talk all the way home, promise. I need some alone time right now, though, okay?"

Dad squeezed my hand, wrapping his other arm around Mom's waist. "Absolutely."

"Sure," Jenna said.

Archer nodded. "Do what you need to do."

I walked past them and out onto the front porch. The steps hardly creaked under my feet as I walked down onto the lawn. I moved to one of the giant oak trees, leaning against it to stare at the school.

I was still standing there when I felt a presence at my elbow. Elodie floated next to me, her red hair wavering around her face. "Hi," I said softly.

"So you're going to be the Big Boss Lady?"

I opened my mouth to make some quippy comment, but nothing came. So I just said, "Yeah. I am."

She gave a little nod. "You'll be good at it. But if you ever tell anyone I said that, I'll kill you."

I chuckled. "Fair enough." For a long moment, I watched her watching the house. And then, very quietly, I said, "If you're ready for me to . . . I don't know, set you free or whatever, I can now. At least I think I can."

Elodie turned to me, her feet hovering just off the ground. "Where would I go?"

"I don't know."

"Would you . . ." She trailed off, and if I hadn't

known Elodie better, I would've sworn nervousness crossed her face. Then her lips moved so quickly that I couldn't make out any of the words.

"Whoa, slow down. My lip-reading skills aren't *that* great."

She drifted closer. "I said, if you're staying at Hex Hall, then . . . I want to stay, too."

I blinked. "For real? You want to stay tethered to me for all eternity? Because if you think for one second I'm letting you in my body again, you've got another think coming."

"I don't want to be in your body anymore," she said, before screwing her face up. "That sounded gross. Anyway, I just want to stay here. For now."

"Why?"

She threw up her hands. "Because you're my friend, okay? Because helping you and your loser crew these past few weeks has been . . . I don't know, fun. And way more fun than I thought I could have dead."

I was weirdly touched, so I tried to keep my voice gentle when I said, "Elodie, I get that. And to be honest, the thought of you blinking out of existence makes me—" My throat closed up, so I tried to turn it into a cough before saying, "But I can't have you tethered to me forever. It's not fair to either one of us."

"Is there any way you could transfer the bond?" she

asked. "All the other ghosts around this place, they're linked to the island. Could you do that for me?"

I thought about it, and my powers hummed through my veins. "Yeah, I could do that. But, Elodie, that will mean you'll be stuck here on Graymalkin Island forever. It'll just be you and whatever ghosts are still hanging around this place."

Elodie vanished, and I rolled my eyes. "Oh, come on!"

But then she reappeared several feet away, on the rise of the hill that led down to the pond. Waving her arm for me to follow her, she floated out of sight.

Heaving a sigh, I climbed the hill, and as I crested the top, I had to shade my eyes against the sunlight bouncing off the water. "Wow," I said, coming to a stop as Elodie hovered next to me. "That the prettiest I've ever seen the pond look. And look, the grass doesn't look so dead over—"

Whatever I'd been about to say died in my throat, and I clamped a hand over my mouth.

Cal walked along the edge of the pond. Well, his ghost did, at least. He was so faint that I could barely make him out, but there was no mistaking his long, easy stride. He knelt down and ran his hand over a patch of the gray grass, and as he did, it bled back to a vivid, emerald green.

He looked over at the hill where I stood, and he lifted his hand in a little wave. I waved back, tears streaming down my face. "Can he see me?" I asked Elodie. "Or is it just you?"

"He sees you," she replied. Then, somewhat ruefully she added, "I don't think he'd give me that particular smile." Then her lips twisted into a mischievous smile. "At least not yet. I do have all eternity to make Cal change his mind about me."

I knew she was joking, but I was serious when I said, "Take care of him, okay?"

And her face was surprisingly soft when she replied, "I will."

In the end, releasing Elodie from me and tying her to the island was a simple bit of magic. But when I felt that little chain of power between us give way, I had to admit I felt more than a little sad.

By the time Archer and Jenna found me, Elodie had vanished again. So had Cal, although the grass all around the pond was green now.

"There you are," Jenna said as she and Archer appeared at the top of the hill.

"Yeah, sorry," I said, walking to stand between them. "Had a lot on my mind."

"I bet," Archer said, wrapping an arm around my waist. "So, you told them you'd do it."

"I did. Do you think that's dumb?"

"I think it's dangerous," he said, turning me to face him. "I think *you're* crazy. But dangerous and crazy are two of the things I love most about you. So, no. Not dumb. Although I am disappointed that your condition for taking the job was reopening Hex Hall and not, I don't know, a Caribbean vacation with your boyfriend."

He lowered his head to kiss me, and Jenna cleared her throat. "Um, hello? Pretty sure vampire sidekick should get some kind of perk, too."

Archer nudged Jenna's shoulder. "Tell you what, when we get back from the Caribbean, she can take you to Transylvania or something. How does that sound?"

She punched his arm, but there was affection in the gesture, and I suddenly wanted to cry all over again. So I stepped back from Archer and said, "Any and all vacations will have to wait until I'm done with the school year." When they both stared at me, I added, "Yeah, that's the other part. When they reopen Hex Hall . . . I'm going to stay here. Just for the rest of the year," I hurried on. "Not like, for life. And college was another part of the deal, so there's that afterward. But, I mean, we'll be able to stay in touch. There are all kinds of spells for that sort of thing."

Jenna and Archer shared a look. "Why would we need to 'stay in touch'?" Jenna asked.

"Well, because . . . Look, I can't ask you guys to

stay at Hex Hall for a whole other year. Jenna, you have Vix, and Archer, you have . . . Actually, what *do* you have?"

"You," he said firmly. "And a whole bunch of holy knights who want to kill me."

"Vix can visit," Jenna said. "And the school will be a good place now, so it's not like one more year will be torture. Although," she said, frowning, "I will admit the place is pretty awful to look at. I don't know how we're going to fix that."

Facing the pond, staring at that green, green grass, I gave a shuddery laugh. "I don't think we have to worry about the island," I said, wiping stray tears with the back of my hand. "It's being healed."

"Well, there you have it, then," Archer said. "Vix can come for a visit, the island will eventually be a heck of a lot less depressing, and I'm not leaving you ever again."

"Yeah, and we still have to deal with The Eye being . . . Eyeish, and me learning to be Head of the Council, which will probably involve lots of boring books and—"

Archer pressed his mouth to mine, effectively shutting me up and kissing the hell out of me. When he pulled back, he was grinning. "And you have an arrogant, screwed-up former demon hunter who is stupidly in love with you."

"And an angsty vampire who will walk into hell with you. Actually, who *has* walked into hell with you," Jenna added, coming around to my other side.

"And parents who love you, and who are probably making out back at the car," Archer said, and I laughed.

"So, really," Jenna said, and looped her arm through mine, "what more do you need?"

I looked back and forth between them, these two people I loved so much. The breeze ruffled the tall grass around the pond, and I thought I could hear Elodie's laugh.

"Nothing," I told them, squeezing both their hands. "Nothing."

# ACKNOWLEDGMENTS

Huge, magical thanks to everyone at Disney-Hyperion, and all the members of "Team Hex." Jennifer Corcoran, you may call yourself a "publicist," but I think "superhero" is also an apt job description. Same for Hallie Patterson, Ann Dye, and Dina Sherman. And of course, the doyenne of Team Hex, my Fabulous Editor of Loveliness, Catherine Onder, whose guidance and wisdom helped me—hopefully!—stick the landing of the Hex Hall series. Thank you more than I can say!

Massive, "Borderline Obscene" gratitude to my agent, Holly Root, for . . . well, being Holly Root. You are the bestest, and I'm so glad Sophie and I found you!

To my writer buds who gave advice, hugs, and when needed, a metaphorical slap across the face while I was writing *Spell Bound*. Chantel Acevedo, Lindsey Leavitt, Myra McEntire, Ashley Parsons, and Victoria Schwab, you all held my hand, which was amazing and slightly awkward. Love to you all!

To my family and friends, thank you for understanding when I was deep in "Booklandia," and not hating me over missed phone calls, unreturned e-mails, and all the take-out dinners.

And last, but never, ever least, the biggest of all thank-yous to my readers. Without y'all, there would be no Sophie, no Hex Hall, no Archer (perish the thought!). Your support and love for this series has meant the world to me, and I'm so happy I have such amazing people to write books for!

DISCARD